CRITICS PRAISE
MELANIE JACKSON!

"MELANIE JACKSON IS AN AUTHOR TO WATCH!"
—Compuserve Romance Reviews

"BRIMMING WITH THE MYTH, MAGIC, AND LORE
OF SCOTLAND, THIS IS A TALE TO CHERISH."
—*Romantic Times on Night Visitor*

"INTRIGUING . . . MS. JACKSON'S DESCRIPTIONS
OF THE CORNISH COUNTRYSIDE WERE
DOWNRIGHT SEDUCTIVE."
—*The Romance Reader on Amarantha*

"MELANIE JACKSON PAINTS A WELL-DEFINED
PICTURE OF 18TH-CENTURY ENGLAND. . . .
MANON IS AN INTRIGUING AND PLEASANT TALE."
—*Romantic Times*

WHAT DREAMS MAY COME

"You aren't real," she informed Dom coolly. "You are a figment of my imagination. And I don't know why you persist in bothering me with these strange dreams. I don't like them. Why don't you ever take me to dinner, or bring me flowers?"

Dom thought about this while watching a blush finally move into her pale cheeks. "You don't like them? Not even a little? But how can that be, my dear, when it is *your* imagination which provides them?" With a small burst of concentration, he made her heavy nightclothes melt away and her braided hair unravel. The bit of mischief made him feel better.

"It doesn't matter if it is part of my imagination. It certainly isn't *all* of it. I want you to go away and not come back until you have learned some manners. And next time bring orchids. They are my favorite." Then, suddenly aware that he had undressed her and she was now standing completely naked in a Highland meadow under a bright June sky, she spun about looking for something to pull on over her nakedness.

"You rotten cad!" she cried.

"Well, yes, I suppose that is factually true by Victorian definitions. But I'm not an entirely bad person for all of that."

"Henry VIII probably said the same thing while he was getting rid of his wives—and he was just as mistaken. Where are my clothes? I want them at once."

"Why? They are infernally ugly. You look like a nun—which you most certainly are *not*, and never were."

DOMINION

MELANIE JACKSON

LOVE SPELL

NEW YORK CITY

For Grandpa Mac and Grandpa Long,
and other missing friends.
We wait for the wheel to turn.

LOVE SPELL®

August 2002

Published by

Dorchester Publishing Co., Inc.
276 Fifth Avenue
New York, NY 10001

ISBN 0-505-52512-7

The name "Love Spell" and its logo are trademarks of Dorchester Publishing Co., Inc.

Printed in the United States of America.

Visit us on the web at www.dorchesterpub.com.

DOMINION

Prologue

Isabella was dead. Beautiful, broken, childish Isabella. Her haunted eyes were closed forever now. Her beautiful voice was stilled.

Dominick looked at the pewter sky filled with silvery doves and wished it black—wished the birds of peace gone. They were a tribute by his grieving vassals to Isabella, but there was no place for lightness or hope in his world. All should be silent and still, as silent and still as the distant grave where his beloved now rested.

Perhaps someday he would be able to face the sun again, to recall with pleasure the time he had spent with his bride. But for now his memories and his guilt were like knives, slicing at his brain, at his heart, at his soul. Almost he had disinterred her, stolen back her body from her jealous brother, Rychard, who had taken her so far

1

away. He imagined the grave through her senses and shuddered at the thought of the pagan sepulcher of cold stone where her family was entombed.

But, he reminded himself, she would never really know that it was cold and dark and lonely there. She would never know anything again. It was just a nightmare, this sense he had of her being terrified of the dark. She was dead; she could not feel anything.

And what could he do if he took her out of the darkness, if he snatched her away from the grave? What could he do but follow his ancestors' ancient traditions and put her on a pyre? Give her beauty up to the heartless, all-consuming flames that swallowed countless pagan souls, destroying what little was left of her forevermore.

He hadn't the courage to ruin what remained of her tiny, graceful body.

Nor could he do as they did in the East and give her body to the sky where birds would pick her bones clean. The very thought made him shudder. He couldn't risk defying the precepts of the Carpenter's religion, those that said Isabella would need her body to live again. He would do nothing that would destroy her physical being and keep her soul from Heaven.

So, instead of acting, he grieved. And he hated. And he and his rage blundered about drunkenly, bruising everything and everyone they touched because he could not hurt the one he blamed for Isabella's death.

He had only loved two things in his life: his mother and his wife. Now they had both died trying to bring new life into the world, leaving him horribly alone, leaving his spirit so wounded that it could barely cling to the life the priests said he must go on living, and which the supposedly grief-stricken Rychard had threatened to take.

Never again! He swore it with every ounce of his wounded being. He would never love anything again. Love could not be trusted. It came in a blinding burst, exploding the senses, sweeping them away, seducing a man into trusting that all would be well.

And when a man's heart and soul were no longer his own, then love was taken away.

Let the priests of Rome talk of God's will and the better life Isabella would have now—and of his duty to marry again. Dominick cared nothing for God's will. He cared nothing for the priests' words. He would never remarry. And he would never love again, not even if Isabella was returned to him in Heaven. The pleasures of the flesh he would indulge, but not the pleasures of the heart. Those he would forget.

The greatest desire that remained in his soul was to be avenged upon the hated Rychard. That man and God together had taken Isabella away. They would take no more—and someday, sometime, someplace, he would see that justice was done. He would have his revenge.

Until then he would serve the Great One's priests by defending the remains of Charlemagne's empire from the Magyars and Muslims. And he would drown himself in infidel blood, in wine, and other distractions of the flesh until he no longer recalled that he had ever loved.

3

Chapter One

Domitien stopped abruptly behind the flowering shrub, which housed some of the City's gray doves, his ears sharpening at the sounds of the Great One's right and left hands talking in the courtyard beyond.

"Domitien must complete the earthly cycle. He has to go back to the human plane and fall in love," Enzo said flatly. "It is the task of all souls, and this time it must be done correctly. The Great One is insisting on it. The pattern must be modified, or it shall be discontinued, the threads snipped off. And you know how the Great One hates a failure."

"But will it ever happen? After Isabella? You know that this trio of souls has never worked well together. The basic design scheme is flawed." Ilia spoke plaintively, his voice nearly overshadowed by the sharp beat of the wings of agitated doves in the bush by Domitien's ear. "It is all very well for the Great One to order this reunion, but you know what will happen. It shall be the way it has always been. Women demand nothing of Dominick—he is always given his fair face and all the flagrant trappings that charm them into imbecility. I swear that the man could sleep while he made love and none of the infatuated creatures would complain."

"You exaggerate—and don't use that name. You know that he prefers Domitien, Dorran, or even Desiderio."

Ilia snorted. "Very well, Domitien then. But don't evade my point. Do I exaggerate? Have you truly forgotten all the hearts that have lived and died at his whim? He might kneel for a time at some woman's feet, pretending to worship at her shrine, but never does he leave his heart as offering. Not once—not a single time in any of his lives—has he ever felt anything more than superficial affection for any of them! And it makes a horrible amount of work for us repairing the damage he does to these other souls. Witness the fact that he never sees them more than once. I don't know why the Great One doesn't send Fate to handle this. She could compel him to act as the Great One wishes."

"Free will, Ilia. You know the Great One believes strongly in free will. And we must be patient. Sometimes love is long in returning to a soul, particularly after a severe trauma. And this time I am confident of success. This woman is different," Enzo said, his beautiful but inhuman voice almost passionate. "He has never lost his love of beauty, and it is with this that he may be redeemed."

Ilia made a rude noise.

"Now, now!" Enzo chided. "I truly believe that she will be able to mold his moods with her sweet murmurs, to shape his thoughts with her song. Why, I have heard her sigh and even that simplest of noises is one long-spun note of the purest music. It is enough to make any flesh-and-blood man long for a love larger than himself, to be the object of such a sigh."

Ilia snorted again.

"This one shall make him weave a garland of heartfelt vows and wear the wreath of love willingly," Enzo insisted. "I have never heard her like. The Great One outdid Himself creating her."

"A lover to 'take from me both my sin and myself?' " Ilia quoted incredulously.

" 'And leave no trace of myself in me,' " Enzo responded. "Yes, precisely!"

"All this with a voice?"

"Not with her voice alone, though it is truly an amazing thing—and you know how Domitien has always liked music. But she is also most conveniently

made in the image of the ones he most greatly preferred."

"Made in the image perhaps, but it will be but a
faint shade of those he pursued in the past. The Great
One simply does not make women like that anymore.
He took them away when he put an end to sublime
poetry and holy veneration through art."

"True." Enzo nodded. "But then, she must be made
differently. He did not fall in love with any of
those—even the titian-haired chanteuse. A pity, for
she would have been a fair match for him with that
fiery spirit . . . but then she wasn't ready to be anyone's great love. Her soul required much reshaping
before being returned to earth, and is still imperfect."

"I recall her. Everywhere she went she left that
horrid musky perfume and scarred hearts bleeding behind her. She was as bad as any plague—quite the
worst of all females. But then, they were all a bad
idea from Eve onward. What was the Great One
thinking? What is he thinking now? He is always so
secretive!" There was a long rustle as Ilia refolded his
arms. A single silvered feather from the being's wing
drifted over to Domitien's feet. The nearby doves
cooed sympathetically. "Still, if this is the Great
One's will . . . Yet I am not certain that beginning
this weaving with a newly modified soul is wise. They
are so fragile when they are still on their first journey
through a life. A soul with a little more experience
of Domitien's past and nature would do better."

7

"Never fear, this woman's soul is still at its core the one he once knew, and she did love him."

"Is it—"

"No, not precisely. That would be asking too much. It is one of the other incarnations that has been . . . strengthened. She is much changed."

Ilia digested this. "Yes. This life she'll start with clean hands and a clear heart. Hmph! Let me see this paragon and the form He has chosen."

"There was only one choice. *Hers*."

Domitien peeped around the cooing bush and saw the silvered Ilia and golden Enzo staring into the scrying glass in the center of the City's main courtyard.

"Ah. I see what you mean." Ilia's voice softened a shade and his complexion turned less steely. "An interesting choice. And she *is* lovely."

"Yes." Enzo sounded wistful. "If anyone can finally dissever Domitien from the wildness of his soul's careless youth, it is she."

"Perhaps, but still—she looks too soft," Ilia complained. "She is a trembling shade that commands delicacy. I doubt she has the strength to move a cold, hard heart like Domitien's, if he is of a mind to be stubborn—which he will be. She may very well be hurt by him instead. Again. Look at their history! We spent nearly a century repairing the damage from their last encounter, and it was not even a long-lasting relationship."

"Do not underestimate this bit of shade." Enzo sounded smug, and he ruffled at the neck and chest just slightly before returning to his habitual golden sleekness. "And she will be 'gifted' before he arrives. We could not send her soul to quest and face judgment if she was not prepared for the journey."

"If you say so. Great romances and their quests always were more your field of interest. Will she remember him though?"

"Not yet. Her memory was cleansed at rebirth. But in time she will recall. The Great One decreed it."

"It would perhaps be for the best if she did not remember. The past can cast a long shadow when it does not end happily."

"She must remember for she, too, needs to be saved. Her soul is part of this horrible tangle of Domitien's past."

"And what of him? What will he recall?"

"Everything," Enzo stated.

Ilia's tone was scandalized. "Is that not giving him an unfair advantage on the earthly plane?"

"He needs every advantage. He will keep his memories—those he allows himself to recall. And he will also retain his seraphic powers."

Ilia cleared his throat. When he spoke, his voice was appalled. "His powers and his memories? And the Great One has already approved of this?"

"Yes," Enzo said happily.

There came a pause as he considered the implications. "If he has his memories and powers, Domitien won't like being made an infant again." Ilia sounded pleased.

Enzo delivered another shock: "He'll not have to be. He needs a grown body if he is to meet this woman—she is already living—and the other in time. Conveniently, there is a soul about to be called back. Domitien shall be given that man's body and life. It is even the type he prefers, the icy blond whippet. It has his face and everything."

"What? Domitien's face was actually given to another?"

"The Great One allowed another to use Domitien's visage, yes. But now it shall be returned for its rightful owner's final visit." Enzo sighed. "Oh dear! That reminds me—I must summon Death and see he makes special arrangements for the soul switch. He won't be pleased."

"Amazing. You shock me. This is unparalleled! The Great one spoils him." Ilia sounded disapproving. "To make Death wait on Domitien's love life—it's unprecedented. And it will make the creature angry."

"Yes, well, Domitien's soul is amusing, and the Great One has a sense of humor. Sometimes."

"I think this venture would meet with better success if he were put into a somewhat less handsome form," Ilia persisted. "A little human suffering and humiliation would do him no harm."

"Perhaps. Though I believe he *has* suffered, being

cut off from the greatest of human experiences. Think of how every other soul he has met has failed to leave an imprint upon him. Not one of his lovers left so much as a smudge on his spirit. There has been no bonding. No love. Not with any being. Perhaps it is unprecedented to send him back with memories intact . . ." Enzo fluttered his wings once, then added to himself: "But whatever we feel, these are the Great One's instructions. Domitien is to be given this Edom Woolcott's body, and is meant for this woman, Laris, in this city by the water."

"Very well then. There is nothing more to say. Shall you tell him the news, or must I?"

"I'll do it. You lack the proper enthusiasm for the task. I wonder where best to start hunting for him. I had thought he intended to visit here today. . . ."

Domitien stopped listening and backed away on silent feet.

So, the Great One was matchmaking again. He got this way every century or so. It always resulted in Domitien or one of the other souls here being sent back to earth to fall in love.

Well, Domitien didn't mind going back to earth— briefly. It had been quite some time since he had known the pleasures of the flesh. The mention of love and its long-absent pastimes quite summoned to memory all the pleasant eras he had passed there. And it sounded like the Great One had chosen a wonderful playmate for him.

Now who could it be? Someone whom he had met before in another life. Someone who loved him— well, they nearly all had loved him, he admitted with a touch of complaisance. But if she was titian-haired . . .

It could be that minx Julia. Domitien was sure that he might eventually have fallen in a sort of love with her if he hadn't died in that stupid duel only a few days after seducing her—there had been the promise of whole kingdoms in that vixen's kisses. And he had certainly been a blond back when the Virgin Queen was on the throne.

Or there was Lucrece. Sweet, naughty Lucrece had been a redhead. He had fond recollections of her and his life in Paris. Though she had definitely come to a bad end during the revolution—quite a fluke, that, her falling off the wall at the Bastille during the liberation celebrations.

But Enzo had said that she was a songstress. That probably meant it was—*what was that ravishing creature's name?* The one in Italy with the demonic temper but the angelic voice . . . ?

Portia! That was who it must be.

Well now. Portia! This could be most amusing. Portia had been a most adventuresome lover, quite the wildest he had ever encountered. He recalled vividly her quivering coyness the first time he had tasted her—and the wound she had left on his back with her tiny dagger when she found him flirting with a rival later that day.

Domitien exhaled slowly and shook himself free of the dizzying recollection.

Portia seemed rather an odd choice for the Great One to make if He was intent on making Domitien fall in love, though. Domitien had been intrigued by her fiery sensuality—so rare in a woman—but hardly affectionate with her. It was hard to feel any gentle emotions with one who was insanely jealous or given to violent sentiments at the breakfast table.

Still, Enzo said that she was less temperamental now. And this woman had to be quite something if she'd made old Enzo sound excited. Domitien couldn't wait to get a look in that scrying glass—even if it did only show him a faint, watery shade of his soon-to-be playmate.

But, he worried suddenly, even if she had been remade in a softer form, was she so wonderful that she could truly 'take from him both self and sin?' Make him fall in love?

Domitien frowned.

That was a tall order. No woman had ever so distracted him, not since—

Domitien slammed the door on the thought and dropped a mental brace against it. He never thought about *her*. She was from *before*, the place of no memory.

He stood still, willing his breath to calm, his fists to unclench. Slowly, the chaos of the stray thought subsided and he was himself again, though less euphoric than he had been.

It sounded as though the Great One meant business this time. He must be in an awfully impatient mood to break the rule and send Domitien back in an adult body and not wait for him and his chosen mate to meet up in the fullness of time. Souls of lovers usually reincarnated together. And He wasn't even going to take Dom's memories before sending him back!

Also, there was this talk of the "other." It didn't make any sense. Why would there be some other soul involved, if this was about Dom finally falling in love? Surely he wouldn't be asked to join souls with two beings? Was not loving one person task enough? It had to be something less important. The other was probably just some minor failure—

Unless it was Rychard?

But no! It couldn't be. That bastard had had nothing to do with Portia—had he? Dom couldn't recall the first time they had actually met—perhaps in battle?—but it couldn't have been in Venice.

Either way, the seeds of madness had blossomed in that one long ago. Surely the Great One had returned him to the clay where failed souls were reworked into better molds. He would not be the "other" Enzo had mentioned.

Dom shrugged uneasily, pushing away the thought of his old rival, and began to wonder if he really could do what the Great One wanted.

He wasn't like other souls. His flaws had not been smoothed away in the forgetfulness between lives. For some reason, the Great One had never reworked the clay of his spirit. He was as he had always been—and that was a man who did not know how to give or receive spiritual love. Ilia was right about that. There had been no one who touched his soul—not friend, not lover. Certainly not a wife or child. There had been no constants, except the hated Rychard.

Dom looked into the distance with unseeing eyes until a small swirl of dove feathers twined about his ankle.

He shook himself from his shadowy reverie.

Failure was not an option. Not this time. That being the case, perhaps it would behoove him to help the situation along—just a bit. He could use the power of the scrying glass to remind Portia of some of the splendid times they had had together. Once he began sending her memories in her dreams, she might be able to open her mind to the past and recall who he was. Things would go a great deal more smoothly if he didn't have to retake old ground.

Of course, this was cheating: meddling with Fate's sphere of control and all. But it wasn't as though he was suborning the Great One's will. Far from it! He would simply be expediting matters.

The first step was to get a look at the scrying glass and find out which city by the water Portia was living in these days. Then he would show her Venice. . . .

15

Chapter Two

The seconds had checked the weapons over carefully, so there would be no cheating there, but Dorran did not trust Reese to conduct this affair with honor. There was only hatred in the man's tiny heart, and he would never have suggested pistols if he didn't plan on making this a killing affair.

And all this over Emilie! The chit had been bedded and forgotten a fortnight ago. Reese hadn't really wanted her anymore; the man had been a good way to forgetting her until Dorran had started making overtures. Playing at seducing her had only been a game for both of them, but the poor fool never had been any good at keeping things in perspective. Now there would be bloodshed.

Dorran grinned broadly. Something inside his soul

made him happy at this duel. As long as the man named Reese's blood got spilled, he was all for it.

Dom touched the deep scratches on his chest and looked out the window beneath the gothic arch in Ca'Grassi. It was impolite of him to neglect his guest—especially considering this was a memory he had conjured and was replaying, sending it to Portia's new incarnation in the world of the living—but in spite of his company he spent a long moment on appreciation of the view he hadn't seen in over two hundred years.

In the distance he could see the baroque roofline of the beautiful Scalzi where the last Doge of Venice was interred. Its classical lines pressed confidently against the blue of the heavens.

Closer at hand was the busy canal, its rippling waters painted gold and bronze and copper with afternoon sunlight, which would soon turn into a harbinging fire of rose and mauve that would paint the western sky with the brilliant warning of the approaching night.

Nearer still were a pair of lovely Cyprus doves, one appearing almost gold in its place in the sun and the other silvery gray as it sat in the ledge's shadow. Both birds were looking into the room with curious black gazes that seemed more intelligent than those of any true avian. They made him feel that he was under observation.

The scene in the bedchamber, he thought with a sudden grin, was very different from the pious ones to be had in St. Mark's Square. It was no wonder that the doves were curious. Let them watch. Perhaps they would learn something from him.

He turned to face the bound Portia. She was awake again and seemed fearfully delighted at her predicament as she stared at him from her position of horizontal captivity, hands tied above her head.

He approached her slowly, stepping over her brocade gown, veiled tricorn, and mantile. The garments had been stripped off in Dom's and their owner's first unseemly haste, and were now wrinkling in a careless puddle of green and black fabric. A few of the small pearls sewn into the gown's neckline had loosened during the struggle and lay scattered on the rug where Portia was now tied. The oyster seeds pressed themselves against the soles of Dom's naked feet, and as he trod carelessly upon them he thought briefly, and most unusually, about casting pearls before swine.

"Domitien," Portia whispered. Her earlier cries of passion and pleading had dealt roughly with her tender throat. Though it made her voice enthrallingly low and mesmerizing, Dom knew that he would have to free her soon so that they could eat and then continue on to the masquerade where she was to perform. However, they had an hour left. That was plenty of time to force a concession from her.

"My lovely Portia," he answered, smiling not quite

kindly, and enjoying the way that the cushion in the small of her back arched her into the air. Her breasts and belly were prettily embellished with small love bites. "What would you have of me now, my titian beauty? Do you concede defeat, or must we fight some more?"

Her voice when she replied was soft, but not soft enough. Her profanity was clear.

Normally, this would have been the opening act of some less than gentle coupling, something dark that Portia sometimes needed when the devil of strange passions rode her. But today Dom swore she would not have her way. He had other ideas of how to punish his prisoner for the marks she had inflicted on his chest.

He stopped long enough to pluck a plume of black ostrich feather from her cast-off hat, and then advanced on his captive.

"Domitien!"

She fought and swore as he tickled her breasts, the backs of her knees, and the soles of her feet. But the battle was against both Domitien and her bonds, and it was unwinnable. Finally, exhausted by her struggle in opposition to them both, she collapsed back onto her cushion, breathing heavily and sheened with perspiration.

Convinced by the languid expression in her eyes that the tigress was truly—if only temporarily—banished, Domitien ceased his torture and finally loosed her hands.

He waited, half expecting a last assault, but his exhausted captive did not attack.

He knelt between her legs and touched gentle fingers to her flesh, preparing her and anointing himself with her essence. It was an unnecessary precaution, a gesture only, for he knew Portia and she would be more than ready; passionate struggle always left her prepared.

Ready to plunge into her, he glanced up at the mirror mounted on the wall. There he saw another, slightly younger Portia gazing back at him with wide and angry eyes.

Laris could not explain her rage at this adultery with her lookalike—this *Portia*, as the man she somehow knew as Domitien called her—but enraged she was. Blindly, insanely jealous. Deep inside she knew this man was supposed to be hers, but he had betrayed her.

In her sleep, Laris frowned in confusion at her unprecedented thoughts. She fully realized that she was slumbering and dreaming unreal things, but that knowledge didn't help. It was like looking into a reflection of a reflection. The world was subtly distorted, but essentially accurate. She was unable to explain why her dream-self thought of this act as adultery, when the woman on the floor looked just as she herself did, but she *did* think it and feel it in her heart. It made her angry.

Adultery, that was a very old-fashioned word—and surely could not apply in any circumstance as she had never been married. And yet it seemed the right term for the moment. Domitien making love to this woman who looked like her—but assuredly was *not*—was disturbing.

Ah! But the situation was not half so disturbing as the man himself, she admitted in her subconscious. This beautiful, terrible creature heaved up from her psyche to make love to her double was causing reverberations all through her mind and body. No flesh-and-blood male had ever affected her this way. This phantasm that her subconscious seemed to know had a terrible but somehow familiar power over her.

As though sensing her perturbation and wishing to end it, the dream man looked her way. His gaze widened as if surprised to see her. He rose to his feet, abandoning the other woman, who collapsed silently into the disturbed linens and faded away.

Naked, he approached the window that stood between them and laid a hand upon the glass. After a moment's intense concentration, he seemed to push through it, and one of the multiple reflections shattered and then vanished.

Her dream man became more real.

Belatedly cautious, Laris retreated.

The man smiled, shaking his head as he stalked

21

her. He paced toward her with the ease of a cat, following her until he had her cornered at the edge of the room.

He reached for her slowly.

Come now! Why the coyness? he seemed to say.

Laris moaned in her sleep as invisible hands slid softly over her cheek and lips, urging her to let go of troubling thoughts and surrender to the enjoyment of the moment and the power he would have to transport her to some other place.

But that couldn't be! He was only a dream, and she could not trust a dream to guide her.

No, not just a dream.

For an instant, it was as though she looked directly into a real man's eyes as he towered above her. They shared a moment of silent communication, his thoughts obviously passionate and urgent, though the message he tried to convey to her perplexed brain was not one she completely understood. It was as though he were speaking in some foreign tongue, forming thoughts for which she had no language.

Too soon.

Then, apparently giving up communication for the time being, he buried his face in her hair. Without his gaze to anchor her she was cast adrift again, lost in stormy dreams, floundering helplessly in the white-frothed waves of a vulnerable and nearly painful attraction that had her all at sea. She floundered until the dream dragged her down into a place of dark and yet somehow familiar passions.

Her needs were not so abstract and strange in that place, though the sensual impulses that were traveling to her came from some unfamiliar byways of emotions that only lived in her sleeping brain. Though she had never consciously known it existed, there seemed to be a well-beaten path to this place of nearly mindless desire inside her.

Laris suspected that somehow it was all a mistake, not truly a place of her own creation but someplace in another's mind upon which she had accidentally trespassed. But that didn't stop the silent dream from unfolding.

The man named Domitien reached for her. The thin fabric of her nightgown did not slow him either. The ribbons were undone and it was pushed away.

Laris had a moment of vertigo and shut her eyes. She could feel the familiar nubs of her bedroom carpet beneath her feet and the cool air from an open window curling about her calves—but when she opened her eyes they said that she was standing on a marble floor in some exotic bedchamber, her body painted by the rays of a setting sun.

She raised a hand to the golden cascade of sunlight that flooded the strange room, but knew it was a miraculous impossibility, existing only in her dreams, for it was really the middle of the night.

"Domitien?" she asked, trying out his name. "Is this real? Are *you?*"

His smile was blinding as he took her into his arms and carried her to the pile of silken cushions where her double had been. He laid her down.

The sheets rustled. She knew she was in her own bed, knew the feel of the pima cotton sheets and the smell of the fabric softener, but the testimony of her dazzled eyes made the knowledge of her other senses seem a lie.

"Where am I?" she whispered. "What is this place?"

He didn't answer, instead soothing her with his touch. He didn't rush now. He stroked and caressed until she relaxed her knotted muscles and then finally moaned with a need that was impossible to conceal.

Yet it was all so relentlessly done, a part of Laris felt as though she were being rushed toward some unidentified end, compelled to passion almost against her will for unknown and possibly dangerous reasons.

The only thing that seemed to give her dream lover any pause was her breasts. Those he studied for a long, puzzled moment, touching them with gentle fingers before he buried his face against them.

"This can't be real," Laris gasped.

She smelled simultaneously the human perfume of arousal and also the scent of dew, the heaviness of atmosphere, which spoke of morning about to break in the real world. Of her life in Los Angeles.

Sensing it too, Domitien suddenly reared up and

pulled her legs about him. He laid a finger against her, stroking gently before he pushed his way inside. There should have been some shock or pain at this abrupt entry. But there was nothing.

She raised her hands. Her fingertips said there was nothing there but air, but her eyes told her that she was touching the ropes of muscle that were her dream lover's now unmarred chest. She raised her hands to his face, trying to wrap them in the pale silk curtain that was his hair, but she held nothing between her fingertips. The nerves in her naked fingers and palms began to cry at the trick and her disorientation grew as she came closer to alarmed wakefulness.

She tried desperately to finish the process, to wake from the erotic nightmare, but couldn't quite manage it. She was snared in this Domitien's world.

He wasn't made of flesh; even now his face was blurring, but he was in her mind. She could speak to him, but he couldn't answer. And he was on her body—in it. His hips hammered at her rhythmically, driving her to climax, but she knew that she was empty. She was as helpless in this dream as the reed before the onslaught of the wind, and it frightened as much as it aroused her.

"Help me," she pleaded with him—right before a strange ecstasy took her.

Laris awoke abruptly, flung from her erotic dream by the power of her climax. She sat up in *her* bed, in *her* room, breathing hard and aware that she was slicked with more than sweat. The aftershocks of fierce coital spasms were still coursing through her.

"Oh my God."

Laris shuddered, staring transfixed at the faint trace of dawn light stealing in through the pane, limning curtains that covered *her* tiny window in *her* apartment in Los Angeles. She had been right about smelling the damp of morning air.

After a moment she thrust back the covers and escaped from the sheets—cotton sheets, not silk—which, impossibly, bore the smell of sex and teased her passion-dewed skin with their clinging cotton folds.

Once standing, she was aware of the familiar nubbed carpet beneath her bare feet, just as she had experienced it in her dream.

Reluctantly, she turned her head. Over in the shadowy corner of the room lay her nightgown, just as *he* had left it, the ribbons at the neck untied and trailing forlornly on the floor.

As I left it! She scolded herself. *It was only a dream. That was all. I was the one who undressed myself and left my nightgown on the floor.*

Uncertain where to go to escape her uneasiness, she retreated to the bathroom to try to banish her dream with the traditional remedy of a glass of water. And then she planned to wash the terrifying, telltale traces of passion away. She would think about things more sensibly when all physical reminders of her dream were gone.

Once she was inside the bathroom, it took an act of courage for Laris to turn on the overhead light and look into the mirror above the sink.

She was relieved to find that it was only a harmless piece of silvered glass, reflecting the usual white tile and the towels that always hung in her bathroom. She looked like herself. There was no other woman. And no dream man reaching for her through the glass.

"This is very strange and scary," she said to her reflection as she approached the sink. Laris didn't mind speaking to her reflection because it was only an optical image, not that wicked, hateful Portia, and not some window into another world.

The thought made her frown. Looking at her body, flushed and damp, she touched her tender nipples once and then her reddened lips before letting her still shaking hand drop back to her side.

Who was that man in her dreams? And who was that woman who looked so much like her and whom Laris was certain she knew? The dream man had called her Portia, and that felt right. But what a strange name! It wasn't one that people commonly used these days. Why had her brain picked it?

And why distort her body into that creature? What was wrong with her?

She continued to stare at her chest, examining it as though she had never seen it before.

The dream man had noticed her breasts. There was one difference between the woman on the floor and Laris, and he had seen it: Portia's areolas were larger and colored like weak coffee. Laris's own were small and the pink of a dusky rose.

She shivered.

"I don't understand this. But it was just a dream! A dream." Laris sank down onto the edge of the tub, unmindful of the cold porcelain on her bare thighs. "I can't be jealous of a made-up woman."

There had to be some reasonable explanation for this nocturnal sensual assault. Maybe she had thought up this Portia so that she might indulge in reckless sexual behavior but not have the normal guilt that would go with it. She couldn't imagine truly wanting to have someone make love to her like that—who would want to be restrained by invisible hands, made completely helpless by a man she couldn't even feel?

But was that just the reply of her training? Political correctness as taught by a feminist mother and modern society? Might this not be some dream metaphor for the emptiness of her emotional life? True, it was not like her to be so indirect and to hide behind symbols, but everyone knew that repressed sexuality was a powerful force and could manifest itself in any number of ways.

Heaven knew that she had been under a great deal of pressure lately. Her schedule was grueling and she was always on the road, sleeping in strange beds, eating at irregular hours, and she had hardly any social life—and no love life at all. She was bound to her job, as shackled as Portia had been, and sometimes as overwhelmed. This was how it had to be if she was to finally attain her goal and find a permanent place with the San Franciscan Opera Company—something that was now within grasp. All she had to do was wow them tomorrow.

In any case, she could not deny that, whatever her rational mind's protests at his high-handed treatment, her body had eventually surrendered to this dream man's—Domitien's—urgings.

Perhaps it was that simple. She had denied herself too long. She had started late and after that first time, when she had loved the faithless Peter in that clueless, unformed way that was sometimes called puppy love, but wasn't anything so harmless when one was twenty-two, she had grown more cautious about staggering into relationships with men. She had learned calculation. And the math for the last several months—even years—had said no lovers. There had been no emotional or physical attachments in her life more demanding than owning a drought-resistant houseplant. Her career came first.

Her watch ticked softly at the edge of the sink, its second hand a reminder of passing time.

Laris stood up.

"I have a rehearsal in six hours," she told her sober reflection. "Then I have to leave for San Francisco. I need to get some sleep—the genuine, restful kind. Tell Domitien to leave me, *and Portia,* alone."

The last words were meant to be flip but they came out tremulous, and she saw that her eyes were more than a little afraid. She feared that the dream had done something permanent to her mind as well as her body. Going back to sleep was an impossibility. Perhaps a shower would cure that.

Feeling sluggish and stupid, Laris reached for the taps. She longed for a return of a three-digit I.Q., and prayed that she was once again in control of her unruly imagination, but down inside she was afraid that she had loosed a monster. Domitien, her creation, had her number now—and she had a feeling he would be calling on her again. Soon.

Chapter Three

They were still counting off the paces when a cry from Lucien warned Dorran that Reese was being his old faithless self and committing the dishonor of cheating at their duel. He tried to turn and fire first but was knocked to his knees by a blow to the back. He wasted his shot by discharging it into the air.

Disbelieving, Dorran reached up with his empty hand to feel the small hole where his heart used to be. Even as he crumpled onto the dewy green where busy ants went about their tiny tasks, he thought it peculiar that he should feel no more empty with his heart gone than he had when the organ was there.

Behind him, the surgeon's carriage horses began to rear and scream with all the hatred and energy that Dorran wished he himself had at his disposal. A smirking, pale-

faced man in a black frock-tailed coat came striding over the green, and a flood of memories washed over Dorran— glimpses of his own past lives ended in similar fashion by a similar foe. Reese. Rychard.

The frock-coated man didn't have his scythe with him, but Dorran recognized him as Death anyway. He said something obscene as the last of his life drained away.

Maeve, in reminiscence, was everything Domitien liked in a woman: long red hair, long legs, large breasts, which he had thought more than once would be fun to bite just a little. And she liked to be tied up with her own stockings. She was astonishing. She was ravenous. She was exhausting. And she was, he'd decided after some thought about his attempts to stir her memories through the last dream sending, possibly the soul that had been reincarnated to inhabit Portia's body.

And he was smack on top of her, mouth to mouth, groin to groin, when she managed once again to push past the recollection of their time together. It should have been impossible, that a living woman should control the dream he was sending her, but nevertheless, in walked the new incarnation of Maeve, or Portia, and his memory blinked out of existence like a candle beneath a snuffer.

Perhaps it was because he didn't currently have a body and couldn't experience arousal with anything except his mind, which was understandably out of practice in dealing with earthly matters.

Laris! That was her name now, he thought, vaguely irritated at having his tidy plans overset again. He hoped that she would not prove so difficult to control when they finally met in the flesh.

He sighed, rolled over on the now empty blanket where the dream image of Maeve had been cavorting with him in the Scottish Highlands, and looked into Laris's gray eyes, meeting her unblinking stare with one equally in command. He didn't want to be harsh with her, but there was no option except that he win this battle; so he made his hard gaze control hers, forcing first her eyes and then her labored breathing to still.

Dom admitted that though he had physical mastery over her dream state now, she still didn't look like a woman who was astounded at the extent of her blessings. She didn't even look appreciative of his efforts to give her back her memory. In point of fact, so far he had failed to stir any fond recollections in her at all. Her mind was completely closed to the past.

That was annoying too. Hadn't Enzo said that her memories were meant to awaken?

Dom wondered briefly if Ilia had somehow anticipated his plan and was blocking Laris's recollection. Surely it couldn't be that Enzo had been wrong and the Great One had paired him with a woman whom he'd never met!

"You aren't real," she informed him coolly, surprising him with the fact that she could still speak while he was controlling her.

Her words were infuriating, yet even in his irritation he noticed again that her voice was a golden river of harmonies, quite the most beautiful thing he had ever heard. He really had to get her to sing for him.

"You are a figment of my imagination," she continued. "And I don't know why you persist in bothering me with these strange bondage dreams. I don't like them." Her voice began to gain strength, and he could feel her pushing back against his will. "Why don't you ever take me to dinner, or bring me flowers?"

Dom thought about this while watching a blush finally move into her pale cheeks. He couldn't tell without looking deeper into her mind if it was embarrassment or anger that colored her. Of course, that didn't really matter. With most women any strong emotion could be quickly turned to passion.

The thought was appealing. He enjoyed seeing Laris with her prim and proper exterior peeled away.

"You don't like them? Not even a little? But how can that be, Miss Prudence, when it is *your* imagination that provides them?" He began to smile as his annoyance left him. Teasing a cold Laris to warmth could prove to be a vastly amusing pastime. And the hunt was half of the fun.

With a small burst of concentration, he made her

heavy nightclothes melt away and her braided hair unravel. The bit of mischief made him feel better and quite ruined her posture of scolding.

"It doesn't matter if this is all from my imagination. I am in control now, and I am telling you that I don't like it. I want you to go away and not come back until you have learned some manners," she said. "And next time bring orchids. They are my favorite flowers."

Then, suddenly aware that he had undressed her and she was now standing completely naked in a Highland meadow under a bright June sky, she spun about looking for something to pull on over her nakedness.

"You rotten cad!"

"Well, yes, I suppose that is factually true by the last century's Victorian definitions. But I'm not an entirely bad person for all of that."

"Henry the Eighth probably said the same thing while he was getting rid of his wives—and he was just as mistaken. Where are my clothes? I want them at once."

"Why? They are infernally ugly. You look like a nun—which you most certainly are *not*, and never were," he told her, studying her body openly. He decided that her slightly smaller, pink-tipped breasts were perfect after all. Really, all that he could find fault with was her disposition.

"I am not going to stand around naked and debate

this. Give me my clothes right now or I am leaving."
She actually stamped her foot at him.

He debated for a moment the benefit of denying
her clothing, but decided to be merciful this time. He
would try seduction and charm first. Forcing a woman
to bend to his will was both distasteful and the last
resort of a civilized man.

"If you must play at modesty, then you may have
a robe," he allowed, catering to her whim. The gar-
ment wouldn't hinder him. He made sure that it was
a very sheer sort of robe, more of a frame for her
breasts and belly than any real covering.

"Thank you," Laris said crossly, pulling on the bit
of silk that appeared on a nearby stand of heather
and trying to secure the slippery panels in place. It
wasn't easy as the robe had no ties or buttons.

Dom congratulated himself for being a gentleman.
And for being sensible even in the face of his annoyance. Short of putting her into a trance, he wasn't
completely certain that he could prevent her from
leaving if she wanted. She felt a lot stronger this time.
Perhaps some memory *was* waking up within her.

Also, at the moment he would have been willing
to wear a horsehair shirt himself if that was what it
took to make her stay put a while longer. He knew
that time for his advance seduction was short, and he
really wanted to discover what it would take to charm
her into remembering their past life, and reanimate
her fondness for him.

"You seem a rather forceful sort of woman. Perhaps you would prefer to tie *me* up," he suggested, rolling onto his back and lounging naked on the blanket, his eyes slitted against the sun.

"What?" Brighter color blazed in her cheeks. Dom decided to supply a slightly cooling breeze. As he recalled, there had been one that June day. Also, some cooing cushats, though he didn't bother to conjure back the doves' bodies; their soft voices were sufficient.

"I don't mind if you prefer to use me," he teased her, adding under his breath: "Especially since you don't have a knife or such a wicked temper this time."

"*Use* you . . . ?"

He gestured at his body, and utterly enjoyed the moment when her jaw dropped and her gray eyes got large. She did everything but sputter. It was the first time that she had really reacted to anything he said, and he was pleased to find this chink in her armor. All it took was the right flame and the moth would always come willingly to be consumed.

"I might enjoy tying you up at that," she finally managed to say. "Especially if it kept you safely restrained whenever I am asleep."

Dom laughed at her. Things didn't work that way, but he didn't consider it his job to tell her so. Besides, she was quite adorable in her naïveté.

Conjuring up a linen cravat, he dangled it like a lure.

"Then come here, my little songstress, and you may have your way with me. I don't bite," he lied.

Laris was aware of the intense sensation building between her legs. The strange arousal made her stomach and heart clench in a way that was nearly painful. It was entirely her own body doing it this time, she admitted. He hadn't touched her. But the tingle had started with his invitation to place himself at her mercy, delivered in that oh-so-reasonable voice. He was the pied piper's lethal tune, destabilizing her reason with his suggestions. Her sleeping brain trailed after his proposition like so many metal filings after a magnet.

His wicked, knowing smile didn't help either.

And why shouldn't she indulge herself just this once? After all, it was only a dream, a refuge even, where she could indulge in some recreational therapy.

And the last time hadn't hurt her.

"Come. You know you want to," he urged softly. " 'Tis bunting time. The grass is high enough to hide us. Come, let us be man and maid together. . . ."

But could she do that? Could she actually kneel, restrain him, then show herself? Parade herself? *Use him*? All with those ancient, knowing eyes of his upon her?

Yes, she decided, she could. Because it was only a dream and no one would ever know.

She was not an indecisive person in life and saw

no reason to be so in her imaginings. Hesitating only a moment to scan the horizon for possible witnesses, a concession to reason that she didn't bother to fight, Laris stepped onto the blanket and bent down to snag the proffered cravat from Dom's long white fingers.

Once again she couldn't feel the wool of his plaid or the grass beneath her feet, or experience the sensation of the strip of linen touching her hands. However, this time the lack of textural sensation was reassuring. It meant that this truly was nothing but a sleeping trance, a conjuration from Morpheus's world.

The man named Domitien obligingly held out his wrists and allowed her to tie him, and then to raise his arms over his head and secure him to a stout sapling. A part of Laris was absolutely appalled at her actions, but an even larger part of her wanted to rub her mouth all over his body, biting all the way down his stomach to his—

She had a brief thought that perhaps this idea was not entirely her own, but dismissed the notion almost immediately. Whose thoughts could they be, if not her own? After all, it was her own imagination that had dreamed this Domitien up, so some part of her, however deeply buried, must have always desired this.

Still, it was a strange and heady mixture of foreign feelings—fiery desire chased by equally fiery shame that raced around and around in her head and body. It made her feel both feverish and chilled.

She looked wonderingly at Dom's pale skin. He

had the lean perfection of a marble statue, but he wasn't so cold and lifeless. Far from it. He seemed to possess a superfluity of life. His almost glowing flesh promised to be as soft and smooth as warm butter, and looked sweet as cream.

Closing her eyes, she inhaled and lowered her face to his chest—

And fell through him onto a nylon carpet.

"Laris, you must keep your eyes open," he scolded, even as her lids popped wide.

Sitting back on her heels, she scowled at him.

"There are rules to this dream?"

"Oh, yes. There always are." Somehow the cravat and sapling had disappeared, and she saw that Dom was busy tracing a fingertip over the swell of her breast where it was trying to escape her insufficient robe. Laris watched his hands with fascination, so distracted that she failed to take umbrage at his next words: "You really are a fetching piece of baggage."

Laris wanted to argue about him freeing himself, but she was hypnotized into silence. She suddenly felt his fingers, and they were traveling up her throat to her lips where he pressed a thumb against them. Apparently *he* controlled what she could feel.

"Your pulse is dancing a wild jig. What naughty impulses were you having, my little nun?" he asked, shaking his head in mock disapproval. "You must really be a very wicked girl to want to tie me up."

Laris swallowed.

"Bring the cravat back," she ordered urgently, her voice not entirely steady.

"No. I think not. We may play that game later if you like. For now—"

"Bring it back," Laris insisted. "Actually, I want two of them."

Both brows arched and the man's thin lips quirked. "Two?"

"It is *my* dream. I want the cravats."

"Little nun, I have something to tell you." He smiled, his eyes sparkling in a slightly alarming manner. For one moment, he did not look entirely human but something otherworldly. "This isn't really your dream."

"Yes, it is," she said stubbornly, mostly because she needed it to be so. If it wasn't just a dream, then something truly frightening was happening—and she didn't want to be frightened. She wanted to tie Domitien up so she could be safe while she . . .

He shook his head, his silky blond hair sliding over his shoulders in a distracting way. She wanted desperately to fist her hands in it but feared that she would not be able to feel anything if she tried.

"I am in control of this dream. You are in my head and you have to do what I want. It is only polite," she persisted, her heart beginning to thunder in belated alarm and not a little frustration. She didn't feel desire often, and did not know how to react when it was thwarted.

41

"I *know* what you want, little nun."

This statement gave her pause. After an achingly long moment she asked guiltily: "You do?"

"Aye, if you are Maeve, then I know what you want. And it isn't to tie me up. Maeve was of a more passive nature. She liked just a bit of persuasion."

Persuasion. She didn't care for the sound of that.

"I thought you said I was Portia," she complained pettishly, pulling away and preparing to rise. Laris wanted to escape before the dream became a nightmare. "Do make up your mind."

"Well, perhaps," he allowed. "But I am more convinced that you are Maeve and simply haven't recalled it yet. You don't seem violent enough for Portia, in spite of your expressed wish to see me bound."

"You think that I'm Maeve," she repeated, watching his lips. "I can't be Maeve. What sort of name is that?"

" 'Tis Scots."

"I'm not Scots. I have never been Scots—"

"Enough! You don't recall yet *who* you've been. We can settle this quickly enough." The man called Domitien rose in a rush. Before Laris could escape him he had grabbed her about her waist, easily flipped her face-down on the blanket and lifted her by the hips until she was pulled tightly against him. Her robe had fallen away and there was nothing between them.

Flesh kissed flesh, and she felt teeth bite down through the hair of her nape.

From the animalistic position, he was clearly prepared to ride her belly to back.

Laris froze completely after the first gasp of shock, the blood rushing to her head and making her dizzy.

"Oh God! Stop this," she whispered to herself. "What is wrong with you—with me?"

After a moment her neck was freed, and she was allowed to sit up slightly. Dom sighed heavily.

"I suppose that I am to conclude from your reaction that you are not Maeve after all?" His hand stroked once down her belly.

Most oddly, she found it soothing.

"Um . . . I think not," she answered, staring straight ahead. But even as she said it, her muscles began to unknot and she moved against him, settling back against his groin where she felt she belonged.

Dom gritted his teeth while he tried to decide what to do. He had forgotten that this encounter would not end in satisfaction for him no matter what action he took. All he seemed able to focus on was that he was feeling tortured and thwarted, and that in any fleshly encounter there was no way he would have denied himself the rightful conclusion to this encounter if the woman beneath him made even the slightest gesture of consent.

"Very well, then, you aren't Maeve. I don't suppose

it matters at the moment. After all, you *were* someone I knew, and we *were* lovers. But I care to do nothing against your wishes. I need a plain yes or no before we go on, little nun. What is it to be?" he asked. His voice was rough, his hands on her waist both warm and hard.

Laris took a deep breath and then another.

"Yes," she finally whispered. "But don't call me Maeve ever again. Or Portia. I am Laris Isolde Thiessen. And in the morning I am calling a psychiatrist because this is more than weird. Obviously I need professional help."

"You will be busy in the morning. You are going to San Francisco," Dom told her, reaching around her to sink fingers into her red curls. "And I suspect that we both shall be very, very busy there."

Laris moaned.

"Why is it that I can feel it when you touch me, but I cannot touch you?" she asked plaintively, attempting to reach back and brace herself on his thighs.

"Because I'm not real," he said, slipping into her. The invasion was slow this time. "Not yet at least."

"No, you're not real, are you?" she agreed, a little sadly. Then she gave herself wholly over to Domitien's ethereal charms.

Chapter Four

Rhys had viewed his rival's taking of Jeanne's virginity as a form of vandalism. The property, once damaged, was apparently then unworthy of any consideration. Daracy looked at Jeanne's bowed head, her titian hair falling down to cover the disgraceful manacles of bruises braceleting her wrists, and knew a rare moment of shame. Her husband had done this because of him.

"You must help me, Daracy," she whispered. "You must go far away and never come near me again."

"I shall help you," he promised, his rage making his voice steely.

And he would help her. Jeanne would be a widow before nightfall. There was no other way he could save her from Rhys's endless retribution.

*   *   *

The lobby was gray, subdued, and tasteful, and filled with equally subdued and tastefully dressed people. On a sunny day it might even appear cheerful with its banks of angled glass overlooking the bay. But this afternoon there was a storm creeping in from the west and its giant clouds had just swallowed the last cataract of golden sun; they were busily blotting out the blue sky as they traveled east toward the mountains.

A number of birds had taken refuge inland, noisy seagulls, shrill starlings, and a mismatched pair of doves, which huddled together on the stony sill above the doors and looked longingly at the pampered trees in the hotel's atrium.

She was here! He could feel her.

Domitien, Edom Woolcott now, turned quickly from the darkening glass and scanned the lobby. It took only a moment to find Laris. Her slightly untamed hair and vivid green dress of raw silk were an antidote to all the tasteful austerity around them. Only her eyes were a good match for the muted lobby, because they were shadowed, and her expression suggested that she was listening to some secret inner music.

Dom shook his head. He thought that he had preferred women more exaggerated in bust and hips, but he had been mistaken. Everything about the more diminutive Laris was ideal—elegant, proportioned for grace, and consistent with his heated visions.

He wasn't, now that the moment of their meeting

was finally upon him, entirely certain of what to say to her. His projected memories of their past life—if either of the two he'd sent had in fact been one of her past lives—had gotten away from him, and he had ended up doing rather more than just sending her a few recollections to jostle her hibernating memory.

So powerful had their first encounter been that, though he had no corporeal body, he had had to cling to the scrying glass to hold himself upright when the ripples of her climax had shivered over him.

And the second had been worse. Or better. It depended on how he looked at it. There had been worlds of promise in that parting kiss given in that phantom Highland meadow. The longing for the real meeting of their lips had all but driven him to distraction in the time that followed. . . .

It was a bloody fortunate thing, he thought, with his new mind, which retained its previous owner's English accent, that his incorporeal being could not actually experience true arousal or satisfaction because he would have disgraced himself before the entire dovecote had it been possible.

As it was, silvery Ilia had been most suspicious of him and of his claims of using the scrying glass for impersonal reasons. He would never have agreed to Dom forging the sorts of bonds with Laris that would allow him mental control over her here on this physical plane.

Catching sight of Death in the hotel bar, Dom waved lackadaisically at the ancient creature and got a curt nod in return. No one seemed to notice him, the bald man in the blue suit who was reading the *San Francisco Chronicle*, but that was probably because he had his scythe inside his briefcase and hadn't had occasion to kiss anybody. Dom found himself thinking that the San Franciscans should be grateful the old continental manner of greeting had been dispensed with in their culture—though the Reaper needn't touch lips to lips with a person to do his deadly work. A cheek or forehead would do just as well.

At first, Death—who always handled Domitien's demises personally, and with unflagging zeal—had been inclined to take umbrage at the change of plans that put Dom into Edom Woolcott's body and left it walking about in San Francisco. But he and Dom had achieved an understanding through the years, and they were able to smooth over their differences while Edom's soulless body slumped emptily on a bench in Golden Gate Park.

Apparently curious to see the woman about whom all the fuss was being made, Death had obviously used his nearest portal to rapidly transport Edom's spirit across the river to the limbo where it would await reassignment, then hurried back to the city by the bay to witness the spectacle of Dom and Laris's first meeting.

Death sometimes had a drinking companion, the very alarming Fate. Dom looked about quickly to see if he could spot Fate with her spidery black hair, but there was no one about wearing her complicated dreadlocks, which weren't really locks at all, but people's fates woven into her ghastly tresses.

Dom, his pulse slightly accelerated and his mood uncharacteristically excited, could have done without Death for an audience. However, Death was better than Fate, and he was fairly confident that he had not lost in the last hundred-odd years the art of making himself agreeable to the opposite sex. He had even remembered to bring her orchids.

Reminded of his delightful mission, Dom turned away from Death and took a step in Laris's direction, prepared at last to inaugurate their meeting—and then stopped abruptly as he encountered a psychic trip line bisecting the floor. It was a faint thing, already dissipating like a contrail on a windy day, but a frisson of familiar warning danced over his spine.

Rychard! He'd know his old rival anywhere. The two of them had killed each other often enough for his aura of violence to be easily recognizable.

His euphoric mood temporarily destroyed, Dom turned slowly and scanned the lobby for his old foe. He couldn't be certain of what guise Rychard might now be wearing, but he had an atavistic apathy for a man with dark hair and a tan raincoat departing through the lobby doors. Wisps of psychic sulfur seemed to cling to him as he stalked for the door.

Feeling the weight of a not entirely friendly gaze upon him, Dom turned and caught Death's knowing eye.

He jerked a thumb in the departing man's direction and raised a brow. Death shrugged, but Dom caught the quick twist of his lips before they were hidden behind the newspaper, and it said that Death knew good and well that Domitien's nemesis was about. And the lack of warning also suggested that Death had no intention of being helpful in the matter.

"Bloody hell."

It was aggravating that Rychard should be here. However, as long as he did nothing to animate the man's memories—or find cause to quarrel—he and Laris should be left undisturbed. Surely there was no existing connection to the Englishman, Edom Woolcott of London, England, and whomever Rychard might be in this life. Edom's memories didn't show any connection.

Also, of course, Dom would make sure that Laris stayed far away from the perverse bastard. He didn't know for certain that she and Rychard had known each other in a past life, but it was possible that they had crossed paths before; and she was exactly the sort of erotic spark that could turn the man's latent but incendiary memories into an explosion.

Dom watched the coated figure travel outside and

down the sidewalk until safely out of sight, then turned back to Laris Thiessen. The lobby was getting busy with visitors returning from the day's outings or leaving for the evening's entertainments, but he caught a flash of vivid green standing at the bank of elevators, and he moved toward it with renewed purpose.

It would be best, he decided, that they meet, greet, seduce, and depart this city in as rapid a fashion as was possible.

Laris had been mentally rehearsing the death scene from *Tosca* and preparing for the moment when she must cast herself off the parapet when her reverie was interrupted by a faintly familiar feeling, which began as a fluttering in her stomach and spread outward rapidly to encompass her entire body in anticipatory unease and arousal.

"Oh, no. Not here! Not now!" she whispered, standing still.

But yes! And now.

Sensing the weight of eyes upon her, she turned slowly from the closed doors of the elevator to scan the hotel lobby. Though her rioting nerves expected to see Domitien, she still gasped in shock as her dream man actually came walking toward her.

He wasn't exactly as he had last appeared in her dreams; he looked more human and real. However, regardless of one or two minor cosmetic differences, she *knew* it was he. It wasn't often that you saw tall, thin, icy blonds that could serve as poster material for the Best of Denmark series walking about in the flesh. Not even in California where the beautiful people liked to congregate.

"Laris. Laris Isolde Thiessen," he murmured, coming to a halt directly in front of her. Three familiar words, her name, but they were fraught with both potential disaster and unexplainable hope.

Before she could recover either her breath or the power of speech, he leaned forward to kiss her cheek and said casually: "So good to see you again, my dear. I hope I am not very late."

Laris laid a hand against her tingling cheek and blinked twice.

Behind her, the elevator doors opened. The man she knew as Domitien took her numbed arm and turned her gently, urging her into the small glass box. He pushed the button for the sixth floor where the hotel restaurant was located.

"Domitien?" she whispered, as though afraid of revealing his identity to the balding man in the blue suit who had at the last minute climbed on board with them. Instinctively, she huddled away from the short, oddly unpleasant male, and Domitien assisted her by turning his body so she was shielded from the man's view.

"Call me Dom, darling. There's surely no need for formality at this point." The tone was mild, the ac-

cent charmingly upper crust and British, but it didn't
fool her for an instant. The hand on her arm was
sending low-grade shocks through her body and the
man's eyes were mesmeric in their beauty. This Domitien—this sexual fantasy incarnate—was about as
harmless as a heart attack.

I should run away from him, she thought wildly, *and
not stop running until I reach Brazil or a vault with steel
doors and armed guards.*

The elevator slowed smoothly and the doors
opened onto a world of glossy cutlery and crystal
vases filled with calla lilies. Her knees were weak, but
Laris could not blame her shaky legs and vague vertigo on the elevator. It was Dom, staring into her
eyes, who was making her dizzy.

As though hearing her thoughts, Dom placed his
warm hand again at her elbow, urging her in a less
than subtle manner to disembark from the elevator.
Too dazed to resist, Laris allowed him to escort her
toward the supercilious man in the gray Armani suit
who was either some minor potentate or else the maître d'hôtel.

"Mr. Woolcott." The man in the Armani nodded
his head, his cool expression changing to one slightly
more welcoming. "Your usual table is waiting."

"Thank you . . . Henri."

Dom's long, strong fingers urged her after the gray-
suited maître d', though their compulsion was unnecessary. Laris was more than ready to sit down

somewhere and have something to drink. The implications of this meeting were battering ruthlessly at her brain, and she didn't feel ready to face them until she was braced with some form of anesthetic.

"Jacques will be with you immediately," Henri assured them, deferring the task of seating Laris to Dom, since he was clearly intent on doing the job himself.

In point of fact, the efficient Jacques was there more than immediately, hovering politely until Domitien was also seated.

"And how are you this evening, sir?" Jacques asked as the trade-off with the man in the Armani was completed with nods and false smiles.

"Excellent, Jacques," Dom answered, his voice now only mildly accented.

"Shall I fetch the menus—"

"No, I believe I know what we'll have." Edom seemed to turn inside for a moment as though searching for some information, then recited: "We'll begin with shallot soup with the bleu D'Auvengue cheese. Then the fennel-endive salad dressed in lavender vinaigrette, smoked salmon with tarragon, and finally we'll have the roast duck—and bring us a bottle of that superb Rhone red I had last time. The duck is strong enough to withstand it, I think. And please put these orchids in a vase."

"At once," Jacques answered, not bothering to write down the order. He was apparently trained to recall all his regular patrons' wishes without such a vulgar memory aid, and he simply took the florist box and departed with a smile.

Laris was not once consulted as to her preferences, yet it didn't bother her because her brain was busy contorting like a ferret after its own tail and wouldn't have been able to do anything so mundane as focus on what to have for dinner. For the first time in years, she felt speechless and meek.

"What were you thinking about just now in the lobby?" Dom asked, his eyes meeting hers and somehow sending a blanket of smothering attraction over her incipient panic. "You looked as though your thoughts were millions of miles away."

"Just thousands," she said slowly, touching her arm. She wasn't imagining it! She could feel exactly where Dom had touched her. Rubbing where the outline of his hand was marked in goose bumps, she wondered if her cheek showed the imprint of lips. "I was in Italy actually."

The bald man from the elevator walked by their table, escorted by an obviously unhappy Armani. Though aware of his passing, neither Laris nor Dom looked up. Tension, attraction, and, on Laris's part, some fear, vibrated in the air between them, invisible to the eye but undeniable and powerful. It was like a lightning storm gathering itself for a discharge.

"Italy?" he asked, his voice and gaze puzzling her

out. "Have you some thoughts, some memories of Italy?"

Laris wondered idly if she leaned toward him whether she would actually receive an electrostatic shock. And whether it would be strong enough to stop her laboring heart.

She laid a hand against her chest in an oddly defensive manner. Dom blinked and then exhaled.

"Does the thought of the remains of Rome make you so very nervous?" he asked, looking down at where she had a hand pressed against her breast.

Laris fought to form an answer. It was difficult because she kept being distracted by her senses and their heightened awareness of Dom.

"Actually, I was thinking of throwing myself off of a building," she finally answered.

"*Throwing yourself off a building!*" he cried.

With an annoyed blush for her silly answer, she explained: "I'm singing *Tosca* tomorrow night at the gala. That's why I am in the city."

Her host sat back and, as suddenly as it had gathered, the electricity in the air began to dissipate. All that was left was a slight tingling that tickled the nerves without frightening her.

"Ah!" Dom's sudden smile was charming, alluring— and not as disarming as he no doubt intended. She remained convinced that this man was somehow dangerous.

"Tell me more about this, songstress. Tell me every

little thing about yourself. I wish to know your entire history from birth onward . . . and perhaps some of what came before, if we can finally discover it."

Jacques appeared with a cart bearing a vase of orchids and two bowls of soup. Though Laris would have preferred to eat in silence while marshaling her badly scattered thoughts, she found herself caught in Dom's gaze. The sight of her twin reflections looking back out of his eyes was hypnotic.

They are not windows to the soul, she thought, *but mirrors that turn my questions outward.*

Dom cocked his head as though listening to her, and then he nodded.

Suddenly, she wanted desperately to be a permanent manifestation in his eyes' icy depths, and this longing for a lasting place in his affections compelled her to answer his questions.

"I was born in Virginia," she began.

They stood out on the balcony of the restaurant and watched the fiery sun setting into the uneasy sea. The clean, cool air smelled of the cold Pacific and white places to the north.

Dom held her securely between his own warm body and the cold metal of the railing as though recalling her earlier words about throwing herself off a building. His arms caged her in a personal, intimate vise, but she was now unalarmed by the contact. Dom would never hurt her. She could tell he had traveled too far to find her.

She watched with dazed fascination as the vanquished sun dyed his pale hands a deep bronze.

"Have a care, little nun," he warned, his warm breath tickling her ear. He added: "We don't want to tempt Death just now."

"Don't you mean *tempt Fate?*" she asked absently.

"She isn't one to play with either," he said equally absently, with a glance over his shoulder at the room behind them. "But Death is a lot nearer, and every bit as perverse if not more so. He is also in a mood."

"I think *you* are the perverse one," she muttered, but without real heat. His voice seemed to keep her usually wary thoughts occluded, and leaning against him was without a doubt the most comforting sensation she had ever known.

"Perverse? Oh, surely not. At least, not yet." Dom shifted his feet outside of her own and rocked once against her bottom. One hand settled on her abdomen, urging her closer. Streamers of heat radiated out from his palm and set her body to pulsing in slow, heavy thuds that were a counterpoint to her racing heart.

Laris twisted and sent him a reproving glance, but he merely grinned at her, unrepentant of his semi-public misbehavior or for disturbing her relaxed mood. The expression seemed to say that he had done much, much worse in his many lives and would again, and she had best resign herself to it.

And that was all true, if her dreams were correct.

"You are missing the show, little nun. Watch now. I promise this sunset will be worth it. See how the birds flee? A storm is coming." He added softly: "How I have missed this. Sunsets are different here."

"In San Francisco?" she asked, though she already knew that this was not what he meant.

"No."

Obediently to the hand on her cheek, Laris turned back toward the sea. Across from them the windows in an office building went from shining crimson to flat black as the reflected light ran off them in a slow, glowing stream. Beyond the stunning cityscape, the sea continued to stir itself to a frenzy.

Hearing a plaintive cry, she looked up at the paling heavens. Wind tickled her face with insubstantial fingers and she inhaled the night breath of the ocean. Hawaii, Alaska, Java—they were all there, traveling on the wind that fanned the waves.

She watched the seabirds racing inland, and marveled at the creatures of the air that moved with so much more grace than any humans would ever have in their awkward mode of earthbound, bipedal travel.

Except Dom. She had to admit that in that moment when she had seen him walking—almost gliding—across the hotel lobby, he had looked like he was something more than merely human.

Suddenly, with a small sting of shock, she realized

that he *was* something more than merely human—at least part of the time. There was no other explanation. He could not have been in her mind otherwise.

"Dom?" she began, feeling again uneasy as something inside her rolled over and tried to wake. She began to shiver.

"Cold?" he asked, running his twilight-stained hands over her shoulders once and then releasing her so that he might slide off his jacket. An instant later it was folded about her, locked in place by his arms.

"You must not be afraid. All will be well," he reassured her.

"What . . ."

His scent rose up from the soft woolen folds of his coat and clogged her senses. Lingering body heat caressed her, breast to loins. Suddenly, primal urges were crowding out all other senses, making them costive. The ability and urge to converse entirely left her, and other compulsions overcame her questions. Yet she struggled against them.

Mutely, she turned in the circle of his arms, staring up at him with wide, slightly dilated eyes.

Dom glanced down at her, read her face, and then his own breath hissed inward, audible even over the sound of sea and rising wind. For an instant, he seemed surprised by whatever he found there.

"This is overkill, but you make it so difficult, my dear, when you fight against this. If you would only trust me and let this happen naturally." Then, look-

60

ing out at the sea: "I suppose that there will be other sunsets for us just as fine."

Laris nodded, not truly understanding and still incapable of speech. Her breath had been stolen and she did not know how to regain it.

Dom looked down at her again and smiled.

"You blush so prettily at nothing. 'Tis a lost art," he added whimsically, touching a finger to her flushed cheek. Then, seeing her eyes dilate and feeling her shiver, he asked: "Or *do* you blush at naught, little nun? What is Laris Isolde Thiessen really like? What does she want? Shall you show me everything tonight?"

Laris's flush only deepened. She felt helplessly tangled in some old longing that had lain dormant many years, but was now awake and spreading its net over her. It was not the want of a moment she felt, but of lifetimes. And a part of her, deep inside where she could still think, was terrified at feeling this mindless, relentless, and inexplicable attraction.

I'm frightened. I don't understand. Help me.

A small dove settled on the railing beside them. It was impossible, of course, but it seemed as if it whispered to her: *Don't be afraid, child. If you are brave, this time you can actually have him.*

Dom said, "Let's fetch your pretty flowers and then retire."

Chapter Five

How had she lived until now? She couldn't imagine how she had endured all the stifling strictures without the hope of seeing him. It still seemed unbelievable that he had noticed her. She was quiet, pretty enough in the way a wren is pretty, but not at all exotic or truly beautiful. But somehow he had discerned her worth, seen underneath her plain face. He said it was her humming that had attracted him, and so she had gladly sung songs for him while he carried her basket. He hadn't needed to. It wasn't that heavy with flowers. But he had insisted. . . .

She went to the garden every day now at sunset with her basket and secateurs, hoping to talk to him or at least catch a glimpse of him. One day he would even kiss her and then—

His laughter, soft and so deliciously disturbing to her

nerves, interrupted her thoughts. Happily, she gathered her skirts and hurried toward his voice. She was smiling as she came through the hawthorn and discovered him wrapped in Camille's naked arms.

He sat down on the edge of the bed, Laris draped across his lap in a living mantle that twined about him arms and legs. They hadn't kissed. Nuzzled, stroked, breathed in each other's sighs—yes. But a kiss, a kiss was one step from an exchange of souls, a great secret to be learned slowly—which was difficult when the other senses, fueled by passionate memories, were rioting and demanding they be fed at once.

Though he wished that he might linger the night, and even a day more, before sating his lust, his body's needs could not be allayed any longer. Conceding to his senses' demands, Dom slipped out from under the curve of Laris's stockinged legs, tumbling her flat on the thick brocade spread, and then rose above her on his knees as though ready to begin an especially devout prayer. He shrugged off his coat, unbuttoned his shirt part of the way, and pulled it over his head. It joined his discarded coat on the floor.

Laris reached up to lay a hand on his chest. In the dim light her fingers were as white as the moon, though not as cold and distant. Though he was not restraining her, she still didn't speak with anything except her eyes. But those were eloquent and passionate even when her lips were held mute.

He undressed her quickly, sloughing off her outer garments with methodical swiftness, but slowing appreciatively as he came to the underclothes she had chosen. It pleased him to find that she wore stockings and bits of silk with lace. He had sensed all along that she had a sensual if shy nature, but the tame nightclothes of her dreams had worried him with their prudish innocence.

He wouldn't have had any notion of what to do with a woman who was not by nature warm and passionate; he was more used to women who came with eyes wide open and arms unfolded.

The thought caused him a brief pang, and he momentarily regretted the influence he had exerted over Laris to bring her to his bed with such indecent haste. It was necessary to bind her to him, of course, but he would have preferred that she came wholly out of desire and not partly from coercion.

Could she be Julia? he wondered. Somehow the question of her past identity was not as urgent as it had been in days just gone by. Whoever she was in his past, she was Laris now: pretty, a bit reserved— at least for the moment—and touched by a divinity in music.

Slowly, he stripped the last of the silk away.

He stared avidly when her clothes and modest fears were finally gone. The pretty flower of her sex was swollen and undefended, a rose with its softest petals just unfolded. He would take care, he promised silently, not to crush it carelessly. She was in many ways like a rose just past budding, or perhaps a ripening strawberry—filled with the promise of summer—but sweeter and fairer by far than either of those things.

He touched her sex lightly, the stroke of a butterfly's wings, no more. But the caress made a slight catch in her breathing and forced wide eyes even wider. There were many notes of passion waiting to be played there, but softly—softly. He would not rush this passage and risk discord.

How she blushed! She was adorable. He saw now that she was not innocent precisely, but still fragile and new. What was he to do first with one so delicate yet sensual?

"A kiss," she murmured at last, reaching for him, her eyes fluttering closed. "Please."

Of course! A kiss. The first secret, perhaps the best. Dom considered himself a master of the art. His kisses were ascendant; women proclaimed him imperator, the palatine of this craft of mating lips and tongues. Yet, recalling all he did of his past triumphs, he was still surprised by what happened when their lips truly met for the first time: Startled to near clarity at the sudden reality of this first intimacy, Laris gasped and half turned her face from him. Her hands clenched, and she buried her face in his neck.

Dom shook his head as though to clear it after a blow, also moved by the power of their kiss. Then he reached back and pulled the tie from his nape. His hair, like streams of moonlight, poured over Laris in a white stream, closing them both into a private world.

"If you must hide, then hide in me," he murmured.

She did not open her eyes, but Laris sank her fists into his hair, holding on tightly as if she feared being swept away from him.

As startled as she at the effect of a minor brush of lips, he thought it seemed best to organize the next sensual assault. Dom prepared by taking her averted face between his hands and laying a restraining leg over her body. Slowly, he brought her lips back to his and resumed the kiss. Little by little, he relaxed his hold over her mind.

The salute began chastely. There was the faint stir of breath, a brush of tender flesh, a taste—that was all expected. But then came a tender sigh, musical as Enzo had predicted, and it serenaded him. He relaxed his own guard, allowing himself a moment of uncalculated appreciation, and in that moment something passed between them.

Laris felt it, too, and opened her eyes, her gaze still and questioning as she looked an inquiry at him.

But Dom did not know what to tell her. He was baffled. It wasn't souls that passed between them, as in an ordinary earth-shattering kiss. He had moved his soul often enough in such a way to know that transition in every form. Instead, something more powerful had passed from her to him, and something from him had gone the other way as well.

It was worthy of pondering, necessary even—but to be done later. In that moment, his body was fixed on rediscovering the soft flesh and wondrous releases that his incorporeal encounters had denied him.

His mouth moved on hers, no longer chaste, and this time Laris let him drag her out into the sea of passion and start drowning her in its unyielding tide. Her softer body pressed itself to his, gladly accommodating his harder form.

When they could bear no more, Dom's mouth left her lips to explore the rest of her body's wonders. He moved unhurriedly to her breasts and then, touching them at last, gave a muted moan.

"Ah, how I have dreamed," he murmured, feeling tremors run through her body and shake its delicate frame. But now he was awake.

Laris felt feverish and her throat was dry. Her breath came hotly. At first she had partly held back from enjoyment of Dom's caresses by a mixture of confused, foreign thoughts and a new, fearful reserve. It was not strange that she had been reluctant to allow this stranger to roam her body at will; what was odd was that his intense admiration had somehow managed to dress her nakedness so she did not feel shy, even though this man was so recently met.

And since she had not forbidden him, he tasted,

nipped, and dined on her at will. His mouth had described her geography with its velvet stylus, writing her wants on some invisible map. It was a tale of exploration that left her skin tingling and her muscles taut.

It was just as it had been in her dreams, only stronger—the difference between a breeze and a hurricane, an eddying current and a riptide.

And then he was inside her—measurably real and solid this time—and the righteousness of him being there was impossibly deep, a stronger desire than any other human volition and not mindful of caution or reason or fear.

Laris was swept along on the tide of his excitement, drawn to a point of pleasure that was near anguish. Carried as he was by the rising exhilaration, his hips moved in a relentless rhythm that reminded her again of the sea.

It was too rough, too swift, too elemental. She thought she could not be ready for the oceans to take her. Laris caught hold of him with hands and legs, slowed him to a less tempestuous pace. The frenzy was prolonged, but only by moments. Before she had time to whisper something of her joyous amazement to him, she was at the trembling crest beyond which there was no control. She fell toward oblivion. Down she tumbled into the ecstatic sea and drowned.

Yet even as she lost herself in the rising tide of the strongest passion she had ever known, a part of her mourned for something that was missing, something she had once had but somehow lost. Or perhaps this feeling belonged to Dom. It was confusing. This was a loss that was hers and yet not hers, and she grieved this missing something as one grieved for the dead.

Dom exulted. He found he liked being petted and stroked and guided by Laris's hands on this new journey to rapture. Though in that instant he would have done anything she needed to ensure her fulfillment— of course he would have—it pleased him to have her demanding and even controlling their union. Passivity would not do in these circumstances. She had to be an equal partner or there would be no chance of trust, no possibility of him losing himself in her as the Great One desired. Now he was going down for the third time and would not emerge until the tide washed him back up on the earthly shore.

When he felt her convulsing around him, he was able to let himself slip free of his moorings and to allow the tides of passion to rise over his head and expel him from safe harbor. Drowning for the first time in over a century was delightful. In fact, it was so delightful that he forgot to keep control and his feelings washed out over Laris in a smothering wave.

He saw something like fear move in her eyes and immediately reestablished control.

* * *

Coming back to herself in the quiet aftermath of the storm, Laris lifted her face from the curve of Dom's neck and spoke for the first time since he had entered her. Her voice was hushed.

"Are you by chance an athlete?" she asked, uncertain of what else to say. Miss Manners had not covered this in her column, and more specific questions did not seem appropriate when she was lying on her lover's nearly concave abdomen and he was still actually nestled within her.

Dom blinked lazily and then seemed to search his memory. His lithe body, though packed with muscle, did not tense as he considered her question.

"I believe that this time I play tennis and polo."

"Ah." *This time.* She returned her face to its hiding place because it felt safer there. For a moment she counted the slowing beats of his pulse.

"Who—what do you do?"

"In what context?" There was amusement in his voice.

"For a living?" she asked from her dark corner.

There was another pause and then he answered seriously: "I own a brokerage firm."

"Oh."

"Does it matter to you what I do?"

"I . . . no. I don't think so." She sighed.

Laris understood that this encounter was not a dream. Nor had their encounters from last night been. Not precisely. Her brief glimpse inside Dom's head during his climax had been too revealing. She could not take mental refuge in that delusion any longer.

But it was a difficult step to accept that she and Domitien had, as he seemed to believe and kept hinting, actually been lovers in another life. None of the things they had done together—wild and strangely wonderful as some of them had been—had sparked a single memory.

Almost, it would have been easier to believe that he was some sort of hypnotist or psychic, and that it was only a contemporary connection that bound them. One could think in terms of decades. Centuries and millennia were harder to grasp.

Of course, whatever the strangeness of their situation, she had been granted her most fervent wish. She had finally kissed him, flesh to flesh, and felt the lips that had, until then, only been phantoms that haunted her dreams. And in that kiss had been both sweetness and cataclysms. There were no clear memories of a shared past, but there were reverberations abounding in her now that would surely haunt her from this day on. Something had awakened. It was that kind of kiss: one that would be felt for hours, even days, maybe lifetimes after it was over.

"I think that I'm getting nervous," Laris muttered. "And about time too. I don't know what's the matter with me. There are so many things I should be asking you."

71

"Yes. But sleep now," he said gently, rolling them both onto their sides and finally removing himself from her body. "Tomorrow shall be a busy day. We'll worry about everything else after your performance is done. Perhaps by then I will have more understandable answers for you."

Laris pressed her thighs together, feeling empty now that he was gone. It occurred to her, though without the expected alarm, that they had not used a condom. The tide of desire had for the first time in her life swamped her from the soles of her feet to the inner reaches of her brain.

She wanted to do what Dom asked, to sleep. But there came a distracting fluttering at the window, heard above the sigh of the wind, which had been forbidden entrance there and was intent on making complaint at the balcony door.

But it was not the wind that entreated so. It was a shiny white moth, Laris saw through slitted eyes, battering itself to death on the cold glass, trying vainly to get at the small light burning on the table.

Laris shivered suddenly. She understood the moth and was dimly distressed for the poor creature. The moth would do anything to get at the light, the heat. It didn't care that the flame would consume it, or that it would be destroyed if it persisted in its quest. It would not stint its zeal, for it was made mindless by its attraction. And so it would be hurt. It would probably die.

72

"Poor thing," she whispered.

Dom stroked his hand down the curve of her waist, banishing most of her worry with the slow sweep of his warm palm.

"You need to sleep, love."

"I can't," she answered slowly, staring at the moth's iridescent wings, but with less alarm.

"You can. Sleep now, little nun," he commanded, and Laris immediately felt her eyes grow heavy and the last of her alarm drift away.

Was it midnight? Nearer dawn? They were still in San Francisco, weren't they? She had no sense of time or place, or even purpose. Her thoughts refused to order themselves, and even her memories were jumbled up with strange dreams. She had lost reason from the moment Dom took her arm at the elevator and kissed her on the cheek.

Laris closed her eyes and gave in to exhaustion. Her last thought was to wonder if love was like a soul—whole in itself and only waiting for the right place to alight. And if it was, had love actually settled within her?

At first they had lain in a sleepy pile—blankets at the peak, then Laris, then Dom at the foundation— enjoying the lingering penetration of her body. But she had not been able to sleep that way, and she needed sleep desperately after the violence of the passion that had passed between them. So now they were tucked on their sides, nestling like spoons with Laris's head sharing his pillow and their bodies pressed so close that Dom had no choice but to drink in her scent and feel her heartbeats as she drifted toward sleep. He wrapped himself protectively around her curves, and tucked one hand over her auburn hair.

Dom felt neither passion nor triumph. He was, instead, thoughtful. He was not used to this lingering in a lover's arms after sex. He usually remained with a woman only as long as good manners demanded, and then fled from her because he did not care to examine the confusing tangle of disappointing and sometimes shaming emotions that came after the rush of climax. But this time he stayed. This time, he had to. This time, lust's triumph was not honor's funeral. The Great One had decreed it otherwise.

Bemused at finding himself in such a situation, Domitien rose slowly onto an elbow and looked down at Laris. He studied her avidly as she slept. Something about her—her voice, her face, perhaps something deeper—demanded a response from him. Even when she was given to Morpheus, she called to him with urgent thoughts. The languid fall of her vivid locks upon the pillow, her soft respiration, the arches of her torso where it flared out at the breasts or the delicate hip with one long leg slightly more forward leaving her sex unguarded—they all said something important, were part of some design, but he did not

74

yet understand the language in which the signs were written. He was certain that he had known it once, but through the ages had forgotten how to read the symbols that were woman. Laris was a riddle.

She was, he realized, a maker of magic stronger than that of mere desire.

As he watched, the strands of her unbound hair that had drifted over her face swayed gently, moved with each soft breath that passed her kiss-reddened lips. The movements were a slow fluttering of human silk whose threads had the brightness of a candle's flickering flame.

Gently, he pulled the wayward strands aside and then placed his own face in her breath's intermittent stream, letting her warm and sweet exhalations wash over him. He could detect faint traces of red wine and something else in her breath stream. Passion? Longing? Whatever it was, it had been contained and concentrated in that kiss.

Dom leaned back, his brows knitting. That was a rather romantic thought, not at all like him. He was suspicious of Romance, of Love itself. Poets had made these two celebrated individuals. They placed them above kings, gave them their own identity, made them gods even. And they could, for some, take on a divine life of their own and eventually overpower all reason. Dom had always, for as long as he could remember, had an aversion to them—an ancient antipathy that seemed to precede deliberately any conscious decision he made about his life and affairs. Yet . . .

He was aware that sometimes a part of him knew a loneliness that had nothing to do with his body, and sometimes, when he drank enough, he and this hidden loneliness would sit together lamenting . . . *something!* He had had *something* once, and somehow or other lost it. He'd lost even the memory of it. But a part of him recalled what had once been there and longed to have it returned so he could again be whole.

Finally he shrugged off the thought.

Whatever Enzo thought about him now being "wise enough to be separated from the thoughtless passions of his soul's youth," he still did not believe in the kind of love that endured even when the hair stained silver, the body grew heavy and slow, and the skin creased with age. He had never lived long enough to see it—had never wanted to live that long.

He wondered what it would be like not to pass from day to day, from life to life, with no earthly master other than passion. What was there to fill the long days when there was not such fickle amusement available, when idle dalliance was not enough?

As though sensing his restless thoughts and wishing to escape them, Laris sighed and snuggled farther away and into her pillow.

Dom looked down at her and wondered about the landscape of her dreams now that he was not there to direct them. Or *was* he there, though not intentionally, even now altering her life's natural course? Might she be dreaming of him that very instant, missing him? Wanting him?

The thought pleased Dom. He found that Laris's mind was very much like the bag—the *purse*—she carried. There were many thoughts packed into a compact space, organized to some pattern that he did not understand but found fascinating. He found himself wishing that he could study her mind as well as her body, and linger over her dreams as an epicure might over a splendid meal, or an artist over a brilliant masterwork.

Perhaps later he might eavesdrop on her thoughts or walk through the landscape of her dreams. For now, he needed to follow his own advice and sleep. Rebirth, though this time not from a womb, was still exhausting. Controlling Laris's initial panic and resistance, learning about his new body and its life and preferences had also been draining. He had to replenish.

Of course, he should be worrying about Death's lingering presence—and that bloody beast, Rychard. *But suffice it unto the day the troubles therein*. He would deal with these things tomorrow.

Chapter Six

Oh, precious time! How swiftly it ran from her. Usually, when she was employed in some mundane task, it was troublesome in its slowness. But when she wished it to tarry so that she might have longer with him, it dressed itself in fleetest wings and fled.

He didn't love her, of course. How could he when the maddening Lucinda and Clare were nearly always there to distract him? But he did like to converse with her. He said she enlivened the dull conversation of the others at this interminable house party. After he had told her this, she began praying that he didn't grow so bored that he departed.

It was perverse, but she was almost glad that Lucinda and Clare were there. Perhaps he would stay for them.

And if she was very careful, no one would ever guess how she felt about David.

Passions grown violent soon died. The poets said so—and she wanted to believe them, for this had been a sweetness that was near to agony. It had to end soon or she would be the one to die of a broken heart.

They stepped out into the lobby. Laris immediately noted the same balding man who had been in the restaurant the night before, and she found herself frowning as she would at a wasp. He was a most peculiar-looking creature. His face seemed tacked rigidly in place—a mask incapable of pleasant expression—and though short in stature, he somehow managed to exude an air of menace.

However, she would not let him spoil her mood. She was connected to destiny and could almost see the future. It was as though her eyes were opened wider than they had ever been—and perhaps they were. She felt wonderful this morning, fizzing like a shaken tonic, and she knew that she was going to give the performance of a lifetime tonight. Her *Tosca* would go down in San Francisco musical history.

Normally, she would have been tense, her nerves so taut that they were a torment. But not this time. Today the planets were aligned. God was in Heaven, and Dom was going to be there to see her at her very best.

Laris glanced over at him again and felt herself color. There could be no doubt that a large part of her strange euphoria was due to him. He might have started as a man of dreams, but her reckless happiness and the small tenderness in parts of her body were a testament to his reality. It was as though he had somehow filled her spirits with helium, made her a gift of mind as well as body.

But that was silliness, just some more pleasant form of lingering illusion from last night, when too much wine and excitement had caused her to imagine things. Sex, no matter how wonderful, could not alter one's whole perception of the world. This was adrenaline and nerves, caused by the approaching culmination of all her years of work and planning.

Dom smiled at Laris, reading her mind not from eavesdropping on her thoughts but from the blush in her cheeks. He had learned that she often blushed at nothing, but this time he was certain she was remembering her wanton behavior of the night before.

She had slipped out from under her dreams and woken him by molding herself against him and murmuring naughty things in his ear with that beguiling voice. He had tried stroking her passionlessly, urging her back to sleep. But it had not been effective because by the time he was coherent enough to speak, his own body was coming awake—stirring itself to greedy attention. And once she had felt this, she had been persistent in her teasing, ignoring his repeated and steadily less stern warnings that they needed to sleep.

But the fact had been that he could not make his tone very severe, for in spite of what was sensible, he wanted to do exactly what she wanted. So he had cracked open an eye and consulted the sky to see if it was anything approaching a reasonable hour. The moon had set. He generously, if somewhat mendaciously, put the time at four A.M. which meant they had had at least three hours of sleep.

"It's the middle of the night," he had complained for form's sake. "Nuns should be fast asleep until dawn."

Laris had only giggled. He hadn't heard the sound before, and found himself charmed out of exasperation by the happiness it contained.

"We really should rest awhile longer," he had said for the last time, running fingers through her hair and then down the pale column of her neck.

Laris's answer had been a small noise in her throat and to reach back with a teasing hand.

He had surrendered then, but on terms. He kept her tucked in like a spoon, only draping one leg over his hip. It was the height of laziness on his part—but damn it! It was almost dawn. He had had an exhausting night and was facing an equally exhausting day, and it was no time for exuberant love play. Besides, she shouldn't be rewarded for resisting his command to sleep. That way lay madness. It was imperative that he remain in control until they were well away from Death and Rychard, and she was completely infatuated with him and would do what he asked without question.

"Dom?"

When she would have tried to turn and face him, he laid a hand on her belly and urged her close. A slight thrust and he was in.

The muscles had rippled beneath his hand, and she stiffened a bit, her voice catching. Recalling her reaction the time he had taken her from behind in a dream, he waited in stillness for a moment to see if it was displeasure or arousal that caught at her breath.

Then she had shivered and clenched around him, and he had had his answer.

He had moved very little at first, letting her squirm and clench and wriggle helplessly for a while before giving in to her pleadings and allowing his fingers to slip down her abdomen and into her curls.

Dom almost laughed aloud at the memory as they left the hotel. He really would have to stop calling her his little nun. No description could be further removed from the truth.

All San Francisco real estate was expensive, but the jewels that crowned her shaky hills were some of the most costly and beautiful gems in the world. The War Memorial Opera House was located at the corners of

Van Ness Avenue and Grove Street across from the Civic Center, which was only a short walk from their hotel. Laris had done some reading after looking into the cost of housing, and she knew that the place where she would perform tonight had been built by Arthur Brown Junior, the designer of the equally magnificent Coit Tower. It contained the same grand, soaring qualities of all great buildings that knew they were landmarks and would last for eons. She adored its gilded arrogance.

The interior was likewise beautiful and aware of its exalted status. Laris smiled up at the ceiling. The hall even wore a diadem to proclaim itself as the queen of all theaters: The broad stage and audience were both overhung by a polished chandelier made of crystal, shards of pure frost suspended in midair fourteen stories above the orchestra. No royal crown on a blue-blooded brow was lovelier.

Laris noticed that they had not stinted on the gold leaf either during restoration. Fort Knox had surely been depleted by the refurbishing of this old house. And this grand abode was to be her home! She was quite certain of it. This theater would not ignore her, nor would the people. She was *wanted* here.

Laris smiled in growing excitement. It was the perfect place to make operatic history. And Dom would be here to see it! At that moment she felt very rich in intangible things.

Her eyes were shining bright as the moon when

she went to meet the musical director and, though it was not meant for him, she charmed him to near senselessness with the joyous passion in her voice.

Night had finally arrived. Excitement floated on the air where it was inhaled and then multiplied by excited hearts before being returned to the atmosphere in concentrated form. Dom swept his opera glasses over the crowd, enjoying each person's intense reaction to Laris even as his mental unease grew.

He had been at the opera house all day. He'd been there for her rehearsals—and to feed her lunch, though she protested the meal—and he had been frankly stunned by what he heard. Even without the excitement of the crowd to encourage her, her voice had been so sweet as to stop the damned in Hell from moaning. She had most certainly been given a divine gift, a unique one. What was it his friend, Byron, had said in that poem?

The devil hath not in all his quiver's choice
An arrow for the heart like a sweet voice.

And with an audience to lift her, Laris had surpassed human magnificence. She was all graceful curves and fire burning on the stage. Her body as well as her voice had been trained to expressiveness. She merged herself completely with the rhythm of her role, telling the tale with body, face, and voice. Music, like the soul, was intangible. And while one could not paint a soul, or sculpt it, somehow it could be found in music's fleeting pleasure.

The audience was realizing this, and the well-dressed multitude was as enthralled with her face and voice as Dom was.

He wanted to resist the pull for it had the potential to outmatch his passionless logic and duty, and in his distraction he might fail to see danger creeping up. But for a moment he allowed the subordination of his mind to his heart. After all, it wasn't every night that one heard a soul. And it was Laris's night of triumph. He was grateful that he was here to see her share it with the world.

Ah, but what none of them know is that the rest of her is every bit as entrancing as her voice, he thought with a trace of smug pleasure. They might guess it from the ardor of her song and the fire of her un-bound hair that seemed to have a life of its own, but they hadn't seen her—*touched* her—breathed in her sighs directly from her lips. Their glimpses of her passion were all pale reflections of the original: counterfeit memories, facsimiles without genuine life.

Enzo and Ilia had been wrong about Laris being a diluted form of some earlier presence. She was a power so concentrated that she could move eyes and hearts and souls to tears.

It was difficult to break away from her spell, to concentrate on anything other than her song, for Laris had drowned out his earlier sense of disquiet.

But there was no evading duty, and Dom continued his visual sweep of the auditorium, arresting his progress only when he saw a half-familiar face in the box across the hall.

Death! The creature was being most persistent in dogging them. Laris had even noticed him that morning, and Dom could see that she had instinctively disliked having him near. If he was not careful, Death's presence might trigger her past memories of decease and frighten her again. Really, Dom hated to spoil his sport but it was time to see about getting rid of him. Surely there was some distant war or disaster that needed Death's personal attention. Perhaps Dom could find a way to speak to Enzo about it later that night.

Annoyed and still disquieted, Dom moved his perusal on to the next box. There he checked a second time. A cannon shot of alarm blasted through him, making him clench his hands on his fragile opera glasses.

Rychard! There was no question of the man's identity. The face was subtly different, the hair a shade darker, but Dom had encountered this scoundrel a dozen times throughout the centuries. He knew his enemy.

Dom said something obscene that didn't accord well with the sublime music rising from the stage. He couldn't very well remove Laris from the theater mid-aria, but he wanted to. Rychard's avid gaze in and of itself was enough to besmirch her.

And he would never stop with just lusting and admiring from afar. He and Dom had played this act out, life after life. This licentious blighter always coveted or destroyed whatever was Dom's. And this time the prize was very fair indeed. Rychard would never be able to resist her. Too, there had been many times in the past that he had only been half sane. Dom knew that he was always wholly capable of violence.

Dom also knew from experience that the Great One did not temper the wind of chance to suit his newly shorn lambs. Laris's innocence would not save her from Rychard if her sacrifice was arranged by Fate.

In fact, Rychard's presence might be why Death was staying so close to them. Perhaps Death anticipated that, despite the Great One's hopes, this life would end as all the others had; and he was waiting happily for the moment of violent bloodshed to begin. How would things end this time if Rychard and Dom again fought? Dom with another hole in his chest? Rychard hanging lifeless on the end of a blade?

No. Dom would not die this time. There was too much at stake. If Fate had plans, she would simply have to change them.

Dom turned back to the stage. Laris was standing on the castle wall, swearing that she would see Scarpia in Hell. He had heard it already that day, but gooseflesh still rose on his arms.

And then, with a last cry that pierced even as it uplifted, she was gone. The curtain came down soon after and the audience broke its trance. Usually decorous, the crowd cheered as well as applauded. They had been transported to some divine place and knew it. Bows were taken. The diva was honored with a sheaf of roses. Up in the chandelier, two out-of-place doves were actually disturbed from their restful postures by the hysterical reverberations below.

Even Death sat stunned and applauding.

As much as Dom wanted to witness all of Laris's hour of triumph, when Rychard left his seat, so did he. There would be no meeting between Laris and this brutalizer of women, not even if it meant killing the man preemptively. The Great One would not approve of murder in cold blood, and it would be an act of human dishonor, but Dom was not about to chance this new incarnation of Rychard getting his hands on Laris.

Onstage, Laris smiled at the audience, but she didn't see the applauding crowd. The lights caught and reflected in the chandelier and were too bright to allow clear sight. Instead, her head was filled up with an image of Dom. She didn't stop to question why his black tux had been transformed into a skirted coat of burgundy brocade and why his tie had become a cravat seated with a large diamond pin.

Something tugged at her attention as she sank into

another curtsey. She turned her head and found Dom waiting in the wings. He was applauding, saying *Brava!* Or that was what it looked like. Laris curtseyed once more, clasping what she hoped was a bouquet of thornless roses to her bosom. Then she allowed herself to be led offstage by the conductor.

Dom kissed her cheek, pride showing in his eyes even as he took out a handkerchief and wiped the heavy makeup from his mouth. Laris touched a hand to her cheek, wondering if he read her amazement that even when his lips were gone the sense of his kiss stayed.

Dom allowed her a few words with her fellow players, but when she would have gone to greet her admirers who were gathering in the wings, he shook his head and guided her quickly to her dressing room.

Frowning, and suddenly ill at ease, she put down her bouquet on the dressing table and waited for the door to close before asking the reason for her hasty and rather impolite departure.

Dom studied her for a moment, clearly knowing he had snatched away a part of her happiness and euphoria, then answered her unspoken question.

"There is someone from my past here tonight. I do not believe that he has recognized me. But he is very taken with you . . . and that is not a good omen."

"You don't like to share with your business rivals?" she guessed. Then she chided: "But that's silly. And, Dom, that is part of my job. Why, he's probably a patron. Most everyone here tonight is. I must go out there and be polite."

Laris took a deep breath and added: "It's important to make a good impression, you see. I should like to settle in one place—here, if they'll have me. I am so tired of being a gypsy. I want a home. That means I must show that I belong here. There are a hundred other girls with voices just as good who are ready to take my place if I don't suit them."

Dom's face softened, and when he answered, his voice was kind and reassuring.

"I understand. And I will normally share you gladly with your admirers. And they will all tell you that you are silly to worry about anyone ever taking your place. But, little nun, this man is dangerous. Not sane. He is a user of women, and a murderer. He may have hunted you in the past. Until we know more about your previous lives and how he knows you, we have to be careful. And he hates me. You need to be wary of him." Dom paused and took her hand. When she only stared in consternation at his allusion to their past incarnations, he promised: "We will find a way for you to talk to your coterie. There is a reception to follow, isn't there? I simply need a moment to speak to the guards about keeping Rychard from you—they call these people 'stalkers,' yes? I'll deal with that while you change your gown, and then I will escort you to the reception and you may charm your audience at will." He paused. "Please do this for me, Laris. I must know that you are safe."

Dom waited, tensed and apparently prepared to do something if she did not agree.

The dresser tapped on the door and entered before Laris could reply.

"Promise me, Laris," Dom repeated. His tone was gentle, but the request urgent.

"I promise."

Dom bowed slightly over her hand, a betrayingly old-fashioned gesture to anyone who suspected the truth of who he was, and then slipped out the door. The dresser, an older woman, smiled benignly and nodded her head as he passed.

"You can always tell the ones that work in the theater," she said with a sigh. "Makes you wish you really lived a hundred years ago, doesn't it, back when they still believed in grand gestures? Bringing ladies flowers and jewelry—those were the days!"

"Er . . . yes. It does sound rather splendid," Laris agreed.

The woman sighed again, and then shook herself out of her fantastic daydream.

"Well, let's start getting you out of that heavy thing. Those gowns weigh more than armor."

Laris allowed the dresser to help her disrobe, her thoughts now as distracted and as wary as Dom could want. In the thrill of performing she had somehow forgotten that Dom was anything other than simply her new lover. His words about a rival from an old life were as bracing and unwelcome as a plunge into an icy sea.

Unable to help herself, Laris shivered. Her imagination, usually not so prone to melodramatic visions, suddenly provided her with a villainous form. He was shadowy, caped, and had midnight-black hair. His face, what she could see of it, was beautiful but cruel. His eyes were not quite human, not quite sane.

"Here, put on this robe," the dresser urged. "You would have thought that they'd have done something with the heating when they were fixing the place up, but the rooms are always either boiling or frigid."

Laris took the robe with a murmur of thanks. She didn't explain that it wasn't the room's temperature that was making her shudder, but rather the conviction that some dark man and Domitien had fought to the death at some time in their pasts. Possibly more than once. Perhaps many times.

And it might happen again. Here.

And Dom thought that this man might have known her as well. He had maybe been a threat to her.

Dom had spoken mildly about talking to the guards about protection, but she was coming to know him now. Dom wouldn't be content with letting the law be their shield if he thought more forceful action was called for. She could not say why she was so certain that these impressions of impending violence were true, but the thought of him confronting this dark man genuinely terrified her.

Chapter Seven

She had always imagined that counterfeiting love for the wrong man would be the hardest lot to fall to a woman. But now she knew it was not true. There was something harder. Hiding a true love was much more difficult. And she had failed at it. She had betrayed herself.

When the appeals to his mind had failed, she had tried to win his heart with the offer of her flesh. And he had finally accepted. But he would not stay. He lad lain with her, and then turned to another on the next day, as if he had never kissed her, never run his hands over her breasts . . .

Trembling with remembered shame, Lotty took up her pen and began to write.

> Small was that wound from Cupid's dart
> But how I bled when it speared heart.

And all the while I cried in need,
Thou applauded and let me bleed.

Two tears, weighted by sorrowful shame and bearing Donald's name, slipped down her cheeks and splattered on her parchment. This grief belonged to him, but he would never know of it. She would never betray herself to him again.

Laris awoke the next morning, her heart pounding, her body as taut as a bowstring. Her cheeks were flushed and wet with fresh tears. She'd *remembered*— and it was painful. The hurt and shame were so awful, so crushing that she could barely breathe.

Dom's hand stirred, tucking itself more securely, possessively, into the curve of her hip. Unable to help herself, Laris flinched and made a small, involuntary noise in her throat.

Instantly Dom was awake, his body tensing, his eyes open to possible danger.

She stared at him with a horrified gaze, wondering if his heart was really as empty as the cloudless skies that were his eyes. What *was* he? Could he hear her thoughts, pounding in her skull, surely every bit as loud as her rioting heart?

"Laris. Calm down, little nun. Everything will be all right. What did you dream?"

"You didn't love me," she whispered, the accusation forcing itself past her white lips. "You didn't care at all. You looked into my face, saw that I loved you, and you used me anyway."

As she watched, something moved through his eyes. His pupils expanded and his irises assumed the glittering aspect of brilliant diamonds. She knew instinctively that he was gathering himself to some action.

"No! Don't you touch me!" She tried to draw away from him, but his arm was an unmoving bar.

"There is no need for you to remember any of this," he told her. "Not if it's painful. I can take it all away again, if that is what you want."

"No need?" she repeated in disbelief. "How can you say that, you—you heartless seducer!"

"You obviously aren't ready to remember." Dom turned his head and looked out of their window.

The light of dawn was parched and comfortless, its heat absorbed by the morning fog. It should have made him appear less vibrant but didn't. Dom carried his own power, his own sun, and he was threatening to eclipse Laris's mind with it. He could reach down into her brain and blot her memories out, maybe burn them away forever!

"You needn't be so *Sabine*, little nun. It was just an *affair*."

She stared at him for a long moment, wondering with a touch of hysteria if he had actually been there for the rape of the Sabine women. Anything seemed possible to her in that instant.

"You can't stop me from remembering. It's too late now," she whispered. But it was more hope than conviction in her voice. He was still worlds stronger than she was. However, she was angry and she was going to try and resist him this time. Her savagely wounded pride demanded it.

"Actually, I can." His voice was even. He turned back to her. For once he didn't soften his words with a smile. "However, I don't think I will, unless you force me to. That bloody kiss we shared started waking your memories for a reason. It must have, because it did something to me too. Maybe it is best that we both remember everything. More of my past is there now, in my head, and there will be more memories all the time. I even have some damned shut-up images that I would rather forget . . . but they keep coming back to plague me. We are probably going to be *forced* into remembering."

Dom ran a hand over his face as though trying to scrub away the stains of old recollections.

Laris looked at him, trying to decide what to do. She looked and looked until she was certain she couldn't bear any more. Body and mind warred to see whose agony was dominant. The fierceness of the pain of his old betrayal was mentally paralyzing, but the sight of Dom's stoic face nearly stopped her breath and wrapped an invisible tourniquet about her wounded heart until it felt as though it were being severed.

"It is always hard deciding what to do, isn't it? But I can help you with this. I know that it is a lot to ask, but I want you to tell me what you know. What you think you understand about your past lives," he said evenly. "It might help both of us."

"No. Never! I'll never trust you." Then: "How could you be so cruel?"

He didn't reply.

"Answer me!" she demanded, the pain of two centuries ago made fresh in her mind. "Will you do it again now? Now that you have flushed out my feeling, will your vanity demand that you leave?"

"No. Whatever you have remembered of our past, I promise that this time it is different." He was still very calm—passionless even. "You are destiny. It is ordained. I am tied to you this time by a will greater than my own."

"I don't believe you. Why should this time be any different?" Laris rolled the other way, trying to escape. But she failed, just as she knew she would.

And this time Dom was not satisfied with just an arm about her waist. He caught a hand behind her neck, fisting it in her hair. He let her feel the strength in his fingers, and the restraint he was using. He could have hurt her, but didn't.

She looked into his hard, unsmiling face. Here he was, her knight, the one she had waited for all her life. And like the knights of old he came with armor and weapons, and the will to conquer. What was he offering her? Palace, or prison?

A strange electricity pulsed down her spine, igniting nerves as it went. She couldn't say with certainty if it was fear or arousal that shook her. A fragile—and hated—sheet of tears filmed her vision. A part of her mind studied her suffering with detachment, perhaps storing up the scene to haunt her dreams later. She did not want the shame of weeping to taunt her. Lotty had cried, and it had availed her nothing.

Laris shuddered at her own autonomous callousness, which would not, for its own pride, allow her weaker emotions the release of tears. What had she become? What monster was ruling her mind?

She tried next to look away from Dom, but could not. She was trapped, locked to this moment with mental shackles as binding as anything made of steel.

He stared into her eyes for a long moment, as though assessing her dream and the ramifications of her new knowledge. It seemed impossible that he could actually peer into her mind, and there was a sense of delicate probing at the outside of this new and very tender memory.

"I don't believe it," he muttered. "Lotty? You were Lotty?"

She tried to tear herself away, though she knew that there was nowhere she could hide physically or mentally that he would not find her.

"Stop," she whispered. "They're mine—not yours. My thoughts! My scars!"

"But I put them there." He shook his head. "Poor Lotty . . . I truly didn't know that she cared that much. She never said anything after that one time. I would not have been so abrupt if I had known how she felt."

"But you still would have left me."

"Left *her*," he corrected. Then, splitting hairs: "She is not the person you are now. And I am not the man that I was then. Poor innocent. Love of the flesh is one thing, but I would never have encouraged such emotional promiscuity if I had understood what it would mean to her. These *affairs* were simply games. We all played them."

Poor Lotty, Laris thought. *She had loved as she did everything—recklessly. She never stopped to think that it was just a game.*

She stared at Dom. "Easily said because you have no heart yourself, and therefore can never be vulnerable this way. Only a heartless person could call what you did *play*."

"Oh, I still have a heart," he answered evenly. "Though I've tried to be rid of it. It is just very withered, and I keep it locked away. But the fact that I do not share my heart does not mean that I cannot be loyal, or that I do not know my duty. You understand about loyalty, don't you, Laris? Lotty certainly did. And in any event, I am not playing now."

Her will began to falter under his steady gaze; little by little she was being unraveled by his clever mind. It took an effort to clench herself against him. But she had to. He peered at her like the ancient mariner, and spoke of duty, probably seeing her as some awful albatross. And she simply couldn't bear it again—loving someone who saw her emotions as a burden. She could not allow his past shadows to darken her heart.

"How could you not know that I—she—loved you?" Laris demanded. "She was too innocent to know that it was a game."

"Probably because I didn't want to know," Dom answered with comfortless truth. "I used to dangle temptation just to see who would rise to the bait. I always assumed that the truly moral ones—the innocents—would not succumb. I am sorry that Lotty got caught."

Laris swallowed.

"I hated you. I think maybe I hate you now."

"I can see that," he answered, and then he dragged her back down onto the mattress where he leaned over her. "But that will change after you have a chance to adjust to the memories, and after you come to know me better."

"Let me go! I don't want to know you better." Again Laris fought against him, but she failed to free herself from his grip.

Yes, almost cheerfully she failed. She didn't in that

moment—any more than she had in the past—truly wish to be free of him. It was the pain she wanted to escape, not the cause of it. All she had ever wanted was his love.

The truth of this thought shook her and sapped her strength. If Duty was Dom's religion, Self-Honesty was hers. Had she—as Lotty—been as he said, emotionally promiscuous? She had certainly allowed herself to care for a man who had a well-beaten path that led to his bed but not to the altar. By the standards of the time, she had suffered the fate that society said she deserved.

Dom seemed to read her thoughts in her paling cheeks.

"Laris, you must forgive. Don't be so harsh in your thoughts. Forgive Lotty, and forgive Donald. For both of our sakes, you must do this. It is the key to moving forward," he murmured. Then he kissed her, not gently, the tight clasp of his hand anchoring her head, his legs pinning her lower limbs when she tried half-heartedly to kick at him.

As always, the kiss was magic. The tourniquet loosened around her heart and she could breathe again. Soon her fickle body, forgetting her mind's anguish, betrayed her by shivering.

Dom lifted his head. His lips looked less cruel than they had a moment before. His eyes had also softened ever so slightly.

"You're trembling now."

Laris swallowed.

"Yes," she admitted. Then added almost bitterly: "But it doesn't mean anything. It isn't the first time I've trembled in your arms."

He smiled fleetingly. It was a twist of the lips, entirely without humor.

"Very true. Nor will it be the last, I promise you."

Laris believed him, and didn't know if this promise made her feel more joyful or terrified.

As soon as Laris stopped fighting, Dom relaxed his grip. Instead of subduing, he let his greater strength cherish her, making an unspoken apology for the wrong of two centuries before.

It was difficult to be restrained and gentle when they touched both mind and body. His desire for her threatened to become carnivorous if not appeased. The taste of her went through him like a shot of whiskey, though Laris was far more intoxicating than any alcohol could be. She was some triple-distilled essence of woman.

Still he restrained himself. He was plagued by a vague sense of guilt, as though he—in this lifetime and not in the distant past—had violated Laris in some manner. This new fastidiousness of nature was annoying. He would have to do whatever he had to do to keep her safe, and he did not like this feeling that he was pulling the wings off a pretty butterfly by plucking out her thoughts for evaluation.

If only she wouldn't fight him.

Lotty! The Great One had chosen sweet Lotty for him. How could this be?

But then, she wasn't really Lotty anymore. She was Laris.

A sense of deep longing crept through him as he looked down at her flushed face. He wasn't certain of what he desired of her, only that there was some great void inside calling out to be filled. The echoes reverberated, painfully stirring to resurrection memories he thought permanently laid to rest.

Dom realized with grim amusement that he would like to challenge the bastard who had brought her such pain and made her welcoming eyes so wary. But though he recalled that Rychard had played a malicious part in unveiling Donald's affair with another woman to the infatuated Lotty, the role of chief bastard and author of her pain devolved upon no one but himself.

Back then, it had all been very straightforward to him. It was all just a game where rules and morality were shaded by one hundred tones of forgiving gray. But for poor Lotty, the matters of the heart had obviously been black and white. First white for purity, and then black for despair and disgrace.

Nor was it fair to blame her for giving her heart, for he had, though without malice, encouraged her. And, in the end, that made his sin far greater than her own innocent misstep.

He had to find the way to tell her, so she wouldn't go on blaming herself.

Dom looked lingeringly at Laris's lips. He longed for the intimacy of her mouth. There lay a passionate bridge, a conduit that would span all anger, the promise of a balm to heal all past betrayals. But he couldn't bring himself to take it again, even though it would be easy enough to overwhelm her small defenses, physical and mental, and force a surrender. He was not here to sack Carthage. He wanted willing surrender.

He recognized then part of what made up that black void inside him. It was loneliness, the enemy that crept into the soul and destroyed from within, making a man doubt every decision he had ever made. Making him believe that he would never know peace again. Making him want to flee his past, his memories.

He was *lonely*. The thought astounded.

And he needed something from Laris, something he could not take by force or trickery. She had to volunteer it with a glad heart.

What was to be done for Laris? For the part of Lotty that remained in Laris? What could be done in mitigation for his wrongs present and past? He had to find some way to heal them.

He laid his past offenses aside—for what reparation could be made to the dead? He *had* done what she accused him of. He had eyed her emotional scars, wrested her memories from her against her will, and made her feel frightened and vulnerable. Amends obviously had to be made to Laris. Balance had to be restored. An eye for an eye, a vulnerability for a vulnerability.

Dom made an impulsive decision. It went against every self-protective instinct he had, but still he did the difficult thing and opened himself up to Laris. He showed her his mind. It was just a small glimpse of his painful loneliness, gone in an instant with his shutters safely back in place, but it was all he could manage.

Yet he was rewarded for this open confession. He could see the instant the reality of his loneliness, his own vulnerability, sliced through the tight knots of her hurt and anger and set her free. Her body and face, as much as her beautiful voice, were trained to display emotion. Though she might try and hide it, her expression was easily read.

"Oh, Dom," she sighed. "How am I to trust? What am I to do?"

"What you were meant to do," he answered. "What *we* were meant to do. If you look inside, you'll see the answer plainly enough."

He lowered his mouth back to hers. This time when they made love, he was as gentle as the sunrise that crept over the windowsill and touched them both with blushing light.

Chapter Eight

She ran through the dawn, sobbing, fearful for her own safety and filled with horror at what she had just witnessed.

He had cut him down! Shot him in the back before the paces had been counted off. Her love was dead! Dead! There was an awful hole in his heart and emptiness in his stilled eyes.

It did not matter that he hadn't died for her but rather for another woman's honor. Nothing mattered now except finding her former rival, Julia, and warning her of what had happened—that her lover was dead and that her husband now carried the mark of Cain.

Dom kept Laris abed until late, insisting that she needed sleep, yet dreams pervaded her slumber for the rest of the morning. Though she learned to control her anguish at the wash of ancient recollections, Laris woke discomposed at meeting herself in these memories.

Even after she rose near noon, her reflections talked to her. They had voices that were subliminal but direct for all they lacked in volume. Her past selves had invaded her brain.

Her orderly, conscious mind could only hold a certain number of conflicting realities, but her dreams were not so fettered by the need for structure; she was allowed—forced, even—to mentally wander through her past every moment she relaxed her vigil and fell into relaxation.

Her mind was like some sort of blossom, one that had been waiting for the right moment to be unfolded. One by one her memories—both beautiful and painful—were being unwrapped and offered up to the light.

Parts of the process were lovely, especially rediscovering the wonder of reckless love in its first deep hours of revelation, when it was all unselfishness and blind trust in another's goodness. There were petals that unfurled happily and reached for the light of awareness.

But there was also petty savagery there, betrayal, dishonor, loneliness, and death—and sometimes *worse than death*. These flawed fronds wanted to stay curled in on themselves, hiding from the light of revelation.

Laris lived many lives in many places and did many things. There were only two constants, but they were lodestones: her ever-failing efforts to win Dom's attention, and the maliciousness of his dark-haired, dark-hearted rival. Both of these things pained and terrified her. They almost overwhelmed the joy of rediscovering her past and the love she had known for the younger, wilder Dom.

Domitien looked at Laris across the breakfast crockery, assessing her mood. The darkness beneath her eyes, as well as within them, bespoke her lack of rest and frayed nerves. Her lips, which had been lovely and even risqué only the night before, were now turned down and bracketed with pale lines of tension. He sensed in her a new hesitation, a doubt about him that was the legacy of her awakening memories.

The sensible course for the day would be for them to leave the city and all chance of encountering Rychard, but he hesitated to uproot Laris when she was so emotionally fragile. He had recemented the broken bonds of their relationship last night, but the concrete of his will was a long way from being set, and gates of memory were apt to open again at any moment and could flood her with more memories of their lost lives.

There was also the pending matter of an offer to

join the San Francisco Opera Company. Dom was certain that the proposition would be made, but Laris was nervous. After last night's performance, and the audience's reaction to it, the ensemble would be idiotic to let Laris get away. Unfortunately she was, like all artists, plagued by self-doubt. He couldn't take her away from what was her life's ambition until it was settled.

Still, she was all but climbing the walls, trapped in their suite with the ghosts of her past jabbering at her. She needed to escape, at least for a while, the confines of the hotel.

Very well then. He would have to find someplace close, but safe, for them to go for the day. Someplace that Rychard would not think to look for them, and perhaps that would make her memories temporarily mute.

"I think that what we need today is a bit of a holiday. You've been under a tremendous strain getting ready for your performance. It is time to *unwind*." He produced the last word with an air of satisfaction. He had always enjoyed American vernacular. "Let's go and do something frivolous."

Laris looked up from her *huevos rancheros*. The spicy eggs and refried beans had congealed on her plate as she played with them.

"A holiday?" she asked, her voice warming even as something that might be burgeoning excitement dawned in her eyes.

"Yes. Let's do something lighthearted and perhaps even vulgar. What would you think of . . ." Dom searched his memory for safe, public things that Edom liked to do in San Francisco. "Let's see, we could be tourists and go down to Fisherman's Wharf—buy a crab at the fish market, pick up some sourdough bread and a bottle of chilled chardonnay, and we'll have a picnic on one of the piers."

"That sounds nice but . . ." Laris thought for a moment and then, wrinkling her brow, said: "Actually, I have the strangest urge to go to Golden Gate Park. I even dreamed about it last night. I haven't been there in ages. We could go to the arboretum, Stowe Lake, and the—"

"Tea gardens," Dom finished for her. The notion seemed a rather good one to him as well, a fact that made him vaguely uneasy. Perhaps the thought of the park was simply a case of him accidentally encountering her dream.

"What is wrong?" Laris asked.

She was now very sensitive to his moods and, unless he cut himself off from her completely, she could not escape feeling a certain amount of whatever emotion he experienced. As tempting as the course was, he knew that it would be neither wise nor kind at this point to isolate her with her thoughts and memories.

"Is there some reason not to go to the park? You don't like the idea, do you?" she asked.

"Nothing is wrong. The park sounds lovely," he answered, shoving both his ambivalence and jumbled memories aside. He would have to get used to Laris sharing a part of his mind, and not allow her presence there to send breaths of uneasiness over his nerves. It wasn't pleasant to feel that he was constantly under observation, but it was necessary for now. He had to keep her mentally bonded to him until she had a chance to bind herself by falling in love with him again—a task made much more difficult with the recollection of her past lives. At the moment she was having a difficult time sorting out new feelings from the old. He had to be patient and alert while she found her way.

"Were you . . ." Laris cleared her throat and asked tentatively: "Did you work perhaps in the park in another life? Is that why you don't want to go there?"

"No, I was never employed at the park. In fact, I was living in Vienna at the time. I do recall when they started working on it though. It was right after the World's Fair exhibition in eighteen ninety-four. It was news even halfway around the world. It's a pity that most of the original art in the tea gardens has been stolen," he added. Suddenly he grinned, pleased to have some amusing memory to share. "There was also quite an uproar when all the expensive imported goldfish disappeared. It seems that prior to the building of a seal tank at the Natural History Museum, one of the flippered beasties escaped and helped himself to everything in the moat. It was probably the most expensive fish dinner in history."

Laris gave him a bemused look. "You remember this? The building of the park in eighteen ninety-four? Even with my own memories, I still can hardly believe this. Not really," she confessed. "In spite of Shirley MacLaine, all this reincarnation stuff just doesn't seem possible. And—"

"I don't blame you," Dom interrupted, rising to his feet. He confided: "I am having a rather difficult time adjusting myself. One usually arrives in a new life at birth, and without any memories of one's past. It is a bit disconcerting to find myself in another man's body with my past lives—and *his* too, actually—very much in mind. Hopefully most of these memories will eventually fade."

"Don't say that!" Laris pleaded, also rising. She laid her napkin on the table with a shaking hand. Her voice was likewise somewhat unsteady, and her thoughts came out logically incoherent: "Please, it's your body now, isn't it? Don't—I just can't think about this. You have to be *you*, not *someone else!* And I have to be me. On top of everything else, I can't be lovers with this other man if he isn't you."

"Hush." Dom made a half step and took Laris into his arms. He rested a cheek on her still damp hair, enjoying the smell of her shampoo and the subtler scent that was her. There was something about the scent of jasmine . . . Someone he had known eons ago had favored a perfume made from the milky white blossoms. In an unguarded moment he admitted, "All will be well. It's confusing and complicated, but we have to bear in mind that the Great One Himself made the arrangements for our meeting. So, with Him in our corner, what could possibly go wrong?"

"The Great One?" Laris asked, her voice barely audible as she clung to his shirt. "You mean *God?* As in the Almighty?"

Dom smiled ruefully and patted her back.

"Yes, there is a master builder. Of course there is, and you can call Him God if you want." Laris looked up and started to ask another question, but Dom shook his head and laid a finger against her lips. "But that is all I can tell you, and probably more than you should know. Some things you aren't supposed to be acquainted with right now. Part of what this life is about is learning to have faith without proof."

Not that he'd had very much success with that part of life.

Dom released Laris and gave her a gentle shove toward the bedroom.

"Go grab a sweater and your purse, and we'll be off to the park. I believe that I sometimes play polo there. And since it's Sunday, there won't be any cars. Perhaps we could rent some Rollerblades. I should like to try in-line skating."

Obviously preoccupied by the thought of Dom knowing the "master builder," Laris gave a long backward glance and then a shake of her head.

"Unreal," she muttered.

He laughed. "Oh, no. It's all real enough. Just very strange at first."

Laris and Dom walked through the dappled sunlight of the Zen Garden, admiring the simplicity of a stone lantern and an old bonsai, which was a perfect miniature of the wind-tortured cedars that grew along the coast.

Dom talked softly in an undertone about the history of the park, about how it was a crazy dream made true by the determination of a brash, young city that was terribly impressed by itself. The area had started off as barren dunes, a wasteland, but was made into a seventy-five-acre oasis because it was nurtured by groundwater brought up by a Dutch windmill in the western end of the commons. Later a second windmill was built, which was used until finally the city had grown enough to have a water system that could support all one thousand acres of the present greenbelt.

The tea gardens themselves had been founded in 1894 when the city was bent on establishing itself as a cosmopolitan metropolis. Laris looked about at the old buildings, feeling the weight of history pressing down upon her. Many of the plants that adorned the gardens' vivid red temple gate, where doves fluttered in and out of their exotic lodging, had been growing there for over a century. Some of the statues in the garden were even older.

Had she been here in another life? Laris was afraid to examine her memories, now mercifully mute, in case she truly had been here and had something horrible happen. She didn't want to come face-to-face with her ghosts in a public place.

Sensing her new disquiet with their surroundings, Dom stroked her neck with his clever fingers until she relaxed and her erratic breathing returned to normal.

They paused at the bridge to admire a windmill palm, which spread out its graceful fans against the clear blue of the sky as it did its exotic dance. The waving fronds that sprang from its thick trunk were at least a century old too. The thought made Laris feel very insignificant until she recalled that, though her present body was still quite young, her soul was even older and more enduring than anything around her.

She and Dom took tea at the Teahouse, watching the shivers of the breeze-tossed wisteria, which seemed bent on shedding its last few fragrant blossoms into their steaming cups. The last petal in Laris's bowl arrived with a splash and a heavy hitchhiker. She quickly fished out the praying mantis with half of her fortune cookie, flicking the large insect into the ferns below with a shudder of distaste.

Dom laughed softly.

"Those are beneficial, you know, even if they do bite."

"They are not beneficial to my tea or my cookie. Look, my fortune is all wet now. I can barely read it." Laris held up the soggy paper. "It looks like it says *Adventure awaits you*. Ah well, I didn't eat a piece of cookie before reading it, so now it won't come true."

"Yes, it does say that." Dom stopped smiling. "And I should not think that you can avoid Fortune by failing to take a bite of cookie. It doesn't work that way." He emptied her cup and, taking a linen handkerchief from his pocket, wiped it clean.

"No? I had always heard that you would not enjoy a good fortune if you didn't eat some cookie first. Don't you want to read your own prediction?" Laris asked, handing him the small dish of sweets. "Yours may still come true."

"I'm not particularly fond of fortune cookies," he answered, but nevertheless took the offering before refilling her tea cup.

"What does it say?" she asked impatiently.

"*Good things come to those who wait*," Dom answered, quickly crumpling the tiny paper. He made no effort to eat his cookie. "Look at the size of that koi. He must be large enough to qualify as a game fish."

"I'm sure the seals would agree with you . . . if they could get over here," Laris answered with a smile for the great orange carp who lazed in the vibrant shadows. Its mouth gaped open and then closed as it breathed.

"What a beautiful day it is," she continued softly. "I've been so wrapped up in remembering that I only just now realized it. I wish that I had brought a camera."

"We will stop for a postcard," Dom promised.

"No." Laris shook her head and sighed. "It wouldn't be the same. I want a picture of *now*."

The eyes should have felt assaulted by the jumble of wild pinks from the azaleas, the reds of the Japanese maples, and the blankets of lush green fern all reflected in the pond, but somehow—perhaps because of the serenity of the waterfall or the pool of water filled with lazy fish—the old gardens managed to convey a sensation of blissful quietude in spite of the crowds that pressed in upon it on all sides.

"It's just so perfectly gorgeous," Laris murmured.

"But not a patch on you," Dom answered, sending Laris's spirits into a state of healthy inflation.

"Shall we be off then?" he asked next. "We've three miles of gardens yet to cover, and they should all be magnificent at this time of year."

Smiling at their obi-clad hostess, she and Dom departed through the gates and rejoined the twenty-first-century throngs.

Hand in hand, they wandered across the road to the arboretum, where they enjoyed the gardens of the world miniaturized into the space of an hour's stroll.

They lingered longest in the Garden of Fragrance where the colorful jumble of salvia, verbena, laurel, and lavender all vied for the attention of both eyes and nose.

Dom, pulling aside the trailing verbena, pointed out to Laris that the beds were built of the stones from a twelfth-century monastery.

"What! How do you know that?"

He laughed aloud at her horrified question. "No, I don't recall the original. As far as I know I have never been a monk. It is just one of the facts I recollect from when they built the gardens."

Flushing, Laris secretly agreed with him. Monk seemed an unlikely occupation for any of the Doms she had met.

They paused once at the exit as Dom stared intently at the fall of white jasmine that twined over the opened gates. He inhaled deeply, a frown on his face. Laris was about to ask him what had caught his attention, but he seemed to shake off whatever memory gripped him and urged her through the arch.

It was a long, rather crowded walk out to the polo fields where Edom sometimes played, but beyond that the Queen Wilhelmina Tulip Gardens were empty except for the long shadow cast by the giant windmill there, which reached toward the setting sun.

Dom guided Laris toward the old building with a sure hand, speaking about the engineering involved in building it.

"Wait," she said, feeling something unpleasant slide down her spine.

"What is it?" Dom's voice was alert and serious.

"I don't know. Something feels *wrong*."

They stood quietly, opening their senses. The first thing they noticed was that the scene in front of them was oddly static, and Laris felt a strong though inexplicable reluctance to step beyond the tulip-edged border where they were standing.

She looked up slowly. The windmill's four giant sails were frozen now, gears locked in place and allowed to rust because the well water they had been built to pump was no longer needed. The weathered wood observation platform, located a third of the way up the tower, was empty of life as it too had eroded over the years until it was no longer safe for people to walk on. Laris had the strong sense that once it was dark the whole mill might collapse in on itself, pulling its rotting skeleton back down into the earth where wooden things should disappear.

And if they were standing too close, they would be pulled down with it.

As if to underline her discomforting vision, the sun passed into extremis, telling them of the lateness of the hour, and it began giving off an evil red light that hurt the eyes. Once again Laris and Dom were bathed in the ichor stain of a San Francisco sunset, but this time it seemed not the red of new passion or heart blood that covered them. It was the red of murder, and it seemed to burn on their unprotected skin, marking them as targets for some large and unkind fate.

"Dom?" Laris whispered, turning her face from the harsh light.

"I feel it." He looked about quickly. "I don't see Death though."

"*Death?*" Laris asked, startled.

"Yes, Death—Pluto, the Ferryman, Hades. The short man in the blue suit from the hotel. He probably keeps a doorway here in the park, and we've blundered into his shadow." Dom gestured at the giant windmill. Its outstretched arms now looked sinister, and she could almost smell the decay that reigned unchecked inside its old wooden shell. "He'd need a permanent portal in such a busy city, and quiet places are not easily come by. This, however, looks like the perfect place. Still, even if this is his lair, there is no reason to feel alarmed."

But giving lie to those reassuring words, Dom turned about slowly, searching the shadows for the cause of his uneasiness.

"Death needs a *portal?* But why? And to where?"

"Even with his many assistants, it is sometimes difficult to get to the souls of the new dead within the prescribed three days after the body's passing," Dom explained.

"He doesn't keep dead peoples' souls in there, does he?" Laris whispered, appalled at the idea of a storage closet for the dead, but somehow accepting the rest of the bizarre premise of their conversation.

"No. It's just a gateway to other places. You've heard the one about the dead traveling quickly? Well, that's how they do it."

Laris was somewhat reassured by Dom's offhand tone and almost reasonable explanation.

"What happens to a soul if Death doesn't come for it?" Laris asked, shivering as some new and unpleasant breath exhaled over her. The musty air smelled like something blown up from a bottomless chasm. The tulip bed swayed unhappily as if it would also like to avoid the unwholesome breeze snaking about them.

"They become ghosts until they are taken away."

"Why—"

"Get down!" Dom ordered, pulling Laris down onto the grass and crawling toward the shallow cover of the tulip garden, which was still shivering violently. Quite against her will, Laris was compelled into Death's red-shadowed domain.

"What is it?" Laris whispered.

She was answered by a sharp crack and a puff of displaced dirt behind them.

"Is that Death?" she asked, crawling up right beside Dom and pressing into his comforting heat. She didn't know what he could do against anyone as powerful as Death, but she still felt safer at his side.

"Worse," he answered. "It's Rychard. The crazy son

of a bitch is shooting at me. How did that wretched whoreson find us?"

"Rychard? The man from the opera last night?"

"Yes. And it seems he's just plain old crazy this time, too." Dom sounded more annoyed than frightened.

"What can we do?" she asked, unhappy that they were under fire, but very relieved that they were facing an only human foe. "There is nowhere to hide out here. No trees to speak of, except those way over there."

Dom glanced back at the ugly windmill, which glowed a sinister red. It wasn't inviting.

"There is one thing we can do."

Laris looked back too.

"What?" she asked, apprehension returning in a rush as the mill's shadowed arms seemed to sway and reach closer to them. "You don't mean to hide in there, do you?"

"I do. We can even use Death's doorway to escape."

"We can, can we? And what if there are dead souls in there?"

"Souls aren't dead. They are eternal—unless the Great One dissolves them."

"That's nitpicking. I don't want to go into the mill."

"What?" Dom's eyes focused on her face. His tone held mild disbelief.

"I don't want to," she said stubbornly. "It's a simple declarative sentence, which I know you understand."

There was another crack of gunfire and the sound of footsteps on gravel.

"Come out, come out, wherever you are," a high voice caroled and then began giggling. "I know you are here, Domitien. You and your whore."

"I should have killed him last night," Dom muttered. His body tensed. "Maybe I can circle around behind him and break his bloody neck. I could leave Death a present in the mill."

"No." Laris laid a restraining hand on Dom's arm, appalled at his suggestion.

"Our options are limited."

Laris swallowed and looked again at the windmill. She detested the sight of it, but anything was better than the thought of Dom taking on a crazy man with a gun.

"Dom?" Laris made herself speak. "About that doorway? We can actually use it even if we aren't dead? It won't hurt us or anything?"

He looked down at her. "Yes, I think so. The road will lead somewhere. It might be Bombay or the South Pole—"

"Or Hell," she pointed out.

"I don't think there is a Hell per se. I know it used to be called Acheron or Hades, but it isn't the way you think. Death might have a home base, and knowing him I'm certain it is unpleasant—but it isn't Hell." There was a third crack from Rychard's gun,

123

and more high-pitched laughter. "In any event it is a chance we'll have to take. We have to get out of the park."

Laris tried one last evasive maneuver.

"Can't we wait for help? Surely someone will hear the gunshots and come. I think the park has its own police force."

"That could take too much time, and I am not certain that they will come here anyway. Death's shadow—around his portals—has a way of discouraging visitors from calling. The police would likely walk right past here and never stop." Dom nudged her. "Start crawling for the far side of the windmill. That must be where the door is."

"Dom, I don't know—" A breath of fresh air exploded over her, bringing with it the sweet smell of oleander. It chased away the earlier foul odors and brought a fitful muttering from the distant eucalyptus.

Dom exhaled in relief.

"Help *has* arrived," he said with satisfaction. "We'll get our chance to escape."

"The police are here?"

"No."

Before Laris could speak again, a horde of doves, wings squeaking with their vigorous effort, launched themselves out of the reddened sky. All but two of the white birds raced toward Rychard. They surrounded and harrassed him. The two largest avians had broken off from the flock and fluttered to the ground near the windmill. They turned to stare at Laris and, except for their different hues, their poses suggested matching bookends.

"We must go now, Laris," Dom ordered, starting past her and catching her arm as though to drag her along. "Follow those two birds."

To underline Dom's command there came an enraged screaming and more gunshots as Rychard fired wildly at the doves around him. Laris picked the lesser of two evils and, hanging her purse about her neck, she crawled into the shadow of Death's rotting portal, led by the mincing step of the two large birds of peace, which had elected to stay out of the battle.

"I guess you were right," she muttered.

"About what?" Dom asked, regaining his feet once they had the entirety of the mill between them and Rychard. He quickly hauled Laris upright and made an effort to dust her off.

"About not needing to eat any fortune cookie to make the fortune come true." Laris rubbed her stinging hands over her slacks, dislodging the few small stones that had embedded themselves in her tender flesh. "I'd say this qualifies as adventure, wouldn't you?"

"Yes, it does. Though I could very easily have stood to be wrong in this instance," Dom admitted. Stopping at the mill's locked door and pulling out an army knife, he picked up the rusting lock and chain and began fiddling with them. The two doves watched him closely, offering occasional coos of encouragement. "Fortune and Fate—those bloody bitches."

"What did your fortune *really* say? It was something horrid, wasn't it? *Beware of men with guns,* or something?" Laris asked, eyes jumping about uneasily as she listened to the battle on the other side of the windmill between the madman and the crying doves. Rychard's hysterical voice was promising to kill them both. Again and again and again.

"It said *You will travel soon.* In Gaelic. That's ominous enough without thinking of it in terms of how the Gaels meant traveling."

"You got a Gaelic fortune in your Japanese cookie?" Laris paused. "Well, what *did* the Gaels mean by travel?" she asked.

"They meant to die, for the spirit to travel to a new life." Dom grunted with satisfaction and dropped the broken lock onto the sill. Without hesitation he put his shoulder to the warped wood and forced it open.

"Ugh!" he exclaimed, recoiling.

The air that rushed out was enough to give anyone pause. It was a mélange of smells, flowers, foods, oceans—and things less pleasant: molding plants, decaying wood, sea rot in every form.

If there had been any doubt in her mind before, Laris now understood that they were entering a dangerous, inhuman lair, and it made the hairs of her nape stand erect.

"Do we have to do this? Break in? Death probably won't like it. He'll be angry, won't he?" she asked, trying one last time to avoid the windmill. "It is almost dark now. We could hide until then—"

"Laris, if Rychard doesn't break in here he will just go back to the hotel and lie in wait for us there. We need to get away from here. After we arrive somewhere else we can phone the San Francisco police and have the bastard detained. There will be plenty of evidence to hold him on this time." *Until I can get back here and break his bloody neck*, Dom added to himself.

"I heard that!" Laris said. "I don't want you going near him. He's dangerous. I remember him. He cheated at a duel and shot you in the back."

Dom snorted at the unnecessary warning.

"Then hear this. We are leaving. Now." Dom stepped into the pungent gloom and then reached back for her.

"Dom! Damn it—"

Before Laris could sidestep, she was snagged by Dom's strong hand and dragged into Death's portal's wooden maw.

"Thanks, Enzo, Ilia. We appreciate the help," Dom called to the birds as he slammed the door shut on the dying sun and closed him and Laris into the dark. He moved around until he found a flimsy bolt and then threw it. "That isn't much to place between him and us."

"I don't like this," Laris whispered, huddling close. "This is an awful place."

"Neither do I like it. So, let's start looking for another door. There has to be one somewhere."

"There are lots of them," Laris said, staring unhappily at the selection of warped wood panels that surrounded them.

Chapter Nine

The grand ballroom was over sixty feet long and half again as wide, and its ornate ceiling made of cerulean tiles was held up by an army of elegant white and gold columns. The base of each column was ringed by a bevy of maidens every bit as jeweled and ornamented as the gilded room in which they danced.

Detlef looked the maidens over carefully, choosing the one he would honor with the first dance on this snowy New Year's Eve. The pretty redhead who hid behind her fan seemed a good choice; her pretty green eyes danced when they peeped over its lace edge.

There were many doors inside the mill, tall and short, wide and thin, and the first Laris opened revealed a strange yet oddly familiar scene. An old man with long graying hair and a white robe sat weeping into his gnarled hands. Beyond the small, nearly empty chamber they could see an opened gate that looked out onto a bleak desert.

The old man lifted his head and, looking toward the desert, began to cry out pained words that Laris could not understand.

"Dom, who is he, do you know?" she asked softly, wishing she could help ease the old man's distress. "What is he saying?"

Dom walked over to her and looked through the portal. He cleared his throat and then translated dispassionately: "O my son Absalom, my son, my son Absalom! Would God I had died for thee, O Absalom, my son, my son."

Laris shivered.

"That's David?" she asked, awed but no longer at all disbelieving of the strange things that were happening to them. "The real King David from the Bible? The one who wrote the Psalms?"

"Yes, that David. This is right after the tragic battle in the woods of Ephraim when Absalom was slain against his orders." Dom intoned in Hebrew: " 'Incline your ear to my cry—Lord, why have you cast off my soul?' "

"What is that? It sounds familiar?"

"That is what would become the eighty-fourth psalm, one of the bleakest passages in the Bible."

Dom leaned over to shut the door.

"Wait. He is so upset. Can we do anything for him? Maybe speak to him?"

"No. I'm sorry, Laris, but raising the dead is not within our power. And nothing else would comfort him. Anyhow, this is history. It cannot be altered. And frankly this isn't something I would meddle with even if I could. After all, there is history and then there's *history*." Dom closed the door quietly, silencing the weeping. "The Great One would see our interference as unforgivable meddling. David has his destiny."

"Oh." Laris blinked. "Yes, I can see your point."

"I have a more likely place for us to visit over here," Dom said, sounding at once more cheerful. He'd opened another door. "Are you ready to see a bit of Europe?"

"I suppose," Laris answered, still moved by David's grief and having a hard time trading her awed yet somber emotions for something lighter. "Someplace closer to San Francisco would be more convenient though."

"Not today it wouldn't." Dom touched her back, guiding her to another door. "Trust me, this is someplace you will want to see."

Laris gave him a puzzled look but allowed him to usher her through the small door.

They stepped out of the windmill and into a busy street shadowed by twilight, and were nearly run down by a rushing pony cart. The diminutive driver never swerved or even acknowledged them as he went trotting by.

"He didn't see us," Laris whispered, automatically moving aside for a group of reeling gentlemen who seemed rather the worse for drink and were commanding more than their fair share of the cobbled way.

"No, he didn't," Dom agreed, taking Laris's arm in a firm grip and pulling her out of the way of traffic that came at them from all directions. "Death's shadow cloaks us here. Makes us invisible. But though they may not see us, it is possible that we may be felt if touched—so have a care."

"Felt?"

"I have noticed that Death's minions are often sensed by the living when they go about their business. Horses and hounds seem especially sensitive to their presence."

"Minions? We're minions now? Well, I'm not collecting any souls to take with us. In fact, I don't think we should be here at all." Laris breathed deeply while staring at the astonishing world before them. It was a place a half step removed from reality. It was like being in a movie, but one where more of the senses were engaged and the action took place all about them. "Dom, where are we? Look at these strange clothes! That is a hoopskirt."

"The interesting question is not where, but when."

"Okay, *where* and *when* are we?"

"We are in Vienna," Dom said. "My guess would be the mid-eighteen-nineties. See over there? That is a coffeehouse I used to visit when I was a youth and craved political conversation."

"Eighteen-ninety Vienna!" Laris stared at him. "Dom! Eighteen-ninety? Truly?"

"Yes."

"And we are standing here . . . But how can you tell for sure what the date is and where we are?" Laris asked. "Oh, the language?"

"That and the fact that I lived here then. I am surprised that you don't know this place though. You came here years ago."

"I did?" She had forgotten. It all looked so different than anything she knew.

"Stop gaping at the people and look about you. Some things have changed, but don't you recognize that opera house?"

"It's the Theater an der Wien," she whispered, looking up obediently at the two-tiered roof and arched windows that were somewhat reminiscent of the architecture from the Italian Renaissance. The two buildings, the one before her and the one in memory, overlaid each other. After a moment of vertigo she was able to marry them both into a single image. "And listen! They are playing *Der Fledermaus*! I always wanted to sing the part of Adele!"

Laris looked about quickly and seeing a break she stepped out into the street, dragging Dom with her.

She hurried up to the imposing opera house and mounted the shallow steps. She was careful to avoid the liveried lackeys who lingered about the door waiting for late patrons.

"I wonder if Strauss is here. Darn it! Why didn't I bring a camera? Look at this place!"

"Careful," Dom cautioned, touching her arm.

Laris stopped abruptly, peering into the marbled hall where a beautiful voice echoed gaily. There was no definite line of demarcation, but she sensed that their zone of safety and invisibility would not extend much farther. Another few steps and she would no longer be invisible and insulated.

Laris turned wide eyes upon Dom and demanded in a voice fraught with frustration: "Do you realize that this may be the great Marie Geistinger singing? That this could be the first time the world has heard this music? And I can't go inside!"

Dom, though ridden by the responsible sense of urgency to find some exit back into their own time, still had to smile at her rounded-eyed awe and distraction.

"When was this opera first performed?"

"March of eighteen ninety-four," she answered promptly.

"Well, it is certainly cold enough for March. The smell of snow is in the air. You may be correct in your assumption about this being a historic date, though I don't recall it particularly."

Laris laughed, half amazed and entirely delighted with the idea. She knew that she should be frightened by everything that had happened to them, but instead she felt as though she were overflowing with sudden good fortune. She might even explode with it—burst into flower like a cherry tree or an early tulip pushing through winter's frozen ground.

Or, she thought with a happy laugh, she could burst into song.

"They can't see or hear us as long as we stay in Death's shadow?" she asked again, making certain of this fact. Her eyes were dancing.

"Not as long as we remain within the perimeter of Death's influence. Within it we can move about at will and probably without even tiring," Dom answered. Then warily: "Why?"

In answer, Laris tilted back her head, closed her eyes, and unleashed her voice at the stony portal.

Though supposedly none of the passersby could hear it, somehow they seemed as if they did, for many froze in place and lifted their heads attentively. Some began to search the shadows looking for the unheard and yet sensed music that came not from within the theater, but out in the street.

Dom's own senses were bathed in the clear, unwrinkled notes that flowed from Laris in a seemingly endless stream. He stared at the delicate column of her throat and was again amazed that such a small conduit could contain the torrent of pure passion that was her voice. It rushed out, this culmination of expression, a giddy accumulation of memories—and it somehow contained violins and trumpets, strains high and low, a true paean of the soul. It was as though her senses were being ravished by some musical divinity, and out poured her answer to heaven. Her clear joyousness pulsed in Dom's arteries and raced through his veins. It was a delicious stroke to the ears and caused an earthquake in his breast.

He had listened through the centuries to all the different siren calls that women had to offer, and he knew that none of them would ever again have the power to completely charm. Laris's voice was the ultimate siren song.

Laris and the great Maria Geistinger stopped singing at the same moment and the theater beyond erupted into applause. After a moment, the people in the street shook themselves free of the spell Laris had unintentionally woven and returned to their evening chores. Mundane sound leaked back into the world, first the sharp ringing of hooves on cobbles and the soft fall of shoes on stone, and then the babble of excited voices, which were suddenly and unexplainably happy as they hurried toward their homes and the pleasures of a warm hearth.

Dom cleared his throat. Laris slowly opened her eyelids and smiled. She was blazing with triumph and pleasure, and he had the oddest feeling that in that moment the sun was not setting into the west, but was actually rising in her eyes.

"The Great One has surely bestowed his blessing upon you," Dom said softly. "I have heard the most beautiful voices of humankind sing on every stage in the world, and none can hold a candle to you."

Laris blushed and looked away. Her eyes were again veiled. Her song-induced radiance began to fade, but not her color. He smiled at her belated blush.

"But I think that much of this is due to you," she told him. "I have never sung like this before. It is as though I am suddenly able to touch parts of myself that were locked up before I met you."

Dom nodded and touched her heated cheek with the palm of his hand. "I think that you were supposed to open up parts of me as well."

"Have I succeeded?" she asked softly.

Dom thought about it. "Yes, I believe so. *Something* is different this time."

"Different how?" she asked, peeping up at him.

"I'm not certain." He shrugged, suddenly uneasy with the conversation. "And this isn't the time to be talking about things of this nature. We must depart before we encounter one of Death's minions. This shadow marks the path they must follow to collect souls of the dying. Your song is likely to have attracted anyone who is nearby."

Laris blinked. "What would happen if we did encounter one of Death's workers?"

"Probably nothing. They tend to be set on a pre-arranged course and nothing sways them. But with Death, one can never be certain of anything."

"I suppose that is true, but . . ." Laris took a step closer to Dom and laid a hand on his arm. Her fingers were warm and real and belied the notion that they were invisible beings. "Could we not look around just a little bit more? When will we ever have the chance to be here again?"

"Laris—"

"Please. We're supposed to be having a holiday, right?"

"Well, then, look at what?" he asked in resignation. "It's all covered in snow and night is falling."

"That way is the Belvedere." She pointed. "It's a beautiful place and I've never seen it in winter."

"Savoy's summer palace—yes, a delightful place. And it would be nice to see Schweizergarten Park again," Dom said slowly, clearly tempted by the chance to revisit his old home. "But I still don't think we should wander so far. I doubt Death's shadow extends so many miles."

"But if this is eighteen ninety-four, then it is the residence of the Archduke Ferdinand. I remember hearing that on the tour. We could actually see him." Laris shivered suddenly, recalling what had happened to the Duke and how the world had been plunged into war soon after his death. "He won't be alive too much longer."

"Twenty years or so."

It then occurred to her that half a world away, construction was starting on the Japanese tea gardens in Golden Gate Park—and that that was where they ultimately needed to be.

"I suppose we should go back straightaway, only . . ." She stared wistfully at a string of carriages up the street, which were discharging their gaily clad fares. Obviously the people were on their way to a ball.

"Only?" Dom prompted, slipping an arm about her and holding her close as though to ward off the cold of the night, which fortunately they could not actually feel as it had begun to snow.

"Could we not have one dance at those people's party?" she coaxed. "Death's shadow should stretch that far."

Dom looked at the ladies in their ball gowns, delicate with their wasp waists and exaggerated sleeves. The snow had not deterred these revelers. The grand residence where they were going to show off their plumage and seek mates was brightly lit within by candles and without by torches, and it threw out its welcoming beacons into the night.

How he had loved to dance! It had been one of the best things about his time in Vienna.

Though he knew that it was unwise to play the moth to this attractive flame, Dom heard himself answering: "Perhaps we might have just one dance."

Blessed with Death's ease of travel, he and Laris arrived in the ballroom only an instant later. As if sensing them, the crowd obligingly parted and let them through the packed foyer and into the ballroom.

Inside, elegant waltz music was played by inebriated musicians at a slightly faster pace than the standard sixty bars per minute, making the dancing seem a bit frantic and wild. Laris could also see that the waltzes were being performed in a stronger style than what she was used to, and that the ladies seemed to lead half of the time, especially on the fourth and sixth turns when navigation on the crowded floor became tricky. And there was a beautiful uplift on the second beat, causing the ladies' skirts to flutter as they rose from the swinging dip. They looked like the most beautiful and colorful birds of paradise on the verge of taking flight.

"Would you care to dance, my lady?" Dom asked, offering his hand.

"I'd love to," Laris answered immediately.

Dom took her into his arms and pulled her tight against his chest, leaving no room between them. His eyes smiled down at her slightly startled expression.

"They don't do polite English waltzes here," he said, his voice assuming a new accent, a slightly Austrian one. "We must move quickly or we shall be taken by the stampede. Can you keep up, or shall I carry you?"

"I believe that I can just about manage the pace," Laris said, following Dom onto the floor and into the exuberant whirl of the giddy Viennese.

The paraffin wax of the parquet floor was very slick and Laris was grateful for her rubber soles. The rest of her clothes did not thrill her, however, once she was surrounded by the silken, flitting butterflies on the glossy dance floor that reflected their costumes almost as clearly as a mirror. Her tailored slacks refused to flutter or swish attractively no matter how energetically she danced. Only Dom seemed completely right.

All too soon, the music came to an end, and Dom was leading her away from the other dancers.

"We'll come back to Vienna for the New Year," he promised, seeing her longing looks and understanding them completely. "We'll rent you a gown and visit the balls."

"Do you think we could eat something?" Laris asked, eyeing the refreshment table, which had been laid out with pastries and tortes lavishly covered in whipped cream. It was only as she spoke that she noticed that her sense of smell was oddly muted and color was beginning to fade from the scene.

"It is too great a risk," Dom said, finally firm about their departure.

Suddenly, all aroma disappeared—there was no perfume, no pastry, no perspiration. Part of the world's color drained away, eclipsed by a sudden shadow.

"We have already lingered here overly long. We must leave at once."

"But—"

As if to underline his words, there was a sudden gasp from the crowd, and a rotund gentleman in a blue coat slipped onto the dance floor, landing heavily on his knees. His face was contorted with pain and flushing in an unhealthy manner.

"Hurry!" Dom said, taking Laris's hand and racing from the mansion out into the snowy night.

Dom pulled her into the deep shadow of a recessed doorway and waited while a tall, black-cloaked figure wafted by. The creature, perhaps sensing them, turned its head toward them, showing them its blank masklike face whose only features were the black holes where its eyes should be.

Laris shivered and did not speak until the dark cape had disappeared inside the recently vacated ballroom.

"Was that a minion?"

"Yes."

"Was it *alive?*" she asked.

"In a sense. They are avatars—images of Death animated by his will. You don't need to worry about it. It has been told what to do and will do it until Death recalls him. Which is fortunate for us as we were definitely seen. Let's go. I want to be out of the windmill before that thing returns with his collection."

Dom started for the far side of the street, and then seeing something there he didn't like, shied away.

"We'll go this way."

As they hurried into the darkness, Laris looked back at the dark patch of walkway Dom was avoiding and recognized an incarnation of Rychard stepping out into the lane. He wore a dark coat with silver buttons, half hidden by a long cape. His hair was cut short and was not so dark as it was in San Francisco, but she knew those awful eyes.

He couldn't see them as they passed on the other side of the street, but his nostrils flared and his thin lips hardened beneath his mustache as though he smelled or sensed something he instinctively disliked.

"Dom," she whispered, suddenly unwilling to chance being heard.

"I know. But don't be alarmed. He can't see us."

"I think he smells us."

"Or senses that I am near."

"We are still in danger, aren't we?" Laris asked, her frivolous mood abandoning her completely. "Even here, we are in danger."

"Yes, we could be, if we left the protection of Death's shadow. Rychard's animus is unending," Dom said, not mincing matters. He came to a halt outside the small alley where they had first emerged. They stood in front of what looked like a storehouse, but there was no question that this was the correct spot; Laris could plainly smell Death's unique stench waiting behind its warped door. "The good news is that I have succeeded in killing Rychard at least half of the time—and it is my turn to kill him again."

"But there is more than one of him," she argued, allowing Dom to pull her down the unlit lane.

"And more than one of me." Dom's teeth gleamed in the dark.

"But not me."

"No. You weren't here in Vienna."

"You are certain of that?"

"Yes. You would remember if you had been here at this time."

"Good! This was fun, and truly I am getting more used to things, but I don't think I am ready to meet myself just yet. That would be somehow unpleasant."

"I certainly don't blame you for wishing to avoid your past," Dom said as they stepped back inside the windmill and slammed the door behind them. "It is unnatural to see oneself while the work is in progress, and frankly not an experience I crave either."

"Well, what now?" Laris asked, staring at the rusted, inanimate shadows that surrounded them.

"We try another door—and quickly. I'd rather not be about if Death decides to handle anything personally. Enzo and Ilia helped us here, and the Great One told him to put me in Edom's body and leave me be, but Death was none too happy about it. And he has been known to occasionally ignore instructions when it suits his purposes."

"Swell. And that minion will likely be back soon too. That poor choking guy didn't look very good when we left him."

Dom grunted an agreement. His head was cocked as though he was listening for something.

"What is it?"

"Nothing. Yet." He looked up and smiled reassuringly.

"So, which door do we try?" she asked again. "This one?"

"Why not?" Dom pulled open what looked like a cabinet and peered inside. "Uh-oh. Not this one."

"Why not?" Laris looked over his shoulder and gasped.

Beyond the small frame was a land tortured by earthquakes and cataclysms. But it was not random rubble lying outside the door. Some of the toppled stones had clearly been hewn by human hands.

Charred and devastated skeletons of what might have been a burnt tree—Laris prayed it was a tree—poked out of the tumbled ashlars. Gray wisps reached heavenward in small but grim eddies.

"Close the door," she said, turning away.

Dom complied. He took two steps to the next door and pulled it open, displacing the intricate weave of a spiderweb.

"Hm, I recall this date well," he muttered, looking

inside. "It was a beastly lot of work. We were all obliged to send serfs and wine as tribute."

"What is it?" she asked, lured over to the door. Laris peered out at the dark landscape. Sky and ground were both painted in hues of gray. "What on earth is burning in those bonfires?"

"Cows. Six hundred of them," Dom answered, shaking his head at the sight of the bright orange lights, which filled up the icy dawn and pushed back the bleak winter. "It was horridly difficult to keep the fires lit once it started snowing."

"Cows? What is this, Texas and the world's biggest barbecue?"

"Perhaps the latter. But this isn't Texas. It is the Yuletide, and this is the wedding of Alexander the Second, King of Scotland, to Margaret of England."

Laris thought for a moment and then said: "That was the thirteenth century, right?"

"Correct. Henry the Third put on a Christmas feast to end all feasts. There two tons of white wine were guzzled—and a ton of red. The Archbishop of York provided six hundred oxen, drawn and quartered, then roasted. The feasting went on for five days in spite of the weather."

"Do you want to go look?" she asked, watching the servants' amazing preparations. "It hasn't started snowing yet."

"No. There was some unpleasantness on this morning. There is no need for you to see it." Dom closed the door firmly.

"Oh." Laris was disappointed, but refrained from pressing Dom to explain.

He pulled open another small door and bent to peer out of it. "Ah!" he said, with an air of satisfaction, which rippled over Laris's skin in a peculiar, though not unpleasant, manner. "This is rather better."

"Is it San Francisco?" Laris asked, returning to Dom's side.

"No. It's Spain. Madrid actually. And I believe that we are standing at the north gateway that is closest to the *Fuentes de las Conchas.*" His accent was fluid and purely Castillian. "Come here, *bella mia.* Observe you this grand place."

Dom put an arm around her and urged her to bend down to the short door so that she could peer out at the beautiful, manicured garden, which basked contentedly in the brightness of a late spring day. The splash from the giant fountain at the knot garden's center was inviting. Beyond the grassy avenue there lay a small but peaceful wood, which stretched into rolling hills thick with trees and was full of restful green shadows.

"Is it our time?" she asked hopefully, searching for some sign—telephone wires, an airplane, the smell of exhaust, or the sounds of a combustion engine—but the only movement and sound came from the youthful stone tritons who were pouring their endless water from the giant conch shells.

"I doubt it," Dom said. He sounded cheerful, in spite of the seemingly bad news.

"Then should we take the time to visit here?" she asked.

"Oh, yes! I rather think we should."

"Why? I mean, if it isn't our time and you are concerned about Death—"

"We have a bit of time to kill while the minion does his job."

"So . . . we should kill it here? It looks awfully hot out there."

Dom shrugged.

"If it is summer, then it will be hot everywhere. It is as well to see a summer here."

Laris stared at him, not trusting his mild tone.

"Dom, what are you up to? Why do you want to stop here?" She stepped closer. "Come on, tell the truth. There is something here you want, isn't there?"

"It is probably just a case of forbidden fruit, *bella*, an unprincipled, irresponsible whim," Dom admitted, taking her hand and turning it palm upward so he could bestow a kiss upon it. "But I always wanted to make love in the *jardines del Campo Moro* at the Palacio Real. Won't you help me make this dream come true?"

When he looked up from her hand his eyes were sparkling.

Chapter Ten

Dona Beatrice looked pleadingly at him as she continued to fan herself in an agitated manner. Aware that it would infuriate his already enraged foe, Don Diego nevertheless raised Beatrice's plump hand to his lips and bestowed a kiss upon the many-ringed fingers.

Releasing the fair, jeweled hand, Diego turned and sauntered by the small group of grandes gathered at the salon door. Ricardo leaned over and hissed at him: "You shall pay for this insult, dog. And for having touched my Angelina."

"The heat has disturbed your brain," Don Diego answered affably, shaking back the lace at his cuffs and stroking his spaded beard. "Best you loosen that ruff and go soak your head for a while."

"I'll see you dead before the day is out."

*"I've no doubt that you shall do your inadequate best,"
Don Diego replied. Then he turned on his heel and walked
away from their wide-eyed audience.*

For a long moment Laris looked at Dom and tried to
keep her heart from turning inside out. She had to
admit that the gardens beyond the small door, while
warm, were not a bad place for a romantic assigna-
tion. But she found herself wishing suddenly, and violently, that Dom would say something about loving
her as well as just wanting to make love. Said as it
was, it left the impression that he would have taken
anyone. It almost sounded like it didn't even have to
be her.

Even though she could sometimes sense his moods
and had seen the loneliness within him, so many of
Dom's emotions and thoughts were still so foreign!
So obscured from her present understanding and even
experience. It seemed sometimes that he wasn't just
from another time, but from a whole other world. She
needed a Dom dictionary to provide translations.

It was also a hindrance that his mind mostly remained closed to her, even though her own thoughts
were there for him to see. It sometimes caused her to
feel naked even when she was fully clothed.

And there were reasons to feel naked. Once again
it seemed that history was doomed to repeat itself.
Poor stupid moth! In spite of her returning memories,

and even though she knew better, she was still falling in love with Dom.

Love! Love so soon? And so carelessly?

But there was nothing inaccurate about this judgment of the outcome of their rapid and strange courtship. History bore testament to her capacity for foolishness where this man was concerned. He had always made her ache even when he made her smile. He had made her gloriously happy, and also caused her endless grief. There was no reason to think that things would be any different this time unless something shook him from his complete self-possession and moved him from emotionless duty—or feckless lust—to actual feeling.

"What say you, *bella?* Will you come play Eve to my Adam in this Eden?" Dom again raised her hand, grazing first her palm and then the pulse of her wrist with his gentle lips. It was an old and gallant gesture. His beautiful, beguiling eyes urged her to say yes.

"*Bella?*" she asked, stalling for time.

"It means beautiful." He shrugged. "It is just an endearment that suits you."

She hesitated, then said: "This is a little different than having a dance in Vienna."

"Yes." He waited a moment and then added: "but you must come of your own free will for I'll not coerce you."

Pride said that she should resist his blandishments. But what was pride? Dom would probably say that it was the Devil's firstborn vice. And she had yielded love to pride before, when her constancy had been tried for too long and she labored under a great sense of wrong. Pride had never brought her happiness.

Of course, neither had love, except for brief moments.

Still, those brief moments, like half loaves, were better than none at all. And they left one with the hope of eventually teaching Dom to love.

And what better place was there to start wooing his shut-up heart than with the one expression of affection that he was comfortable with? She could hardly ask him to explore the uncharted territory of his heart for her if she was unwilling to set aside pride and to make the journey with him.

Perhaps it was foolish of her. She should wait and consider carefully the implications of what she was doing now while her thoughts were not fogged by passion. But that was not who she was or ever had been.

That thought brought her a measure of peace.

"I suppose that it is inevitable. We have been brought here, after all," she said softly, relaxing her guard and allowing her thoughts to merge completely with Dom's.

"Ah." He inhaled sharply. "You do trust me a little then."

"Yes, I trust you now, however stupidly."

"Well, then . . ."

The Best in Love Spell Romance!
Get Two Books Totally FREE*!

**PLEASE RUSH
MY TWO FREE
BOOKS TO ME
RIGHT AWAY!**

Enclose this card with $2.00
in an envelope and send to:

Love Spell Romance Book Club
20 Academy Street
Norwalk, CT 06850-4032

All at once, her senses sharpened. The world beyond the doorway brightened, the water sparkled, and spring's perfume drenched the air. Death's shadow faded to a pale, almost unnoticeable gray.

Dom smiled swiftly, his teeth a flash of white in his wicked face. "I adore your logic. Indeed this must be divine inevitability! It has practically been ordained by the Great One—and therefore should not be resisted. Come, *bella*, I will show you some of my world and we will wash some of Vienna's unhappiness away."

Without waiting for further invitation, he pulled her out of the dark windmill and into the fragrant garden. He found a patch of brilliant sun and then tugged her close, fitting his mouth over hers in a single possessive motion, which had the ability to blot out protests of mind and body alike.

Laris didn't bother resisting. Instead, she moved her tongue over his and arranged her body so that it was melded to his from breast to loins. She let the soul kiss happen, and was glad for the desire it inevitably called to unfold itself and wrap around her senses. She reveled in it and willed him to feel it with her.

Dom groaned as he finally broke their kiss.

"Laris, *bella*! I do not know how it could be, but I always seem to crave more of you. I have you and have you, but still want more." Dom's fingers tangled in her hair, bending her head back so that he could nuzzle her throat. His eyes closed in bliss and he touched her as a blind man might, his lips and other senses functioning as eyes.

Other senses.

At this thought something turned over in her mind and she was vaguely aware of some distant voice chanting, making an invocation perhaps. Or perhaps it was monks at prayer. Whatever it was, it was peaceful and soothing and belonged in the air on this warm spring day.

As though called, Laris looked up into the empty blue sky and strained to see something there—a cloud, a bird, perhaps a kite.

Or an angel.

"Dom, there is something . . ." she began, staring more closely at the strange pictograph appearing in the sky. After a moment, she realized that it must be a formation of birds. That was symbolic of something, she was certain, but her overwrought senses did not allow for rational thought.

"Come with me now. There used to be a blanket hidden in the fork of that tree." Dom's eyes snapped open, claiming her attention.

When she did not immediately respond, he swept her up in his arms and strode impatiently toward a leafy bower, making his order to follow moot. In spite of his words, he was not relying entirely upon her free will.

Wisely, Laris did not ask who had hidden the blan-

ket in the tree. She had made peace with the fact
that Dom had had many, many lovers over the course
of his lives. It helped as well that Dom had said that
he *had always wanted* to make love in the gardens.
That suggested that whatever the damning preparations, his plans had never actually come to fruition.

He released her long enough to secure a rather
dusty rug and to spread it out in a shady grove, but
then he drew her back again, pulling her tight against
his body, rocking her against him as though he could
somehow turn them into one being.

They sank down onto the rough wool, crushing the
grass and dry twigs beneath the rug. Laris was dazed
and trembling at the sudden onslaught of desire, an
emotion that she realized she was receiving directly
from Dom. He had dropped his guard enough for his
arousal to show through, and the rising tide of this
desire quickly drowned out the lovely singing in her
head with an older, stronger song that told of the
elemental things that passed between man and
woman.

She reached for him eagerly. The silky cascade of
his silver-blond hair curled about her fingers and
chained her fists.

His own long-fingered hands undressed her and
then caressed her body, touching in precisely the
right way, telling Laris that he was also feeling her
thoughts and desires, and acting upon the knowledge.
She did not try to hide herself from him and in grat-

itude he gently, skillfully stroked her, arousing her to a fever pitch. As her skin heated, a strong scent of jasmine filled the air.

Above them, a dove cried softly and sunlight breached the curtain of the trees' shady limbs gilding them with an almost heavenly glow as Dom sank into her, mind and body.

The overwhelming passion was almost enough to obliterate the familiar loneliness and grief that seemed to overwhelm Laris, flowing from Dom's mind.

"We can stay for a quick tour of the premises," Dom said. "But we must be ready to leave the moment that someone dies. I don't want another run-in with Death's minion."

"Of course," she answered, but her tone was absent. Laris was staring in amazement at what Dom called the *escalara de honor*, the stair of honor, in the main hall of the Palacio Real. It was something out of her childhood Cinderella fantasy. She had come swooping down just such a staircase in her daydreams, wearing an enormous ball gown of gold brocade.

The great room around them echoed with her whispered words. There was space abounding and at present no other humans there to fill it. She had seen many of the castles of Europe on her travels and dutifully admired their architecture and history, but they had always felt like well-preserved museum exhibits, faded and without the strength to truly have an impact on the imagination. But this palace was not some memory of stone, cluttered with jaded vacationers, laden with cameras and chatter, and perhaps some equally faded ghosts who had forgotten who and what they were. It was a home—a royal one—and a seat of power. Kings, who caused thousands to tremble at their words, had walked here.

The tapestries on the walls were unfaded. The frescos were bold with heavenly blues and still retained the artists' energy and religious devotion. There were no carefully placed cords, or alarms, or guards to hold her back from the overwrought bronze sculptures, the tortured furniture, and the enormous paintings on the wall. No one would stop her if she wanted to pet the marble lions that guarded the twin stairs.

Unable to help herself, Laris tested the acoustics by singing a few phrases from *Lakme*.

Dom almost groaned with pleasure at the swell of her voice as it filled the great hall. As always, she sang with luminous joy, as if her veins were filled with lightning storms.

"*Bella*, we haven't time for a concert—but how I wish that we did."

Laris smiled happily. "I know. I just wanted to test the acoustics while everyone is at their siesta and the building is quiet. That is where they are, isn't it? At siesta?" She paused. "This is an amazing room. I can't believe that you lived here once. When I was eight or nine I would have given anything to live here."

"Yes. They are at siesta," Dom acknowledged. "And I am glad that you like this room. Come to the dining hall. *That* is a truly amazing, if indecent, sight." Dom took her arm in a gentle grip that did not break in on her dazed appreciation.

"Where is the dining room? Downstairs?" she asked as they passed quickly through the high floor where ancient horse armor was displayed beneath an arched ceiling of dark wooden beams. The exhibit was so real, with the feathered plumes nodding as they passed, that Laris half expected the metal parade to gallop after them.

"It is just here. This is the servants' entrance, but it is closest." Dom pulled back a heavy arras and waved her inside.

"I don't believe it!" Laris breathed, her eyes assaulted by the gleam of pure gold that seemed to drip from the ceiling onto the expanse of linened table where it puddled in enormous dishes. Even her fantasy ball gown hadn't glistened like this room.

"All the plunder of the New World brought home to please the king," Dom agreed, taking a seat at the head of the table and sprawling in the elegant seat. He picked up a goblet and examined it as though recalling when he had seen it last.

Laris counted seventy-eight chairs at the board in the dining room where there was as much gold laid on the tabletop as gilding the ceiling above.

"Gold plates and cups . . . Is it all real?"

"Oh, yes! Kings, the divine rulers by will of Great God, do not stint themselves with tawdry thrones or humble dishes. After all, great princes need great playthings." His voice wasn't cold, but Laris caught a sudden chill.

"Is there a throne room?" she asked suddenly, wanting to be away from the dining room and whatever it was that was upsetting Dom.

"Of course." He rose languidly, his regal posture a mismatch for his contemporary clothing. "This way. But in its own way, *this* is actually a much grander space."

Laris soon understood what Dom meant. The throne room was lined in red velvet and filigreed silver strapping, which must have required an army of servants to polish. There was a gold canopy over a delicate throne guarded by four golden lions who rested their paws upon orbs that represented the world and Spain's mastery over it. But there was no whimsy here.

"It's like standing in a giant jewelry box," she breathed. Then, with annoyance: "Darn it!"

Dom laughed softly.

"Regretting the lack of a camera again?"

"Aren't you? This is astonishing! What time is it? I mean, what year? Do you know? Would there be a portrait of you someplace? I'd love to see you in fancy dress. Did you have one of those spade beards?"

They moved back to the dining room and Dom said, "Of course I had a beard. I was always fashionable. Let's see . . . it is difficult to say with any assurance exactly what the year might be. Early eighteenth century certainly. Perhaps—" He was interrupted by a servant bearing armloads of flowers, which she laid upon the expanse of gilded table and began to arrange in a tall vase.

A second girl entered behind her. In another moment the room had filled up with busy people.

Abruptly everyone had awakened from their siestas and were back about their work, dozens of soft feet padding everywhere on the parquet floor.

Dom pulled Laris out of the path of the busy servants and then stared fixedly at one of the young girls who had a love bite on her throat, which her veiled hair failed to cover. He said softly: "Angelina Serrano . . . So! It is *that* day."

"You know her?" Laris looked at the petite, dusky beauty and tried not to feel jealous. It was difficult because she fully realized that she had climbed aboard a brakeless train that was riding downhill toward some unknown destination. Her only choices now were to enjoy the ride, or put her hands over her eyes and start praying for deliverance.

Dom shrugged. "After a fashion. I should have realized it when we saw the dining room. It is the twenty-first of May, seventeen hundred and fourteen. This is an important occasion for France."

"For *France?*"

"Yes. The war is finally over. And victorious France has placed Philip of Anjou—Philip the Fifth—on the throne here in Spain. He is the grandson of Louis the Fourteenth and quite obedient to his family. This is when Spain lost Belgium, Luxemburg, Milan, Naples, Sardinia, Minorca, and Gibraltar—all because of the war. Sad to think of all our efforts going to benefit the French."

"The war?" Laris wracked her brain trying to recall any great wars in 1714.

"But none of that is important tonight," Dom went on, waving a hand. "This is a great banquet to honor the ambassador from Greece, Philip's first guest of state. The ambassador's name day was that of Saint Constantine, and Philip was inclined to be generous rather than Catholic on this occasion. He could afford to be. By this time the worst of the Inquisition's activities had wound down and he was able to do this without church reprisal or too much public outcry."

"Saint Constantine?" Laris asked, puzzled by Dom's rather fixed expression and hard voice. He had never previously evidenced any interest in politics or formal religion.

"An Orthodox saint . . . and an inoffensive one." Dom quoted softly: " 'Having seen the image of Your Cross in the Heavens, and having, like Paul, received a calling not from men, your Apostle among Kings placed the care of the Royal City in Your hands, O Lord.'"

"That seems harmless enough," she ventured.

"It is." Dom turned to her. He thought for a moment and then said idly: "If you like, we can go and watch the parade of guards. I didn't see the procession last time and should like to watch it."

Her senses came alert. "Why didn't you see it? Were you working somewhere?" Laris frowned and looked about at the shadowed room, which suddenly felt darker and colder. She drew in an alarmed breath. "Someone is about to die in here, aren't they? That's why Death's door is open to this place."

"Of course." Dom was watching the servants, waiting for an opening when they might safely leave the room.

"Is it you?" she asked apprehensively.

"No."

"Rychard?"

"Don Ricardo Alverez. But no, it is the ambassador's son, fifteen-year-old Agamemnon, who will die tonight. Of course, Ricardo was doing his level best to be sure that I died this day as well. I don't see a clock, but Ricardo and I, Don Diego Ysidro, are likely engaged in a duel even as we speak."

"You and Ricardo are fighting a duel? Now?" Laris's voice rose. "Where?"

"Sí. Would you like to watch Diego and Ricardo duel? It is better than a portrait, I assure you." Dom's mocking gaze dared her. "It would not be so dreadful. Neither of us died this time—and I did take him rather neatly."

Laris bit her lip. She was horrified at the suggestion, but also intrigued. When would she ever have a chance to see such a duel again? And if Dom didn't die . . .

"All right. Let's go observe this duel. You are outside somewhere, I take it?"

"Yes, but we needn't go outside into the heat. It should all be plain from this window."

Dom walked to the heavy drape and pulled it aside. Bright sunlight flooded the room, partially dispelling Death's shadow.

"Watch how clumsy this pass is," Dom said with indulgent scorn. "Rage is not a good companion in such a fight. Concentration and a level head are needed for good swordplay."

Laris joined him at the many-paned window and looked down on the two contestants. If there had been a formal salute between them, she had missed it. Blades were already clashing, glinting in the bright sun.

"Why fight at midday? It's madness. You'll both get heat stroke."

"Don Ricardo forced the quarrel. I had no choice in this matter. You will notice that there are no seconds here. It wasn't a formal *duello*. And he was already quite mad, though not from heat," Dom agreed. "Ah!"

Laris winced as the two men nearly touched chests before breaking away. It was a hard fight, both contestants clearly set on avenging whatever grievances had brought them to the field of battle. Ricardo was savage and wild with his thrusts, his attack filled with fiery hatred. Laris saw what Dom meant by needing a cool head; Ricardo's angry assaults often made his passes go wide.

Diego could have ended the duel at any time had he been satisfied with merely wounding his opponent, but clearly he wanted to do more than draw first blood. And he was willing to play with his murderous partner until he found just the right opening.

And then the moment arrived. Ricardo overextended on a particularly savage lunge and, while he was overbalanced, Diego was able to strike his blade away and bring his adversary to his knees.

Laris watched as Diego's sword hovered over Ricardo's heart. One thrust to the heaving chest would end his life, and it was apparent to her that Diego wanted to kill his opponent.

However, after a long moment, he made a quick slash at his opponent's cheek and then stepped back, dropping his guard.

Ricardo raised a hand to his face as though disbelieving that he had been hurt. Blood seeped between his fingers.

Laris couldn't see Diego's face from their vantage point, but she noticed a softening in his posture. Battle lust had left him.

"Why didn't you kill him?" Laris asked, turning to look at Dom. His expression was likewise closed to her.

He shrugged carelessly. "Once I drew blood the battle had to stop."

"That isn't the reason," Laris said softly. "You had him at your mercy. Why did you stop?"

"It did not seem right to leave a body in the garden where it might be found by the ladies. Also, it might have disrupted the feast." He added dispassionately: "In any event, leaving him to live with that badge of disgrace was a most fitting revenge."

"I see. So you were not overcome with compassion for a madman, or just plain having scruples about killing someone?" Laris pressed, wanting him to think about his answer.

A sudden movement in the trees beyond the courtyard caught both their eyes. A dark-cloaked figure emerged from the woods and began ghosting toward the conch-shell fountain.

"Certainly not. One couldn't afford compassion or scruples around Ricardo, for he had none himself. However, it seems that Death anticipated another ending for our endless fight." Dom turned from the window and let the heavy drape fall. "Come. We will go and watch the palace guard's parade, but then we must leave. Death or his minion shouldn't come around until after nightfall, but he sometimes likes to sit in on grand parties and spoil people's enjoyment by spreading unease."

Laris shivered. If Death's minions were so frightening, what must the creature himself be like—when he wasn't parading around as a bald fat man? When he was coming to collect a soul?

"But I still don't understand this hatred between you two. Why do you and Rychard hate each other so much? How long have you been killing each other in these stupid duels?" she asked, her voice vexed. "Surely it can't be because of some woman. How could some ancient and probably meaningless love affair breed such lasting enmity? Surely you were fighting over something large—maybe a disagreement over religion?"

"I don't recall why we fought. It could be as you say, a matter of religion. Yet I am fairly certain that it was a woman that first caused our quarrel. Surely that was the case in many subsequent lives. And I don't think that I was ever religious, so what else is there to fight over really?" Dom answered, but his pleasant and slightly amused voice was still as distant as the hills of Rome.

"You truly don't remember why you started fighting?" Laris demanded, appalled. She tried to force herself inside Dom's head, but the shutters were closed tight. She was learning to judge the intensity

166

of his reaction to an experience by how much of his thought and emotion he could block from her.

"Dom!" she continued, her voice filled with vexation. "But that's ridiculous!"

"Isn't it? Yet I really don't recall the cause of our quarrel. It was all a long time ago, and I don't remember anything from that time if I can help it. Now come along. The palace guards truly are worth seeing. There are thirteen pure white stallions, a dozen blacks, and ninety perfectly matched bays, which are trained in formal steps. You shall like the uniforms as well."

Laris allowed Dom to guide her from the room, but she was beginning to feel the pangs of renewed frustration. As usual, Dom's avoidance of the subject of his emotions and thoughts was complete. In spite of all they had shared, the barriers around the topic remained intact and she did not seem able to breach them with words.

Her resolve to tear down those walls was growing ever stronger. He'd even said that she was meant to open him up somehow. If only she had the key to unlock his mind and tongue so that he could share these strange and confusing mysteries with her!

But if there was a key she had not yet found it, and it was beginning to look like she would have to pry open his thoughts with bare hands and naked teeth. And she would be forced to do this. She realized now that, until he was able to open up to love, there would be no end to their suffering. For her, there could be no end of pain because there was apparently no end to her love. It would go on century after century, even when it was unrequited. There was no middle ground. It all turned on Dom learning how to love, because it was love that would save them. Or destroy them.

However, terrifying as this newly discovered proposition was, she couldn't count this trip as a total waste. What they had shared in the garden had been wonderful. And she at least now knew where to begin her quest for understanding. It was obviously in the time in Dom's past that he refused to recall, the time when he and Ricardo started their eternal quarrel.

She wondered uneasily just how many centuries back the conflict had been born. It also made her wonder in a broader sense about the Montagues and the Capulets of history. Perhaps it was not separate individuals who were caught up in generational familial quarrels. Maybe it was just that the same angry spirits kept reincarnating in the family line and carried on their previous lives' hatreds.

Then, when one day the quarrels stopped, she had to ask herself if it was because the souls had finally found peace, or if the Great One simply got tired of their squabbles and did away with them.

The thought made her shiver.

Chapter Eleven

Donazella Diana assumed a tragic air and began to sing young Lorenzo de Medici's favorite song:

> *Youth is wondrous but how fleeting*
> *Sing, and laugh, and banish sorrow;*
> *Give to happiness good greeting*
> *Place thy hopes not on the morrow.*

Doffo was not unappreciative of the pretty scene Donazella made, seated by the elegant fountain outside the gray palazzo, but he refrained from answering the fair singer's come-hither glances with so much as a smile; the jealous Seraphina was standing close beside him. The little black-haired witch was not beyond making a very public scene.

*   *   *

Dom and Laris pried open the next door inside the rotting mill and looked out hopefully at a dark, narrow alley that was lined with a series of rickety structures abutting one another in a confused tangle of fitted stones and beams.

So tall and thin was the space between the canted buildings that wrestled for liberty, that passage between them was left in perpetual shadow, and this made it difficult to discern what was natural shade and what was Death's old business trail.

There was no way for Dom or Laris to judge the temperature of the day, standing as they were in the heart of Death's sense-obliterating shade, which did not allow for many normal human sensations. But a short man cumbered up with rolls of bright fabric went staggering by wearing a coat of what looked like worn squirrel skin, suggesting that though the strip of sky above was blue, it was still cool enough to be late winter or early spring.

"Okay, so this probably isn't the twenty-first century," Laris said, trying to sound blasé but not entirely succeeding.

"No. I know this place though," Dom said, taking her arm in a gesture that was becoming characteristic, and rather reminding her of a parent grabbing at their toddler before crossing a busy street.

The thought made her smile. Of course, Dom was right to be concerned. She found herself forgetting in moments of exhilaration that there actually was some danger attendant to their ventures, and was apt to rush toward whatever had excited her imagination. This traveling through history was heady stuff.

"Should we be stopping here?" she asked, but purely as a matter of form. Their other stops had been fascinating and she was swiftly losing her fear of encountering Death or his tenebrous minions. Even their unpleasant meeting with Rychard in Golden Gate Park was nearly forgotten. It seemed as though it had happened weeks, perhaps even months or years ago.

There was also the possibility of learning something more about Dom. Perhaps this was the place where his avoidance of love began.

"Where are we now? When are we?"

"Florence—and I believe March of fourteen eighty-eight." Dom also sounded rather pleased, and there was a suggestion of excitement bubbling out from him. His control was again being relaxed and his memories were reaching for her, waiting to add color and texture to the scene before them. "If this is true, and the shadow goes the right way, then there is someone here you will want to meet. Or at least see."

"The pope?" Laris guessed, trying to think who might be in fifteenth-century Florence as she stepped carefully out and over the worn cobbles. "The Medici? Romeo and Juliet?"

"Sorry, no Romeo and Juliet."

The channel running through the middle of the cobblestone street brimmed with many-hued liquids, which Dom knew to cause olfactory distress in those who could smell them. These gutters had ruined more than one pair of his shoes as well. That being the case, he did not try to conjure any olfactory memories to share with Laris.

"Do you speak Italian?" he asked suddenly.

"A fair bit," she admitted. "In any event, I can sing it. But I haven't a clue what these people are saying. Is it some Florentine dialect?"

"Yes, but I believe that I can—ah!" Dom concentrated for a moment, reaching out for Laris with his mind. Her nerves rippled pleasantly. Gradually the babble from the streets took on coherent order, and Laris was able to understand the vernacular.

"How can you do that?" she asked. Her voice was curious and awed rather than angry at his mental intrusion. "It's amazing. Miraculous even."

"It is something peculiar to Death's shadow, I think. My powers are growing stronger. Our bond is growing stronger. It seems I can offer up my body's memories of this place and make them real to you." He shrugged, but Laris could tell that he was pleased with his gift to her. "I suppose that it is some sort of minor miracle."

"You lived here then?" Laris asked, staring about

172

them in fascination. "What did you do in fifteenth-century Florence?"

"As little as possible." His voice was a well-bred drawl, his expression insufferable.

"Dom!" she chided. "Be serious. Is this where you lived?"

He grinned at her. "No, I didn't live here, but I visited often enough on business." He well recalled the vexatious hazard of the Conica of San Michele where the dyers guild plied their trade. He had bought many a length of fabric from them to please his greedy mistress, Seraphina Beltraffio, when he visited the other guilds. "As for my occupation, I was a minor nobleman with an appreciation of art and an unhealthy interest in politics. At least, I was interested in my early years. Later I became more cautious. I didn't engage in trade myself because it was considered ungodly and mainly left to the Jews."

Sensing that she was straying close to something painful and that Dom was about to close up on her, Laris changed the subject. "So about the pope, or the Medici . . ."

"Seeing either is possible," Dom answered. "But that is not whom I was thinking of paying a call on."

Laris, who had been teasing, blinked a few times.

"We could actually see Lorenzo de Medici? He's really here?"

"No. Old Lorenzo is dead. The Duke of Florence rules here now, and he has woven a net of treachery in which he is now ensnared. We won't be going to visit him."

A church bell began to ring. Dom looked up.

"Ah! Do you hear that? That is San Gervasio. I know those bells well. I visited often to watch the master at work," Dom murmured, stepping out into a slightly wider street where an old man bearing a basket of eggs nestled in straw pushed rudely by them.

Overhead, a large crone in widow's weeds was descending a steep ladder from the building's roof and forced them to step back or be enveloped in her skirts.

"Sons of perdition! Vile demons trying to steal my eggs," the old man muttered angrily, glaring into the air at the crone and then looking over to where Dom and Laris stood. His eyes remained unfocused as he addressed his curses to the wall. He stomped on without stopping to pass the time of day with the old woman.

"I find no joyance in old age," the crone complained to herself, taking up the unhappy conversational thread that the old man had started. "Clamber up, clamber down—all for this 'lady.' Take the milk of a black jenny, they say, and infuse it with anise and asparagus root. Add the bulb of white lilies so it will restore her complexion. Much I care about that! What is to restore my knees? Snake grease is so expensive! Look at her, up there on the roof . . . tinting her hair with saffron and ox gall and gold. One thimbleful of her gold dye to sell, and I should have no more knee problem this spring."

Curiosity aroused, Laris looked up, hoping to see the woman who was dying her hair with real gold. Sitting at the edge of the roof was a woman in black with long golden hair drawn up through the crown of a straw hat. The extravagantly long tresses were allowed to fall over the wide brim like a golden veil that completely encircled her and hid her face from the sun. A maid was moistening the strands with a sponge affixed at the end of a long and slender stick. Beside her was a tripod from which a stream of nearly invisible steam arose.

"Who is the golden idol?" Laris asked, staring at the false, metallic hair, which glittered magnificently in the morning sun.

"Duchess Beatrice." Dom chuckled. "She looks a bit like a golden spider, don't you think? It was rumored that she tried to poison her husband with tainted peaches when she discovered that he had written poems and love letters to another woman."

"Her husband would not think it so nice if he knew her locks were also washed with a potion of bird droppings and bear claw," the old crone commented as though she were privy to their conversation. She leaned against the dirty wall, a hand to her breast as she caught her breath. "Take away the perfume of civet and rose water and he'd know it soon enough. This one is pure poison."

"You knew all the best people, Dom. Not that her husband shouldn't have been poisoned for being a cheating cad," Laris added fairly.

The old woman, finally having restored her breath, stepped into the street and hobbled away with much twitching of shawls and disgruntled grunting. One bit of fringe touched Laris on her bare arm as she passed, and it set up a phantom tingling.

"I will never get used to this," Laris complained, rubbing her skin briskly. "Being here but not really being here."

"I should hope not. This is not a life that I would wish anyone to lead for long, being half dead to our senses and condemned to look forever at our pasts." Dom shook his head. "But come along now. There are some things of true beauty and wonder to see here."

They set off again into the labyrinth. Laris was grateful that Dom knew where they were going. The dark, patternless alleys connecting one into the other without even an occasional sunlit square to break up the monotony seemed like a rabbit warren to her.

The world was feeling rather claustrophobic and filled with unfriendly people when suddenly, from out of one of the ugly narrow doors, there came a soft singing:

"*O vaghe montanine e pastorelle.*"

Dom smiled and began to hum.

Without conscious thought, Laris looked into

Dom's mind and then also began to sing about the lovely shepherd girl who lived in the mountains.

Dom blinked and stopped humming.

As had happened in Vienna, the people milling about them paused a moment to look into the air as though seeking some divine explanation for the almost inhuman music that touched their minds if not their ears. And after a moment of pleasant puzzlement, they shrugged and then went on their way, looking rather more cheerful as they resumed their daily tasks.

Dom took her hand and squeezed gently. They walked briskly until the other woman's voice faded, and then Dom stopped to consult the ground.

"We cannot go the direct route," he said impatiently, straining to see the barely visible course of Death's trail. "But I believe that—yes! This way will take us to the back alley of the church. Here we shall find him, if we hasten. He came here nearly every morning."

Dom hurried them around another tall building and stopped at a small age-darkened door. He forced open the miniature panel and waved her inside. Laris squinted into the great darkness inside the corridor, which finally opened up into a small, lighted chamber.

"Don't worry. There is nothing bad inside now. Almost no one comes here anymore," Dom assured her, laying a warm hand in the middle of her back.

"Whither thou goest," Laris muttered and stepped inside the gloomy passage.

"That's my girl!"

They went down a long, windowless hall and then stepped out into the dim light of the nave of a small stone church. Laris examined it carefully as they walked. It was a humble building, the pews plain and the walls free of any art except a large crucifix and a gleaming white statue of a robed woman.

"This isn't what I expected of colorful Florence," she told Dom. "It is almost Calvinistic."

"Yes. It was one of the churches stripped by Savonrola. An artist—a genius—has been hired to restore it to proper splendor. Careful now. I cannot tell precisely where Death's shadow lies in here because the building is so old and faded, so step with caution. If you begin to smell things or feel a change in temperature, retreat quickly."

Intrigued, Laris nodded.

Standing before the marble statue of the Madonna was an elderly man with light blue eyes and a silvery beard topped by long wavy hair, which was also beginning to silver. It was a fine face, almost feminine in its lines, and at the moment meditative.

"Who is it?" Laris asked, feeling that she should know this man.

Dom smiled. "An artisan, one of Florence's best. Watch him."

After a long moment of distant thought, the man

turned to a roll of stained leather he had laid on the altar steps and began unwinding it. Inside was a selection of metal instruments and assorted parchments, which he set aside with a careful hand.

"I am waiting, Madonna," the man said softly. "I have been here since the night sky turned from deep blackness to translucent blue and the cocks began to crow. Thou wert inclined to come to me before. Why not now? I have not drunk wine for a month and have shunned all women. I am as pure as I may be and yet still be a man. Come out now into God's sweet morning light and be revealed," he coaxed. Then, with a sigh: "So, you are to be cruel today. Then I must in turn use math instead of magic to conjure another of you."

He turned up what looked like a pair of calipers with his rough and spatulated fingers, and he began to measure the damaged statue's serene features and record the numbers on a sheet of parchment.

Another small moment of near recognition sparked in Laris.

Shivering, though not with cold, she looked closely at the jumbled papers. Mixed in with the artisan's notations, there were some sketches of the skeletal structure of a bird's wing and what looked like the drawing of a helicopter.

"It is Leonardo da Vinci!" she whispered in joyful disbelief, taking Dom's hand and pulling him a step closer to the aging artist. Her footfalls sounded loud in the silent room, but the old man didn't notice. "It's really him, da Vinci! I can't believe it. Dom, you knew him?"

"Yes, this is the great Leonardo," Dom agreed, allowing her to bring them closer. "He came here after Moro paid him off. Restoring the church was a belated ducal bribe to God to keep the French from invading Lombardy. We became acquainted then."

"Moro?" Laris asked, reluctantly distracted from her unblinking study of her favorite painter.

"The duke. He rightfully feared that the triple alliance of Venice, the pope, and the king would curtail his power over the city."

"Oh." Laris knew she sounded blank, but Dom's words didn't mean anything to her. "I feel very ignorant sometimes. None of my past memories are about great things—wars or politics."

"It was only a small thing that happened here. There were no great battles for the history books," Dom said kindly. "It was just rather important here in Florence at this time, and for these people. It was all because the fears of dukes and kings were visited heavily upon the lesser mortals who lived under their rule that I remember it at all."

"I'm sorry, Dom. I must seem very historically uninformed to you." Laris turned from da Vinci and gazed up at his shadowed face. "But I am learning as we go, and I'm glad to have the chance to see where you lived."

Dom shook his head. "No, you are *not* ignorant. And I find you a breath of refreshing, modern air. One not obsessed or tainted by the ugliness and regimentation of the past. For you, this is all joy and adventure, and it does me good to see it through your eyes. It translates a somewhat less than happy time into something lovely." He smiled gently. "So, go on. Look your fill of the great man at work. I wish that you could have watched him painting."

Thinking of the artist's work, she asked: "It was magic? Seeing him paint, I mean."

"It was divine alchemy of some sort. Almost he could capture the essence of the soul of his subject and put it on canvas. He worked with a focus—with an absorption that I have only ever seen in one other person. The Great One almost never bestows such gifts on mortals."

"Who else did you know?" she asked, distracted and trying to imagine anyone more gifted than da Vinci.

"You, of course." Dom smiled at her obvious surprise and then took her shoulder and turned her toward the artist. He gave her a gentle shove, warning: "We can't stay long though."

She frowned in vexation.

"Darn it—"

"Yes, I know," Dom said sympathetically. "I wish you had a camera too."

Laris laughed and took Dom's hand, and then crept

forward on silent feet to the very edge of the deeper shadow and leaned out recklessly. She might have gone on even then, but she was brought up short by a pair of doves swooping close overhead. They beat at her warningly with soft wings and then raced back upward to settle in the lofty rafters.

Da Vinci looked upward quickly and then turned toward them, his distant expression fading rapidly and being replaced with one of alert wonder.

"A vision. God and the Madonna be with me! And who art thou?" he asked softly, his keen eyes probing the darkened corner as though he could truly discern their outline. "Not a saint surely. Ah! Is it an angel of music I listened to in the street perhaps? I swear that I heard one earlier. Will you not sing again for me? Or stay that I may take your likeness?"

Laris's breath froze at his words.

"Dom?" she whispered. "He sees me."

"Your foot," he warned. "It is in the light."

She looked down and saw that one toe had trespassed an inch beyond Death's boundary and was gilded with stained daylight, which had crawled up her body and gently illumined her in an eerie golden glow. Suddenly, she was aware of the chill air that filled the church, the smell of old torches, and the scuff of the workmen passing by in the street outside the church's massive iron-bound doors, which had been left ajar.

The artist's eyes followed the length of her brightening arm to where it still clasped Dom's hand.

"And an angel of darkness as well," he said. "But not always of the darkness, I think. Strange angel, thou hast the look of one recently departed from Florence, a Doffo Masaccio by name. If it is thee, Doffo, or his shade, then I have a message for you. It is from a lady, one sore distressed by your abrupt departure from her orbit. 'Remember,' said she, 'that the heart cannot be denied forever—not even the heart of one turned to an angel.' I had not understood what she meant until now. But it is plain that music touches us all."

With a low grunt, Dom pulled Laris back into the shadows where the light gradually faded from her body. His face looked suddenly strained.

"Angel? Where hast thou gone?" Leonardo called. After a long moment he said sadly: "Perhaps these old eyes have deceived me at last. Madonna, how I am to finish your likeness if I cannot see?"

"You were this Doffo? What happened here?" Laris asked with another shiver. The cold was fading from her body, but not from her mind. She was recalled to her goal of discovering more about Dom and whatever it was that had turned him from love.

"We are leaving," Dom said, his expression grown tight and angry. He was withdrawing from her mind, taking sensations with him. "This isn't a safe place anymore. In truth it never was once the bigots had control of it. I should not have brought you here."

"Wait," Laris pleaded, laying a hand on his arm. The muscles beneath her palm were tensed, and she stroked them briefly. Looking up into Dom's shadowed eyes she said: "Please wait. We can't go yet. He seems so unhappy. I want to sing something for him before we leave."

"Laris, it is kind of you but . . ." Dom began, only to stop when he saw her face. His own features softened a shade, and he relaxed slightly. Long lashes veiled his eyes. "This is utter foolishness—dangerous as well. We should *never* have been seen. We could alter everything about his life—about the history of this time. If Leonardo talks to anyone, there will be tales of Doffo's ghost haunting Florence."

"But it's Leonardo da Vinci, and he wants to hear me sing. You said yourself that this man was touched by the Great One. And maybe we were *meant* to be here," she said, as if that clinched the argument. Which it apparently did, for Dom only nodded before turning his back on her and going to stand in the door where he served as a sentry.

"Hurry. I do not know what may happen now that you have stepped out of Death's shadow, but you can be certain that it won't be anything pleasant if he catches up with us."

"We have avoided him so far," she said encouragingly.

Dom snorted, his rigid back eloquent disapproval.

"We've avoided his minions. Death is worlds more persistent. So do make haste, *bella*."

Laris pushed the new worry from her mind. She cleared her throat and then inched as close to the edge of Death's silhouette as she could without again violating the boundary.

For a moment she could not think what music to offer this great man who thought her an angel, but then with a shrug and a small smile of mischief she began to sing the only thing that occurred to her, Musetta's *"Quando me'n vo soletta"* from *La Boheme*:

> *When I walk alone*
> *Through the streets,*
> *The people stop to look*
> *And inspect my beauty,*
> *Examining me*
> *From head to toe . . .*

Dom choked once and then laughed softly at her choice of songs, but Laris did not turn to share the smile she felt moving through her mind. Her eyes were fixed on the artist, who had grown still at the start of her song. He had cocked his head attentively, listening as a dog might. After a moment, she saw his body sway, and he took a small lilting step.

"Ah, kind Madonna," he sighed. "So, you relent and let the angel sing."

Then the artist danced to her voice.

After the last note of the song had died away, Leonardo turned to the shadow where Laris stood and said blissfully: *"Gratzie, angelina mia."*

"Prego, Leonardo," Laris said softly. Then she blew him an unseen, but perhaps not unfelt, kiss.

She turned back to Dom, smiling happily. "I wish we could stay awhile longer. He would like *Der Fledermaus.*"

"No, you don't want to stay," he said. He took her hand and laced their fingers together. He was smiling again but his extremities were unnaturally cold.

"Dom?"

"I have been reminded by our painter friend that this was a very harsh place where people lived short, hard lives. It was better when the Medici still lived and there was some courtly elegance." He spoke quickly, trying to explain. "You would have enjoyed seeing their treasury—the cellars where they stored pearls like bits of grain and scooped them out with ladles, where they kept leather sacks of gold and gems—but now it is the duke's city, a city headed for turmoil. We've already had our Bonfire of Vanities and Anathemas, and the Ordeal by Fire. And there will be more before long. I don't know the precise date but I can feel it coming."

"Dom." Disturbed by his agitation, Laris laid a hand against his cheek and rose up on her toes, thinking to kiss him. Staring into Dom's eyes and looking with all her senses, she had a brief vision of a long scaffold piled with faggots and three men, stripped and coffled there with nooses and iron chains.

"*Sepro te ab Ecclesia militante,*" a faltering voice muttered, saying the words of excommunication that would send Girolamo Savonrola, Domenico Buonavicini, and Silvestro Maruffi to death. One by one they leaped from their ladders and let the kindly nooses strangle them. Then there came the leaping fire, which grabbed first at the mobs around the dead priests and then at their intended victims. Greasy smoke roiled into the air.

At the edge of the crowd there stood a beautiful woman—Seraphina.

Laris shuddered and looked away from her lover without kissing him. She put her hands over her eyes and took a slow, deep breath, trying to clear her lungs of remembered smoke.

She no longer wanted to know what had become of Doffo, for she knew that she could never bear it if that was also his fate.

"You're right," she told him, shaken to her core. "It is time to leave this place. I'm sorry I made you stay."

"Laris!" Dom gathered her into his arms and rocked her gently. His hands ran soothingly up and then down her spine. Once again, his emotions and memories were contained behind his mental wall. "I am sorry. I forgot for a moment that you could see it, too, if I got careless with Doffo's memories. Please try and forget this horror. I swear to you that he did not burn with Savonrola. Doffo was too much a sensualist to have embraced that movement."

Dom did not tell her how Doffo had actually died, knowing that the tale would distress her nearly as much as the snippet of memory she had inadvertently seen.

"Forget it? How? How does one forget people burning?" she asked.

"I don't know," Dom said, sounding almost helpless. Then: "Perhaps you could think instead about watching Leonardo dance for you. I swear that the brilliant old man never danced for another soul! It is entirely possible that he shall someday paint your portrait into a frieze. Certainly he shall remember you until his dying day. And maybe beyond it. Surely that is a great legacy to take into another life."

Reminded once again that they had all lived more than one life, Laris tried to put things into a larger perspective. There was also the fact that she would never discover what she needed to about Dom if she kept flinching away from his memories.

She was silent for a moment as she reordered her thoughts, and then she lowered her hands from her face and faced him.

"You've been shielding me from your bad memories before this, haven't you? Just here? Or everywhere we've been? Was life at the Palacio Real horrible too?" she asked of his shirt, in no hurry to pull away and see any more of harsh Florence in the fifteenth century reflected in Dom's eyes.

"The Palacio was my home. As often happens, it was also at times a prison."

"I see." Though she knew the answer already, Laris still asked: "Do you keep things from me all the time?"

Silence.

"Even when we make love?" she asked, upset at the idea showing in her voice. "Do I get to feel all of you then, or do you still hide the important parts from me?"

Dom hesitated, then said: "There are some things better not shared. You can understand that, can't you, after today?"

Laris nodded. "Yes, I can understand that. Some of your memories are horrible. But I also know that there are some things that are better shared, however painful."

"Those things—the *good* memories—I have shared with you. Even before I arrived here, I tried to share them with you."

Laris nodded again. "Yes, you did. And I thank you for them with all my heart, thank you for sharing them with me. I think that perhaps they were important. Maybe even critical. Perhaps this all is. And I should like to have some say in what you keep from me. I've been handicapped this whole relationship, asking you to open up to me when you can peer inside me at will—and I hate feeling like the beggar maid. This affects my life too."

"I'm trying to open to you."

"Are you? Truly?"

"I promise that you have seen more of me than any person ever has. It is probable that after another week in your company I shall be unable to keep anything from you," he complained sorrowfully, obviously hoping for a smile.

Laris lifted her head and looked fully into Dom's eyes. They were veiled now, and would be as long as he willed it, but she had seen them naked and knew what was there in his memory: not just the distresses and horrors of past lives filled with brutal men, but oceans of sadness and seas of loneliness so profound that he had given up trying to reach the shore of normal existence where others lived and loved.

It wasn't that he didn't believe in love, she realized. It was that he didn't believe that there was any hope of love for *him*. She wanted to throw him a lifeline, to build a boat that could withstand the sea of memory and rescue him before he gave up entirely and drowned—and she drowned with him. But she was not certain how to go about it. She had tried before in many lifetimes and always failed.

Dom, too, was doing some gazing and assessing of what he saw. Laris's wide eyes spoke of both the expectation of love and equal expectation of pain from him. He feared that, as more of her memories returned to her, the fear of pain would grow. And when the pain got too large, she would pull away from him.

Of course, there was one thing that might stop the memories. Perhaps no more recollections of past lives would be sent to them if he could finally do what the Great One wanted.

Could it be that hard? Others fell in love all the time—sometimes many times in a single life.

Looking into the gray depths that led to Laris's soul, Dom asked himself if he dared let go of will and sensibility, if he dared to give her what she and the Great One wanted. Could he actually tumble down the steep-sided abyss that was the great love she sought when he did not know there would be anything other than loss waiting at the bottom? Could he truly do that?

Once there, he was certain that escape would be impossible. And he knew that he would not survive another defeat like the one that he felt sure had ripped a hole in his soul centuries ago.

And then there was the matter of having to reveal himself—all of himself—to her. He did not know what lurked in the darkest corners of his mind, behind the doors of memories he had bolted shut. What if she saw the truth of who he was and did not love him in return?

His fists clenched in her hair as if clinging to an

anchor while a storm of possibilities washed over him, some wonderful, others terrifying.

It is all a matter of faith, he told himself. The faith he had spent lifetimes denying. He had had centuries to think on this, and ample time to plan for Laris's advent into this new life. And still he did not know whether to flee from her and try some other trick to avoid the possibility of a fatal loss, or to let go and surrender to whatever fate awaited him.

Full of the agony—and the more pedestrian emotion of annoyance—at his irresolution, he decided once again to postpone any decision about what to do. This was not a step to be taken in a moment, or without due reflection. He knew of no time limits the Great One had set upon him. He and Laris had their whole lives to resolve this matter, to find a compromise that wouldn't mean his—and her—destruction if he miscalculated. He did not need to decide anything while standing in the shadow of old death and disappointment.

Above them, the doves cooed sadly. Dom looked at them, his face grim.

At least, he didn't *think* that the Great One had set any limitations upon them that would make an immediate decision necessary.

The golden dove bobbed its head slowly from side to side.

Dom, thinking of how Death had lingered near, frowned at this new worry. He looked in question at the two birds who perched in the rafters.

The doves stared back, apparently mute, or un-willing to help him with this question. Which was only to be expected. The Great One believed in free will.

"Come on, little nun," Dom said, forcing his hands to let go of her hair. He brushed his lips over hers once, drinking the sweetness as a temporary anodyne to his worries, and then he stepped back. "Let's go see what is waiting behind those last two doors in the windmill. I can't believe that Enzo and Ilia would have sent us into one of Death's damned gatehouses unless there was some hope of salvation there."

He didn't add that sometimes what the Great One saw as salvation could appear to the ones being saved as heartless suffering.

Chapter Twelve

"*Madre de Dios!*" Manuel whispered, and then looked about guiltily for Father Alvarez. The precaution was unnecessary; the priest had died the day before, succumbing to the same fever that had claimed so many others. In any event, Desiderio could readily forgive the blasphemy when they were faced with the virulent green of the endless vegetation the starving men had been ordered to fight their way through.

The windmill was more cheerless than ever. Reluctantly, Laris tugged on the rusting latch and opened the door that was the second to last. Even as she touched the cold, powdery metal, she could tell by the especially thick shadow leaking under the frame

194

that she was not going to like what lay on the other side of the warped wood panel.

But perhaps, painful as it seemed, it was the sought-after answer to Dom's rejection of love. Maybe the solution to all their woes was waiting beyond this old distorted wooden door. She wouldn't know until she braved whatever lurked in the uncanny shadow.

"Laris," Dom cautioned, "let me do that."

"I can manage." In a rush of bravado, she threw the panel open.

"Oh, no."

She knew the scene outside at once. It was the fen near Stirling Castle. She had seen a reenactment of the Battle of Bannockburn there two years ago when attending the Edinburgh Festival as a guest artist. Unlike Vienna, the battlefield had not changed with the passing of the centuries, and she knew it well.

Of course, the reenactment she had attended had not used real blood, and she had not been permitted to get so close that she could see the eyes of the men lying on the marshy ground and see the sweat that ran from their bodies in gory sluices. She had not watched their bloodied shirts ripple under the caress of the soft breeze, which fondled the fallen as though they were its dearest friends.

Her view this time was not so comfortably distant. She was separated from the slaughter only by the width of a doorway.

Though she could not smell or actually feel what was happening to the men beyond the entryway, she nevertheless comprehended the full horror of what was taking place there and was frozen by it. It was death—massive death—with all the frightened souls of the slaughtered colliding one into the other as they tried to understand what had happened to them.

If there was ever a place that Death should be present and orchestrating, this was it. He had to be somewhere there outside the door.

An ax whistled past the entrance and landed with a dull thump. A man with long red hair jerked once as the weapon was then pulled from his chest, and he did a half turn and landed on the ground. He wore Dom's face.

"*Saorsa*," the man whispered as he reached out a trembling hand toward the bagpipes that had fallen at his side. He was able to lay a bloodied finger upon them before his arterial torrent ebbed low and his beautiful, pain-filled eyes went blank.

"No," Laris whispered, starting to reach through the door for the dead Dom who lay on the other side.

"The piper's dead!" someone said, shock and rage present in equal measure in the hoarse voice.

"Close it," Dom ordered, turning his back. "Don't go out there. Just shut the panel."

"No. Maybe I can do something," she whispered. "He might not be dead."

"You can't do anything, Laris. He's gone. Close it."

But she couldn't shut the door.

Absurdly, given the screams of battle, the hum of carrion flies still filled the air, louder even than the ringing of battle steel.

Then a voice began shouting: "On them! On them! On them! Drown them in the river!" And thousands of screaming bodies wrapped in muddied plaid went running by.

Suddenly a black-cloaked figure was in the doorway. It reached down for the piper, but seeing Laris's own extended hand reaching through the door, it turned and gripped her also.

The head swiveled an impossible number of degrees until the blank face looked her way. The empty pits it had for eyes faced her, but there was no life in them.

Laris gasped. She was cold—so cold. The minion's brittle white fingers were laid over her pulse point, and they were sending icy poison through her body, down her arm back up through her neck, heading for her heart, which it intended to still.

"No!" She jerked back, falling over on the floor.

"Enough." Dom spun around and without looking through the portal, he reached past her and quietly closed the door.

"Oh God," Laris whispered, cradling her arm to her chest.

She opened her mouth to tell Dom what had happened, but he spoke first, forestalling her.

"It was a rout from then on," he said quietly. "The English were drowned in the river almost to a man. Bruce actually won Bannockburn with very few casualties. It was a great victory for Scotland. It was an honor for every man who died there to give his life for this cause."

Warmth returned to her body. Laris, at last able to move, pressed the heels of her hands against her eyes and tried to rub the grotesque images and fright away.

"They are getting worse, the doors," Laris said, too upset to mind her grammar.

"I am sorry that you saw that. But it's just the past," Dom said quietly. "A shadow of something that happened long ago. It is like I told you in Florence. You must not let these things affect you. All that matters is the present and who we are now."

"It's just a memory," she repeated, looking down at her wrist. There wasn't a single mark to show that Death's minion had touched her. She might have hallucinated the encounter. "But, Dom, it happened to *you*. And you remember it! How can it not affect you?"

"No. It happened to Duncan. This is just like . . ." He thought for a moment, then went on with an analogy of something that he himself had never seen. "It's like a movie. It can't hurt you if you don't invite it in and make it real again. You simply have to close it out. These memories are convenient pegs that one is tempted to hang old feelings on. But the temptation must be resisted, or at least the emotions you choose to display must be chosen with care."

Laris shook her head.

"This sort of past-life experience is why we are stripped of memories when we are reborn." Dom made a gesture of helplessness. "We were never meant to accumulate so much sorrow. You must not take it to heart."

"But you haven't been stripped of memories. And neither have I. Or, maybe I was before, but they are coming back now."

"True," he agreed. "This time I wasn't erased. But the same logic applies. We must ignore it. Forget it even, if at all possible."

Laris stared at Dom, wondering if he truly believed what he had just said. His expression gave nothing away. Dom's beautiful eyes might as well have been lined with lead shielding for all the emotion they provided her.

"But isn't that what happened to you long ago? Something so bad that you couldn't let it back into your mind? Isn't it still affecting you? Is this the thing that turned you from love?" she asked, her own eyes filling with the tears Dom would not shed for his earlier incarnation.

"No. This wasn't it."

"But what in the name of all that is holy could be worse than this?"

He stared back at her, eyeing her tears in bemused

incomprehension. He touched her cheek, smoothing it with his thumb, but he did not open his mind to her.

"You seek strange things and cry for the wrong reasons." He tried to explain something he had never put into words. "Laris, you will not believe this, but there are worse things than dying. Living in continuous fear, or worse—living without hope is much worse. Or I always found it so. In fact, there is only one thing worse than living with no hope, and that is living with it and having it betrayed."

"Living with hope is worse than dying?" Laris asked. She then nodded once, next shook her head. She was getting nowhere trying to approach this from the outside. Yet every time she tried to reach inside Dom, to understand his view of the world, she ran smack into the wall of isolation that ran around his innermost thoughts and feelings.

And that caused her to wonder what he saw when he looked over his walls and into her own mind. Was she his opposite, a coke furnace blasting out painful emotions he could not share? She did not have his ability to hide her thoughts at will. He had to know what she was thinking and feeling. He had to know what she was planning for them.

Did he view her desire to know all of him, for them to love and have a future together as some sort of snare, a trap or weapon that would take away his protective armor and leave him vulnerable? Had her love for him over the years seemed like a pressing invitation to go skydiving without a parachute? Was it an abrasion to his already damaged soul?

If that were the case, if they were so opposite in thought and nature, what hope was there for them?

"I found it so. Hope is often cruel." Dom finally looked away from her and gestured to the door. He did not try and read her thoughts, perhaps sensing that they were too painful to share. "Duncan believed in the cause he fought for. He lived a long life and died honorably and without regret. Don't shed tears for him. I do not."

"I am not crying for Duncan," she said cryptically, lowering her eyes and forcing her tears to stop. Her gaze when she looked back up was calm but rather bleak. Perhaps it was time to try constructing some walls of her own.

"If not for Duncan, then who?" Dom asked in consternation as he offered her a handkerchief.

"No one," Laris said, refusing the linen with a watery sniff. "I am just tired and a little hungry. Let's get on with this before I collapse. I just want to go back and get on with my life."

Dom frowned as he looked her over, assessing her physical state even as he refused to view her mental one. Laris forced herself to meet his gaze and tried not to think at all about the creature who had grabbed her. "Very well. Let's see what this last portal offers. Perhaps something else entertaining."

"I hope not. While it's been instructive, touring your old pleasure palaces, I don't think I am going to learn anything more since I'm so tired. Can't we just go back to San Francisco? Surely it's safe by now. We've been gone for hours—maybe days."

Dom's touch was again light on her cheek, and he stepped closer. Losing her battle with nerves, Laris closed her eyes. She didn't want him seeing any hint of what was in her mind, and she did not want to risk seeing any more of his thoughts until she was calmer and had a chance to think things through.

Death's minion had touched her. What did that mean?

"We don't get a choice about when lessons are taught," Dom said. "The Great One ordains and Fate makes a calendar. All that we humans can do is refuse to learn from them."

"One would have to very obstinate."

"Yes, but that isn't a problem for either of us, is it?"

"No," Laris admitted. "At the moment I feel very stubborn, and I can tell that you do too."

Dom paused at her bitter words. "Rest for a moment. You are tired. I can look at this alone," he said gently. "Indeed, that might be best. Why don't you wait for me over there?"

And what if Death is waiting for him outside that door? a voice inside her head asked.

"No." Laris drew in a deep breath and slowly exhaled. She opened her eyes. Her voice was dreary but firm as she said: "If you can bear to see all this horror, then so can I. Let's see what our last *lesson* of the day is. Maybe we'll want to learn it after all."

Dom shook his head; he knew this might well not be their last lesson. The Great One always had the last word.

He knelt down by the final door and reached out a steady hand.

Laris had to admit that living without fear or hope had seemed to make everything very easy for Dom. How convenient to have no dread to make you a coward, to face no risk of being disappointed. Perhaps she *should* try to emulate instead of change him.

The last door in the windmill was barely more than a cupboard draped in an old tarp, which they had to pull aside in order to see through.

"Oh!" Laris said in surprise.

The view on the other side was gorgeous in a fecund and primitive sort of way, and completely foreign to Laris, who had never seen streamers of cloud tangled in a jungle's creeping grasp. Everything was very quiet. It seemed a huge improvement over the last scene they had witnessed, but she could tell from Dom's groan and annoyed curse in some foreign tongue that once again they were someplace he had lived and hated.

"Where is it this time?" she asked warily, peering out at the lush canopy overhead, which seemed unnaturally silent and as eerily still as a photograph. *Or a movie without a soundtrack.*

The sky seemed to shimmer, causing Laris to have a moment of vertigo. Though her body did not seem to recognize any physical discomfort while in Death's shadow, her mind was reaching some sort of emotional critical mass and crying out for a rest.

"South America somewhere. Ecuador probably. Perhaps Peru. They didn't have countries and borders as such when I was here."

"And that would be when?"

"The year of our Lord and His Most Gracious Majesty King Charles the Fifth of Spain, fifteen hundred and thirty-two. Of all the useless and bloody dangerous places for this door to open up on, this is by far and away the worst of them." Even with the English accent and moderate tone, the whiplash of true annoyance was evident in Dom's voice. His mood was also eroding. Apparently he wasn't enjoying revisiting the brutal landscapes of his past, whether they could hurt him now or not.

Laris closed her eyes, hoping that the darkness would have a calming effect upon her fraying nerves. After their visit to Florence, and her brush with Death's minion, all she wanted was to return to her own time and the sybaritic comforts of a five-star hotel. Traveling the world of Dom's past existences was getting tiring. However, she didn't complain. Sifting through the ashes of his lost lives had to be even worse for him.

She just prayed that it was not all a purposeless exercise. In spite of her claim to obstinacy, the day had kicked the stubbornness out of her. She didn't know about Dom though. Could he face more? His capacity for obstinacy was greater than her own.

"What were you doing in South America?" she asked in an effort to distract Dom from his irritation, and to supply some context to her reeling thoughts. She needed some information, some labels to explain where they were and what was happening. Her normally quick wits were foundering in the sea of mental weariness, which she feared was close to the ocean of despair.

"Soldiering. Briefly. The climate was not kind to my compatriots, and we did not thrive here."

"You were conscripted?"

"No, I *volunteered* to come in search of gold. Desiderio was young. One should not expose the young and weak-minded to temptation."

Laris felt momentary satisfaction in discovering the answer to why the golden dishes at the Palacio Real had bothered Dom.

She thought next about his reply and then shook her head. This wasn't the time for another history lesson or a philosophical debate about the follies of youth. Whatever she was supposed to learn, it wasn't that lusting after wealth was a bad idea.

"Should we take a look anyway? Just in case it actually is the twenty-first century and we are at the edge of a Club Med resort?" Laris asked, wishing that her senses of smell and taste were not deadened by Death's miasmatic shadow. A whiff of cigarettes or gasoline would be very reassuring and would spare them the need of venturing out into the jungle to search for signs of civilization.

"It is about to rain."

"How can you tell?" Laris asked, stirred to momentary curiosity. "Can you actually smell ozone?"

"I can predict the weather here because it is always either raining or getting ready to rain in this cursed place."

"Well, we could take this tarp to use as an umbrella," Laris suggested, forcing herself to sound brisk. She tugged the dusty fabric that had covered the doorway free of its rotting cords and folded it into a square that would fit inside her purse. "We wouldn't get so very wet. Anyway, it's only rain, not boiling oil. Let's get on with it."

If they were not venturing back out the first door to San Francisco again, she was willing to look at anything if it would get her out of the windmill. She did not want to be there when the dead from Bannockburn started to arrive.

"You can only say that because you have never been in a storm here. This isn't our century and the nearest city, if you could call the overgrown ruins by such a name, is a long, long hike away." Dom spoke patiently, making no move to help her with the tarp. "You don't want to go out there."

In spite of herself, Laris again found her interest piqued. She looked out at the symphony of greens and tried to imagine hiking through it.

"An abandoned city? How many hours of hiking is it exactly?"

"That rather depends." Dom's voice was dry as he turned to inspect the windmill, looking for some door that they might have overlooked.

"On what?"

"On whether headhunters are chasing you."

Laris smiled briefly and then realized that Dom wasn't making a joke. "Oh. There are really head-hunters here?"

"Yes. So, you see why I don't think that it would be wise to venture out? In this gloom we could easily miss the edges of Death's trail and expose ourselves to the dangers of this horrid place. Little though I like the idea, I think we must go back out the first door and see what awaits us. We must discover what has happened with Rychard. Perhaps you are correct about the passage of time outside—"

In answer, a violent blow was struck at the mill's door and it burst open under the impact. A crazed and bloody Rychard stood swaying on the threshold, his shadow stretching before him like a black net. His lips were peeled back showing his teeth, and he still had a gun in his hand, though his arm was now badly punctured and bleeding heavily. His legs were cut, too.

It seemed impossible that Golden Gate's serene tulip garden should lay beautifully empty behind him. Home was only twenty feet away, and yet they couldn't get to it.

Rychard's scary eyes focused on them, and he raised his gun. Dom did not bother telling Laris to run. He simply planted a hand on her behind and shoved her out the tiny door. He was less than a moment behind her, probably spurred to near-inhuman haste by the report of the gun exploding in a confined space. Rychard's shrill scream of rage was an added spur.

"Fate, you bloody bitch!" Dom said angrily.

"Is Rychard worse than headhunters?" Laris panted as Dom dragged her to her feet and they sprinted for the jungle's ineffective cover, which threatened to be more of a trap than a shelter. Roots hidden by a thin cover of leaves thrust themselves out of the ground at the perfect height for snagging fleeing shoes.

"We'll soon find out."

"How many bullets can he have in that thing?"

"Too many. Now save your breath and run!"

They found a path of sorts that veered off to the right. It was little more than a wide cleft in the fractured rocks, but as it was bulletproof, free of obstacles and large animals, they took it gladly.

Laris wanted to look back and see if Rychard was gaining on them, but decided that concentrating on not falling was probably the wiser course of action. Seeing the bullet with her name on it before it hit her was not an experience she desired. Unlike Dom, she couldn't think of anything worse than dying.

They ran on without pausing, and eventually the sounds of pursuit faded behind them. They finally slowed their pace to one less grueling, and then, as their lungs demanded it, they stopped to rest in a small patch of greenish light made by a recently fallen tree that had torn a hole in the forest's dense canopy. Leaning against the boulders that surrounded them, sharing short, fragmented breaths with Dom, Laris finally noticed that she had a headache and was feeling dizzy.

"I don't know what's wrong with me," she began, putting a hand to her head. The air was thick and suffocating and made every breath a labored act. "I suddenly feel horrible, like I have a hangover."

"Altitude sickness maybe," Dom answered. He did not appear nearly as winded as she felt, and Laris envied him his matter-of-fact strength. She felt rather like a defeated conquistador who had just run a ten-mile footrace in a heavy metal helmet that was two sizes too small and had become embedded in her skull.

Before she could think of anything else to say, the bit of blue sky overhead disappeared, and with a crack of ear-assaulting thunder, it began to rain—a rain that was wetter and harder and more omnipresent than anything she had ever seen or felt or even imagined.

And she *could* feel. The water was drenching her clothes and crawling over her skin like some living, clinging slime, conclusively proving her unhappy suspicion that they had stepped out of Death's protective shadow and were now enjoying the full effects of an Amazonian rain forest.

She didn't bother unpacking the tarp. It would not do any good against such a deluge.

"Damn it. I can't believe this is happening." Laris put her hands to her temples and began to rub them. Her throat ached, and her eyes burned with sudden unshed tears that she flatly refused to release. She and Dom were alive, unhurt, and together. She had a headache and was tired, but that was nothing to complain about.

Yet.

"Poor Laris. This has been quite an adventure for you."

Dom's hands covered hers, taking up her gentle massage. With a sigh of contentment, she leaned against his chest and rested her head on his shoulder. Standing close to him, listening to his heart, she thought the rain didn't seem so bad.

"Are we lost?" she asked, her voice forced to calm

even though water was running into her mouth and eyes.

"Not terribly. The trouble is not retracing our steps, but running into Rychard—or someone else—if we do."

"I don't want to see Rychard or *someone else*. But what then do we do? We can't stay here," she said definitely.

"No, we cannot. Not with dark falling," he agreed. "We are going to have to find some way to circle around this hill and get back to the ruins from the other side. And if we're lucky enough, maybe something will eat Rychard."

Laris considered the "hill." It looked more like a mountain to her, taller and stronger than any fortress ever built. It was covered in enormous plants that all but hid the sky from them. And the trees probably had giant snakes in them. As well as headhunters.

You said you wanted to know all about Dom's past, a mocking voice reminded her.

And so I do, she answered.

With that, Laris pushed the undermining thoughts firmly aside. It was time for a show of intrepidity—for Dom and for herself.

"Ruins? Is that what we were in? I didn't notice."

"Yes, but modest ones. It looked to be some sort of storage building. The *Indios* used to have them along the trail to their sky temples so that the priests could stop for food and rest when they made their annual pilgrimage to the shrine."

Laris raised her head and looked at Dom. Raindrops starred his eyelashes, and his hair was plastered against his skull.

"You said we might run into someone else? Who were you thinking of? The Indians?"

"Possibly. Or *mis compañeros*." Dom didn't look happy, but he did not appear frightened either. Laris took heart from this.

"*Compañeros?* Do you mean the other conquistadors you were with? We might actually run into *you?*" Laris asked with a touch of excitement. "But wouldn't that be good? They would be some protection from the headhunters. And maybe Death's shadow would be nearby."

"I have no doubt that Death's shadow is near them, but no, this would not be a good thing."

"But why not? You could talk to them—tell them some story."

"Because having a second me—a nearly exact twin—show up would likely cause consternation among the men. They were simple people, superstitious and frightened."

"And violent," Laris added, thinking of the scene in Florence.

"And violent," Dom agreed. "They'd likely kill us both immediately."

"They would kill a woman—just like that?" she asked, appalled.

"No, I mean that they would kill Desiderio and me out of hand. You would likely be raped first. That was the approved course of action for many men when presented with heretical women." Dom's tone was even as he delivered the bad news, but she could see something moving in the back of his eyes, something hard.

Laris pinched the bridge of her nose. "Okay. Then I suppose that trying to find your friends is not an option."

"No. Not unless all else fails. I'd sooner meet up with a pack of *quiexada.*"

"And what are those?"

"Wild boars." He looked at her as though puzzled. "You didn't know this word. Is it because your mind is closed to me now?"

"I guess it is. I can't feel you now either. Maybe because we aren't in Death's shadow anymore." *Or is it because Death's minion touched me?* she wondered.

"Perhaps this is for the best," he murmured. "My thoughts are not likely to be pleasant ones."

"No, I imagine not. Mine aren't any too happy either."

"Still, it is strange. And I would prefer that you have my knowledge of the jungle. There should be some residual tie that I can use—Laris, look at me."

Laris stared into Dom's eyes, not afraid of the cold

fire of resolution that burned in his gaze because it couldn't touch her heart.

"Nothing. Your mind is truly shut to me now." Dom's brows drew together. "I do not like this at all. You should not be kept from me. Something—some-one—is interfering with us. It is like there is some shadow cast over your mind."

"Let's worry about it later," she suggested, as her head continued to pound. She didn't mention that it could be some lingering effect from her encounter with Death's minion.

"I shall. There must be some way of remedying this. But first things must come first. We must leave this place immediately. I do not want you exposed to its dangers once night falls."

Perhaps it was foolish, given their situation, but Laris was suddenly very confident that they *would* find their way back to the windmill. Dom was furious. And an angry, thwarted Dom was likely a determined one.

"Well, at least we have this tarp. I have matches, too, so if we find anything dry we can have a fire." She patted her purse. She added with feigned cheerfulness that belied her exhaustion: "And I have a couple packages of granola bars, so we can have lunch—dinner," she corrected herself, noticing how the darkness was beginning to press in on them.

Dom nodded and even managed a grim smile. "I

am finally glad for your bag. Come. We must find the cave before darkfall."

"The cave? You know where we are, then?"

"Yes."

"You were here before? That's terrific," Laris said, genuinely enthused. "This way we won't get lost."

"Yes, it's terrific that I've been here before," he agreed dryly, setting off into the jungle. "Stay close behind me and try not to make any noise. This place looks empty of people, but I assure you that it is not."

Dom—Desiderio—had promised himself that if he made it out of the jungles of South America alive he would never set foot in their green hell again.

Of course, he hadn't made it out alive. Perhaps that was where his plan had gone wrong.

He loathed the jungle, its constant fetid damp that prevented sweat from ever drying from the skin, where every breath was drawn with effort and sat heavily in the lungs like stagnant water. And he detested the stinging insects, which burrowed into every inch of exposed flesh. And then there were the *carangageiros*—the giant jumping spiders that took birds as their prey and sometimes tried for humans as well. Most of the native plants were also hostile.

The native humans had left a lot to be desired too. By the time Dom's mission had arrived, the local populations were firmly entrenched against the European invaders. An understandable reaction, Dom had to admit, given that they had been little better than robbers and murderers come to feed off the New World. But it had not made for a pleasant or easy campaign.

Fortunately, he did know more or less where they were, and therefore which way not to go. However, there was no guarantee, in spite of his brave words to Laris, that the path he had chosen was actually any safer than the one where his friends were making camp. And he did not have a machete to clear a path if the way became overgrown with plants. That would slow them to a crawl or else force them onto the trails made by animals.

All he had in the way of utensils was a pocket-knife, a money clip, loose change, and a handkerchief—none of which was likely to prove very useful as either tools or weapons. And they would likely need both before very long. The jungle was treacherous. It—

"Dom," Laris whispered sharply and then drew in a sharp breath. "Oh God! Dom!"

Alarmed, he spun about, just in time to see a velvety brown fer-de-lance drop onto Laris's shoulder. Its triangular head was aimed at her breast pocket, its body trying to find purchase on her neck.

Without thinking, he grabbed the deadly serpent by its tail and flipped it back into the green vines with a snap of his wrist.

"Oh God," she said again.

The rescue happened so quickly that Laris's face was still draining of color when the danger was gone.

"Was that . . . .?" she asked faintly, sinking to her knees as darkness clouded her vision.

Dom knelt beside her, holding her up so that she wouldn't fall into the leaf mold. There were many vicious insects on the ground that she would not want in her blouse either. Above them, the rain kept on, assaulting the canopy overhead with liquid missiles, which the broad leaves then drooled down upon them.

"It was just a small snake," he said comfortingly when his own voice returned to him and he could trust it not to betray his alarm. "It was just the cloud forest saying welcome and look sharp."

"*Welcome?* With a viper? It looked . . . like a poisonous one . . . I saw on a nature show," she told him, taking several deep breaths through her mouth. Her body had begun to shake in reaction.

"You must trust me to know what is safe and not safe," Dom told her in a bracing voice, even as his hands ran over her, assuring himself of her well-being. "When a snake falls on you from overhead, it is apt to look very dangerous, but that isn't always the case."

"And that one wasn't dangerous?" she asked. "Really?"

"No, it wasn't that dangerous," Dom lied without compunction. "It might have bitten you, which

217

would have hurt, but it wasn't poisonous."

"Oh." Laris straightened and made an effort to collect herself. She clenched her fists against their trembling and took another slow breath. "I feel so stupid, overreacting like this. I just never had a snake fall on me before. It startled me."

"Well, I have had it happen, several times, in fact. And it is always disconcerting. Especially if it is very large or fast."

"I can imagine." She shuddered with distaste. "This happens a lot? Snakes just fall on you?"

"And spiders. It happened more often than I cared for. Disgusting creatures." His tone was fastidious and almost made Laris smile. "But I can take care of any number of simpleminded reptiles or insects, so you needn't fear anything as long as you are close. And I will find a way for us to join thoughts again so that you will be able to protect yourself."

Dom drew Laris to her feet, checking her complexion before he released her arms. It was difficult to judge anything in the fading light—everything was painted with the same unattractive green pallor—but he could see that there was more color in her cheeks, and her lips were not as bloodless as they had been moments before.

"That's my girl. Buck up now. We must go on. It is only a little farther," he said encouragingly, though he did not in fact know if this was true. "And then we can rest and eat. We need to do both."

"I am all right now," Laris assured him, pulling her purse back up onto her shoulder and straightening her spine. She tucked in her shirt. "Let's go find that cave and have dinner. I think you're right. Suddenly I'm starving."

Dom suspected that she was lying. Terror did not cause hunger, but rather the opposite. Still he admired her for the show of strength. He allowed himself a brief hug and a quick prayer of thanks that the deadly snake had not bitten either one of them, and then he set Laris from him. There was no time to further express his gratitude that their time together had not just come to an end. He had to get her into a shelter and let her rest.

He had to keep her safe! Somehow.

It was bad enough that in the past he had stolen her dreams of love and romance. He could not live with himself if this tour of his long-ago foolishness and stubbornness ended up stealing her present, most beautiful, and gifted life as well.

As Dom began pushing into the labyrinth of green hazards, moving rather as Daniel must have through the lion's den, he hoped fervently that the hill on this side of the stone bowl they were in proved to be as cavernous as the one on the opposite end of the hollow.

Of course, a ubiquitous supply of shelter was the only thing he wished to have in common with the mountain caves to the east. For it had been in one of those caverns that he and his companions slept on the night the *Indios* had attacked them, chased them into the jungle, and then, having pinned them against the mudflats where the crocodiles lived, they had slaughtered them to a man.

Chapter Thirteen

The green around the cave's mouth was dark and impenetrable, and growing more ominous as the light faded. The monstrous trees with their heaved-up roots were wreathed in a variety of parasitic plants, many of which were very beautiful, but which Desiderio had discovered could not be trusted either because their leaves were caustic, the nectar was poisoned, or because they were guarded by terrible armies of stinging ants that could chew through any fabric and even leather.

One of Desiderio's companions spat contemptuously and turned his back on the green hell. Another made a rude gesture, the force of which was ruined by the sight of his Adam's apple's erratic jerking up and down.

Desiderio was more cautious. He backed into the cave without making any insult and did not take his eyes from

221

*the silent jungle. It was too quiet. The cicadas had ceased
their shrilling. The hummingbirds and monkeys had disappeared. And there was an odor of wet decay beginning
to overpower the smell of living things. He feared that in
spite of the silence, they were far from being alone in the
wilderness.*

*More than any other night he had passed in the jungle,
tonight he was wishing himself elsewhere.*

Laris saw only two other animals on their way to
Dom's cave. One was an angry monkey who rushed
by them, hurling simian insults in a screeching voice
as it hurried on to some destination. The other was
a black jungle cat that paused to examine them with
soulless green eyes before it padded by on utterly silent paws. Laris had always thought jaguars beautiful,
but she discovered that they were also frightening
when the iron bars and deep moats of the zoo were
not around them.

The gulch she and Dom traveled finally narrowed
until the trees on both sides of the divide had grown
together overhead. Laris was certain that the gap
would close completely and they would be forced to
retrace their steps; but the stone finally relented and
just as Dom had promised, they came across a cave
about twenty minutes later.

Laris did not at first recognize it as a cavern. Its
low mouth was blocked by a fall of rubble, creating
a partial barrier against the cold, silver rain, which

sluiced off the slope above the cave in a clear water-fall.

There was a skeleton of some poor creature that had obviously been trying to escape the cave when it died, but as it was washed completely clean and had no odor, Laris did not find it overly distressing. As nature "red in tooth and claw" went, it was a fairly gentle demonstration of where they were.

Though the rain was coming down harder than ever, Dom paused outside the cave and sniffed suspiciously at the dark opening.

"No bats," he said at last.

"You can smell bats?" Laris asked, head averted as she spoke because she was tired of swallowing the odd-tasting filtered efflux that was a mixture of rain and bitter plant sap.

"Their droppings. It should be all right, but wait here a moment while I investigate. Don't move from this spot," he ordered, ducking slightly and entering the cave. He disappeared immediately into the shadows beyond the thin spill of water.

There was no noise except the rain, but Laris had the uncomfortable feeling that she was not alone in the downpour. She looked around quickly, but there was nothing there.

Still, she had the feeling that she was being followed, observed.

"Dom?" she called softly.

His answer was an indistinct murmur.

Laris, who was nervous as well as weary of the rain drumming on her head and running into eyes and mouth, chose to interpret his reply as an invitation and quickly followed him into the cave. She didn't bother to try to avoid the spill of water off of the mountain. The gentle waterfall could hardly make her any wetter than she was, and there wasn't any way to get inside without passing under it.

Dom took her arm as she entered and forced her to a halt in the vaguely illuminated area at the front of the cave.

"Patience," he cautioned. "Remember that we are no longer protected by Death's shadow, and we may not be the only creatures who have tired of the rain and come searching for shelter."

Laris froze, looking about with trepidation. It was one thing to tiptoe into the lions' den when you thought no one was home. It was quite another matter to come calling when the lions were in residence and possibly in the mood for dinner.

The light was dim inside the cave and showed them only the front of what was obviously a fairly deep cavern. The floor sloped gently toward the back of the stone hollow and was surprisingly flat, as was the ceiling, except where it had suffered the cave-in near the mouth. There it was ragged and uneven in color.

The floor around them was dry and littered with what looked a bit like dried twigs and leaves, but might also have been insect husks and cast-off wings.

At that moment, she did not particularly care which it was, as long as it burned well.

They waited patiently for a minute or so to see if there were any warning growls or hissing, but no sounds, hostile or otherwise, issued from the back of the cave.

Dom finally relaxed his posture and let go of Laris's arm. "I believe that we are alone."

"Then let's make a fire," she said, shivering as her alarm faded away and the unnatural chill ebbed back in. "I am really feeling the cold right now. I thought rain forests were always warm."

"Not at high altitudes. You have also had a shock." Laris looked quickly at him as he spoke. "That snake probably scared ten years off of your life."

"The snake . . . Yes, it scared me."

Dom, who was still glancing about with a slight frown between his brows, finally nodded to himself. He ran a hand over his face in a vain attempt to dry it.

Before their run from Rychard, Laris thought, they had been dealing with the challenge of old perceptions and facing emotionally charged memories. As wrenching as the experiences had been, they had had some choice about whether to participate. They had not been forced through any of the other doors or, indeed, even out of the safety of Death's protective shadow. Now the choice was gone and they were left with harshness of this past reality.

So just deal with it, Laris scolded herself.

Dom nodded his head again, but didn't move.

"Is something wrong?" Laris asked aloud, also looking about again, though she didn't notice that anything inside the cave had changed.

"No. Not that I can see. It is just rather odd that there is no sign of animal occupation. In spite of the hill we are circling, we are in a bowl here and the bottom of it gets very wet. Much of it is a dangerous mudflat that smells as if all the victims of the plagues were left to rot there. Excepting the crocodiles, the animals avoid it in favor of higher elevations."

"Crocodiles? Are you kidding? At this elevation?"

"No, I do not jest. It was most unexpected. They are not particularly large." Dom's tone was neutral. "In any event, this cave should be prime real estate."

"I suppose you're right," Laris said slowly. "But I don't see anything, do you? There would have been water trails if anyone had come in after the rain started."

"You are correct. There is no sign of animal occupation on the floor. That leaves only things that fly or burrow." Dom shook himself. "And there obviously are no bats in here, and nothing except man will burrow through stone . . . so I am worrying over nothing. Why don't you work on the fire while I gather some leaves for a bed and see what I can find for our dinner?"

He reached with difficulty into his damp pocket

and removed his Swiss army knife. He waved it at her in mocking salute.

"I shall return anon, my lady."

"Like Caesar, you go forth to conquer?" she asked, striving for lightness when she felt none.

"But yes! Let us hope that I don't have to conquer too many trees to find what we need."

"Can't we just sleep on the tarp?" she suggested, thinking of how high Dom would have to climb before he could reach any broad leaves, and what creatures might be lurking up there. In the jungle, very little could grow on the gloomy bottom of the forest floor, and all the living beasts had moved up into the air. She recalled seeing a program on the nature channel that focused on the many amphibians that lived their entire lives up in trees, never once touching the ground. It wasn't a life she would like at all.

Dom shook his head and reached for Laris's mussed hair with his empty hand. He smoothed back the tangled locks with a gentle palm and then brushed his thumb over her eyelashes, which were wet with drops of rain.

"I don't recommend it. Sleeping on stone has a way of making one feel decades older. And it is very cold because it eats up your body heat without ever giving it back. Don't worry, I know which plants are safe and am very good at climbing trees." He kissed her forehead. The salute was chaste but not passionless.

"Please be careful," Laris said, wrapping her arms

about Dom's waist and squeezing him tightly. She forced herself not to argue with his decision, but was unable to forestall one last warning: "Watch out for snakes, especially the big ones. And also . . ."

"Yes?"

"Just watch out. For everything."

"I shall." Dom managed a lopsided smile as he began to wring out her sopping hair. "I have grown accustomed to this body, and plan on finishing out its life somewhere civilized."

Laris watched the thin stream of water from her hair as it pattered on the floor and wished that Dom had said that he planned on living out the rest of his life with her. To say anything else seemed like tempting Fate. However, she knew that this wasn't the best moment to inaugurate a discussion of relationships or semantics.

It took an act of will, when there was such a divergence between the desires of the heart and the mind, but she eventually let go of his waist and stepped away. Her lips were forced into something resembling a smile.

"It's getting dark," she said, folding her empty arms about herself, hoping the inadequate gesture would comfort and warm her. "Better hurry. I'll have a fire ready when you get back."

"Yes." Dom, perhaps hearing something in her tone, gave her a searching glance before turning back toward the outside. He paused at the cave mouth and looked over his shoulder. His manner was frighteningly gentle when he said: "If for some reason I don't come back before dark—"

"You will!" she said swiftly. "Just don't go real far. Promise me. And call me if you need help."

"Yes, I will be back. But if I am delayed for some reason, I want you to stay here for the night and then backtrack to the ruins. Use the door that leads back to San Francisco. Don't wait for me. I'll come when I can."

She stared at him, not wanting to understand what he was saying.

"Promise me that you'll do this, Laris. You must. I need to know that you will be sensible."

"What about Rychard?" Laris protested. "Won't he kill me if he sees me? I should think hiding here until you come would be better."

"It would not be better. Rychard might not kill you," Dom said. Then added softly: "The jungle surely will, though, and not as swiftly as a bullet. Hard as it is, you must be sensible."

Laris forced her lips to move.

"I—I promise I'll be sensible."

"That's my girl." With those words, he was gone through the silvered waterfall and out into the danger of the coagulating darkness.

"He'll be back. Soon," she reassured herself as she stared at the streaming water. "He's been here before.

He knows what he's doing. And he wouldn't leave me if it wasn't safe."

Laris, suddenly feeling all the cold and wet and cumulative weariness of their many adventures, began digging in her purse, looking for her tin of safety matches. She had promised Dom a fire and there would be one. With it they could hold back the night and terrors that waited in it.

Being careful not to drip on her tinder, she scraped the odd bits of distasteful detritus on the floor into a largish pile and then set a match to its edge.

As she had hoped, the tinder burned well. As she had feared, much of the fuel was dried insect husks and smelled less than appealing as it transformed itself into needed heat and light. Still, it was fire, and it would serve as a beacon for Dom and also to keep any large animals away. For that reason, she found it the most beautiful fire she had ever seen.

Slowly and carefully, since the leaping shadows distorted the floor's surface, she searched the front part of the cave, seeking more twigs, dried vines, and sticks for her tiny fire. It did not take long to gather up everything that could be found within the radius of the fire's orange luminosity, including the dead animal's bleached bones.

It made her feel slightly ill, particularly after Florence, but she put the skeleton's tiny pieces in the fire as well.

Though her headache had eased, foraging consumed her last measure of strength. Laris told herself that she dared explore no farther. The black of the cave was like no other she had ever seen, and it frightened her at a visceral level. She had been camping as a child, but never without some ancillary equipment like camping stoves and lanterns. Without a reliable source of light, she didn't dare venture into the dark depths of this cavern. She might fall down a shaft or into a chasm. Dom would never know what had become of her. He would go back to the windmill and leave her, alone, in the dark, forever.

A violent shudder tore through her body.

Drained and increasingly uneasy, Laris slowly spread out the tarp and then emptied her purse onto the dusty canvas. Most of the contents were of no use. She could not see a need for perfume or lipstick. But not all her clutter was useless. In addition to the granola bars she had two packets of brown sugar, one of honey, and one of taco sauce, three salts, a small box of mints, a few wet-wipes in foil packets, and an unopened package of tissues.

The last item was very welcome as Laris suddenly realized that in addition to all her other human bodily woes, she was again subject to the call of nature. Her bladder was paging her.

"Damn it all. Not now," she pleaded. "Can't you see that it's raining?"

But her body wasn't listening.

After returning everything to her purse, she looked

once about the cave hoping for some miracle of plumbing, or at least an artifact that might serve as a latrine. But finding nothing that looked remotely like a bathroom fixture, she resigned herself to the unpleasant fact that she had to make one last trip out into the rain.

The distasteful task seen to, Laris returned quickly to their shelter and took off her clothes so that she might wring everything out and start the seemingly impossible process of getting dry. It had to be done. The cloth of her shirt and pants had become a clammy cocoon, and she feared that, her body might be transforming beneath it. At the very best, she was shriveling into an albino prune. At worst, she could be playing unknowing host to several forms of fungi, leeches, and parasitic insects.

Feeling anxious, she stripped, making a careful examination for bites or green stuff on her body. It was a relief to discover that she had not actually turned into a hothouse for alien plant-life and was not hosting any of the larger parasites.

Her underwear was made of lace and light microfiber, which dried out quickly, but her sweater, blouse, and pants were cotton and inclined to hold doggedly to their moisture even when she was brutal with her twisting. There was nothing for it but to spread them out and hope the fire lasted long enough to banish the moisture.

Laris was still debating whether she was colder sitting about without clothing or wearing the damp garments when Dom returned to the cave, dragging a variety of broad-leafed ferns and what looked like giant withered green beans behind him.

"You're back," she said, not caring that it was an obvious thing to say. Relief flooded through her, making her dizzy, and she rushed to greet him. It had belatedly occurred to her that maybe the lesson she was supposed to learn was how to survive without Dom. "I am so glad that you're back!"

"Just like a bad penny, I always come back," he agreed, dropping his collected flora in favor of holding Laris's body tightly against his own.

"Ouch—what is this?" she finally asked, reaching for the hard lumps that pressed into her ribs and breast. "Is this the very latest in Amazonian fashion? Rock-stuffed shirts?"

"That is dinner. Or perhaps dessert. I needed my hands for other things." He chuckled and stepped back. His abused shirt was quickly unknotted to reveal some prickly looking fruit.

"You might have warned me. I think I'm bruised from your dessert."

"Sorry, *bella*," he said, clearly unrepentant. "But as they say, true love is true pain, yes? And these 'rocks' will keep us from going hungry. Besides, what did you expect of me when you threw yourself into my arms? I have never turned you away."

"Hmph!"

She didn't ask him if he meant his flippant remark about true love.

"And what are *these* things?" she asked, picking up the yard-long withered sticks.

"More dinner. They are seedpods," Dom answered, spreading the leaves out to drain. He handed her the knife, eyeing her sheer bra and panties but refraining from comment. "Cut it open. There are seeds down inside all those white fibers."

Bemused, Laris sat down on the tarp near the fire and cut a long slit in the leathery pod. As Dom had said, there were fat seeds inside the thing, which surrendered themselves after a little digging.

Cautiously, she sampled one and found it pleasant if rather too bland for actual excitement. There was no danger of these particular seeds finding their way into a trendy salad bar unless they were treated to roasting and glazing with exotic spices.

Laris laughed suddenly.

"I can improve on this," she said, reaching for her purse and removing her various condiments. She held them up to the flickering light so Dom could see them. "What is your pleasure? Hot sauce? Honey? Salt?"

Dom came and sat down beside her, studying her packets and then her smiling face with a certain amount of amusement but also admiration.

"I wondered what you kept in that bag."

Laris tore open the taco sauce and smeared some on one of the seeds.

"Not bad," she said, offering one to Dom. The ritual of eating was making her feel better, and it seemed to chase off some of the cold.

"No, not bad at all," he agreed. "Give me the knife and I'll prepare the fruit. We may wish to use some of your honey for this as it is not very ripe. Anything truly sweet was already half eaten."

"What *are* those?" she asked a third time. "They certainly are ugly."

Dom shrugged as he halved the tough skins.

"We called them *dulces*."

"That means sweets, doesn't it?" she asked, recalling the limited Spanish she had learned while linked to Dom's memories.

"Yes." He cut three horizontal lines in the fruits' flesh and then three vertical ones. Putting down the knife, he forced the skin inside out so that squares of yellowish flesh were forced into the air. He flicked away the black seeds, tossing them into the fire where they hissed and then exploded with tiny pops.

Carefully, he licked the juice from his knife, grimacing at the tart taste.

"More honey?" Laris asked, reaching for the brown packet.

"That would be best," he said, folding up the tiny blade and shoving it with difficulty into his wet pocket.

"You may want to take your clothes off and wring them out while we still have a fire. I think they'll dry faster that way."

Dom nodded and stood, though he was clearly not enamored of the idea of being without the minor protection of clothing.

Laris pretended not to watch as he struggled out of his clinging pants.

Dinner over, they made up their leafy bed and then talked quietly in the growing darkness of their lair while night fell over them. It came with a thick cloak that was blacker, and more smothering in its silence, than any night Laris had ever seen or heard.

"How did you come to be in this forest? I know you came after gold, but what about the army?" Laris finally asked, watching unhappily as the fire died down. There was no more fuel to feed it. "Surely it can't have been to subdue the native population. There couldn't be enough population out here to bother with."

"No, we were not here to consolidate power for the throne or to save heathen souls." Dom's voice was reflective and a bit bitter, though his expression remained unchanged in the dimming firelight.

"What then?" she asked, lying down and snuggling into his arms. She pushed back her unease with his warmth and the sound of his heart beneath her ear.

Dom sighed. When he spoke his voice was as lulling as a song, but his words were hardly the stuff of bedtime stories and lullabies.

"It truly was all about gold. Pizarro had run mad. Gold fever was upon him and rotting his brain. He had seen these life-size statues of gold pulled out of the tombs in Peru and began to dream of the wild rumors of this fabled city of El Dorado. He finally came to believe that there was an *Indio* empire there where the king actually gilded himself in gold dust every morning and where the streets themselves were paved in the precious metal. It did not take much to inspire the other men to greed—especially those who were new to the land and did not understand how savage it could be." Dom shrugged. "After several months the thousands of native bearers were dead, the horses had all been eaten, and we were all on the verge of starvation.

"Pizarro was too busy torturing the *Indios* for information to care about what happened to the rest of us. We were months away from any city and surrounded by barren lands, so we split up into foraging parties in the hope that one of the groups would find some food. My group came here."

"And?" Laris asked softly, not certain that she wanted to know the answer but feeling that she must listen to anything Dom was willing to share about his past.

"Some of the Imara were friendly and shared their food, and a few of Pizarro's men made it back alive to tell the world about their adventures. The rest were not so fortunate."

Understanding what Dom meant, even with her present psychical insensibility, Laris nodded once and then changed the subject to something more hopeful. She did not want to think that somewhere nearby there was another Dom who was hungry and in grave danger. Maybe his fate was justice, but it was also merciless. She understood that history should not—perhaps could not—be altered, but the temptation to attempt it was awfully strong.

"We have had enough of sad things," Dom said. "And the night is no fit time to speak of them in any event. It's like calling ghosts or summoning the things that go bump in the night."

"Yes, that's what it's like." Thinking of Death's minion, she nodded briskly. "Let's only talk about cheerful things for now. Tomorrow can take care of itself."

So, instead of the past's disappointments and horrors, they talked then of favorite foods and music, of cities they had visited and friends they had known. Though they never spoke directly about the future, or their plans beyond the next morning, Laris, lying there in Dom's arms, was able to forget the dangers of the things lurking in the darkness beyond the cave long enough to begin to trust that they would live to have a future. Perhaps even one together.

The thought made her smile as she fell asleep.

*   *   *

Dom was awake for a quite a while after Laris had tumbled into an exhausted dream. He still found her to be the triple-distilled essence of all that was good and feminine, but at the moment it did not inspire him to lust. The fierce protectiveness that filled his brain allowed no space for any other emotions or desires.

He would save her from this! He made the vow silently but solemnly as he stroked her tangled hair. Whatever it took, whatever sacrifice he had to make, he *would* save her from this sweltering fecund hell of his past.

Chapter Fourteen

Unseen, but perhaps sensed, by the other animals who were seeking shelter from the hunters, a small band of exhausted men staggered on in the darkness, trying to hold off the night and its many great terrors with a few smoldering torches and weary prayers.

They had come to this jungle with gargantuan appetites for gold and conquest, but none of that greedy vision remained to sustain them. Their aristocratic veneers had been stripped from them long ago, and they were wearing various wounds, some new and crimson, some old and turning green.

Behind them were the Indios. In front of them was an expanse of evil-smelling mud where they knew crocodiles slept.

All they wanted now was to escape, but that did not

seem likely. A few of the men began to weep. The rest
were stony-faced and resigned. Two others melted into
the underbrush and tried to slip away.

Laris could not actually see the sun rise, but she
watched the light outside fade from black into gray
and then finally green. The air filled up with the min-
gled scent of decay, damp earth, and flowers. And
something else, a smell that was vaguely familiar and
somehow unpleasant.

Though she had not set her mind to the path of
consideration, nevertheless her half-waking thoughts
were being guided someplace where enlightenment
seemed possible. Bits and pieces of their recent experiences were fitting themselves together and a
broad outline of meaning was appearing at the back
of her mind. There was a pattern here and it was
embroidered on their souls, the stitching reinforced
by centuries of repetition. This trip they'd taken to
all Dom's pasts was somehow tied in to the Great
One's hopes for Dom. And Rychard. All the souls
that were in this loop.

Didn't it *have* to be?

Also, Dom had been in his natural habitat while
in Spain and Vienna, wearing his old personas comfortably, but the further back in time they journeyed
the less at ease he was. He seemed lost now, somewhere between who he was in Florence and the man
he became in Spain.

She hoped the person he was now would be canny enough to avoid anything that could kill them.

And strong enough to kill anything they could not avoid. Assuming, of course, that the thing that attacked them was actually killable.

Laris frowned.

But this wasn't all about Dom. Somehow she played a role in this puzzle of lives, too, but so far she had been unable to determine what her part was.

It seemed impossible that she, like Dom, wouldn't have to be robbed of her comforting blindness and have unwanted insights forced upon her. She knew it was going to be unpleasant when this happened. Personal insights always were painful.

Yet, she could tell this uncompleted pattern of their souls had to be altered and the work finished. They had failed thus far because the combination of forces was always the same. Dom was what he was, and so was she. Something would have to change in order for them to break the cycle.

Change *was* coming.

A black-winged butterfly fluttered by the mouth of the cave, moving in jerks and starts and looking like some exotic blossom tossed in an eddy. Only there was no eddy to toss it about because the air about them was utterly still and breathless. It reminded her of something else, some creature large and unpleasant.

Laris lowered her eyes from the mouth of the cave

to the ground and watched with dazed incomprehension as a sea of green confetti moved over the cave's previously barren floor. There was divagation in the emerald tide only at the edge of the tarp, but even there she could see activity. The old fabric twitched spasmodically at the edges and shivered everywhere else, telling her that something was moving beneath it.

It was like being on a raft in the middle of a lake filled with miniature water lilies, she thought with bemusement.

Then as her brain swam its way to the surface of full consciousness, it dawned on her that they were surrounded not by water but by ants—*stinging ants!* They were carrying in small pieces of severed greenery. And the insects were now busily cutting their bed up beneath them and carrying it away to some nest in this cave.

"Dom?" she whispered.

He grumbled and started to roll over. Laris stayed him with an urgent hand. The abrupt contact brought him immediately awake.

"What's wrong?" His eyes and voice were cold and focused.

"Ants," she said unhappily. Then, when he didn't immediately react, she added: "Millions of them. They have us surrounded. They're eating our bed."

"*Ants.*" Dom slowly raised his head and peered over her shoulder. He whistled between his teeth.

"They would explain why no one else is using this cave. The rain must have driven them back last night."

"Are they *bad* ants?"

"In these numbers? They are all bad." He thought for a moment and then asked, "Is there anything left of the fire?"

Laris craned her own neck and looked over to where her impromptu hearth had been. It also was covered in a boil of leaf-bearing ants.

"No. No fire. And no rain either, at least not right now."

"A flood! A flood! My kingdom for a flood," Dom muttered.

A sharp pain stitched through Laris's hip. She tried not to move, but the floor was feeling very hard and her limbs were beginning to ache from the strain of keeping absolutely still. She closed her eyes and tried to think of something constructive. If Dom wanted a flood, she would gladly have traded everything they had for a can of insecticide.

Then she blinked and started to smile.

"Okay," she said. "We don't have fire and we don't have rain, but how about poison?"

"Poison sounds delightful. You have some hereabouts?"

"Maybe. I have *something* that might work."

"You have something that might be poison?" he asked, wariness plain in his voice. "Where?"

"I have poison in my bag. Can you reach my purse? I think it's behind me near my head. Open it up and look inside it for my perfume. It is in a small silver bottle."

"You want your perfume?"

"Yes. I once saw a friend use her cologne to kill yellowjackets and even spiders. Maybe it will work on ants as well."

"It kills wasps and spiders, and you put this poison scent on your body?" he asked, surveying the floor with an unhappy eye as he dug cautiously inside her handbag. The ants were very large and red in color. Their large mandibles and the sheer number of them were terrifying. "Not that I am not grateful to have this perfume, but whyever would you wear such a scent?"

"I'm not a bug. I like the smell just fine," she said impatiently. "Anyway, it isn't the scent that kills bugs but the alcohol and oils. It covers their skin so they can't breathe and then confuses their sense of smell with a stronger odor. With any luck it'll wipe out their trails and make them retreat."

"Or perhaps it will make them frenzy." He pulled out the small vial and sniffed at it cautiously. "It makes *me* want to frenzy. Or swoon. Are you certain this is poison?"

Their eyes met and for a moment caution was lost. Laris swayed forward, thinking only of touching lips to Dom's half-smiling mouth.

Pain intervened again.

"Ow!" Laris looked down at the shivering tarp. One scout had clambered up on it and taken an experimental bite of her finger. She crushed it angrily.

"No, I'm not certain of anything," she said, returning to practical matters. "So we had better be ready to run, hadn't we? Unless you think that they'll go away when they get all the leaves?"

"No, they won't stop with the leaves," he said, and Laris knew that he was thinking of that stripped skeleton they had burned the day before. "They are simply saving us for *afters*. Now that one has come up here, others will soon follow."

"Well, I don't fancy being some ant's dessert. Shall we go?" Laris wiped her wounded finger on her slacks, hoping being rid of the ant's remains would stop the growing sting. It was frightening to think what hundreds or thousands of bites would feel like.

Dom pulled the cap off of her perfume and handed Laris her purse. They sat up cautiously, being careful not to crush any of the tiny bodies working under the tarp. He reached out a long arm and squirted the ants working at the edge of their bed closest to the cave's broken mouth.

As Laris had predicted, the ants that were hit with perfume did a quick writhing dance, squirting their own acid into the air as they died. As a bonus, those near them pulled back a few inches, either disturbed by the scent or their dying comrades' toxic outpourings.

"*Brava, bella*," Dom complimented, giving the vial another pump. "Killing ants with perfume. I should never have thought of this. I could have made use of your ingenuity on my last visit here. But I suppose that I must content myself with having you and your arsenal here with me now."

"I have no camera, but I do have poison. The world's most expensive bug spray—one hundred and sixty dollars an ounce," Laris answered, starting to smile until she smelled the mixture of acid and perfume boiling up from the floor. "Ugh! That's awful. What kind of bugs are these?"

"That's eau de dying ant. Still, there are worse odors in the jungle."

"I hope I never smell them!" she answered, pulling a sleeved arm over her lower face and breathing shallowly through her mouth.

Slowly Dom rolled to his feet and then reached back to help her up. The air was somewhat cleaner up near the ceiling. Laris took her hand away from her face and then rolled her shoulders, trying to ease her stiffened muscles so she could run if she had to.

She wished passionately that she had thought to replenish her supply of aspirin when she'd changed purses for her trip. She was going to need something for her muscles. As an effete child of the modern age, she was not used to sleeping on stony floors.

"Are you ready?" Dom asked.

"Yes."

Cautiously, they stepped out onto the cave floor, crushing hundreds of tiny convulsing bodies and spraying more perfume as they went. Around them, the unsprayed ants continued to carry their bits of leaf into the black cavern recesses, but disquiet was clearly spreading.

"It's a good thing we dressed last night," Laris muttered, hanging her purse around her neck. "I wouldn't want to be doing this in bare feet. Ant bites really sting."

"Fortune seems to be favoring us . . . in a limited sort of way. For a while last night I thought we had been marked by Death, but perhaps the tide of ill luck has turned." Dom spoke as he stepped carefully over the rubble barrier and then turned to help her climb the low wall. "There don't appear to be any ants out here, but it still seems wisest to move on immediately. They might decide that they like your perfume after all and come out for seconds. Ants can, and do, travel widely in their search for food."

"Or they might come out just to retaliate. I don't think the colony is very happy just now." Wave by wave, the swarm was turning to face them. A horrible clicking filled the air.

"Best keep this handy." He handed Laris back her perfume bottle and then rubbed both hands over his face, feeling the growth of his new beard that appeared as little more than a silvery shadow.

"Bah! What a stench! A little behind your ears was nice, but this is horrible." He wrinkled his nose while he scrubbed his aromatic hand against his pants.

"The heat and travel may have ruined it," Laris volunteered. "I don't recall the scent being this pungent. Of course, I don't usually use it in such large doses either."

"When we get back to San Francisco, I shall get you some perfume that does not kill insects. An attar of jasmine or honeysuckle perhaps."

"It's a date," Laris said, shoving the bottle into the top compartment of her purse where she could reach it easily. She had no intention of wearing that particular scent again. It would always remind her of being lost in a hostile, foreign land.

Once they were away from the caves the shrill calls of the cicadas again filled the damp air. Presently they were joined by the songs of some invisible birds that serenaded Dom and Laris with eerie arias as the two worked their way around the edge of the hill, searching for a way back to the ruins and the windmill portal.

Laris found herself looking about for a pair of oddly colored doves, but there was no sign of those familiar birds.

They saw no sign of any humans either, but every once in a while they would pass a mound of vine-covered stones that had about them a vague suggestion of symmetry. It seemed unlikely that the jungle's current inhabitants would allow their monuments to fall into disrepair, so it seemed probable that they were passing the remains of an even older civilization.

Feeling peckish, Laris dug out her granola bars and offered one to Dom. He nibbled at it cautiously at first, but finding it tasty he soon had the rest of it devoured. They had mints for dessert. It wasn't really an adequate meal, but it had the benefits of being readily available and not requiring preparation.

Laris was growing more accustomed to the fetid miasma of smells that made up the rain forest floor, but she did not enjoy their outing. The altitude made exercise enervating, even though Dom was careful not to set a difficult pace and she was able to keep up without growing dangerously winded.

"Will we be able to circle the hill today?" Laris asked, enjoying watching the play of Dom's muscles as he walked ahead of her. It was the only thing that she was enjoying about the morning.

"I hope so," Dom answered. "If we don't encounter any difficulties we should—"

He stopped abruptly in a small patch of hazy light that shone through a hole in the forest canopy.

"What is it?" Laris asked, lowering her voice and pressing up against him. Dom reached back for her, settling a hand on her hip.

"I've found Death's shadow."

"Oh—that's great!" Laris appreciated the irony of

her words even as she said them. She tried to peer around Dom, but his hand stayed her.

"Perhaps." Dom didn't move a step as he examined the greenery around them.

"What do you mean?"

"Where there is a shadow there are also people, usually dying. But not always right away. And it was my experience that all those who inhabit this clime are of a less than friendly nature. If they are still mobile, we probably do not want to see them—and certainly we do not want them to see us."

"Oh . . ." Laris leaned against Dom's slightly damp back, feeling the fatigue in her legs. She didn't allow herself to complain but did ask: "But if we are cautious?"

"No. I don't think so. This shadow also does not lead the way we want to go. In one direction is Rychard, and in the other the mudflats on the basin's floor."

"We couldn't perhaps cut across it and use it as a place to rest for a little while?"

"Perhaps. But I don't know how wide it is, and I would not want us stranded in it if Rychard is near. It would be too easy for him to find us. I also wouldn't like to waste the daylight on something that will only lead us astray."

"None of the shadows before were very wide," Laris pointed out. "And it could take a lot longer to go around. Besides, maybe you and I could reconnect mentally within it."

As if to lend strength to her suggestion, the world got dark and it began to rain. The sudden cannonade of the morning deluge that found them through the trees above threatened to beat their skulls flat.

"I never knew that rain could hurt," Laris muttered, missing the tarp they had left behind. "I think I hate this place."

"You are not the first to feel that way." Then Dom said something else in a dialect she didn't understand and pulled them both into Death's shadow.

Immediately, the painful sensations ceased. Also immediately, she could feel Dom in her head. It was as though some electrical circuit had closed and his thoughts were again channeling down her neurons, giving her enhanced senses and knowledge.

His mental attendance had become such a constant background for her thoughts the last few days that, foreign as it was to have someone else's presence in her mind, she found that she had missed him when he was gone.

Dom weighed her weariness and assorted body aches, doing his best to mask his own misgivings about being back in Death's shadow where the past could touch them in unexpected ways.

Laris knew of his unease, not by what she felt, but by the parts of him that were still closed to her.

"We'll wait out the storm here. But watch carefully." His voice was flat, but she could sense the caution and wariness that was within him as he searched the surrounding ferns.

This elaborate caution probably meant that it wasn't a good time to try peeping into his brain and discovering if he was still standing on the brink of his emotional abyss, arms pinwheeling while he decided whether or not she was worth taking the emotional plunge.

Laris sighed as she temporarily abandoned that line of thought and also began to scan the jungle, though she was not certain what she was looking for beyond snakes, vindictive ants, or headhunters.

She frowned at the tangled vines around them. She should have loved the rain forest with its clean streams and beautiful fecund greenery. It was one of earth's last unspoiled Edens. But it was all so foreign and terrifying. It wasn't quaintly exotic as all the nature shows suggested; it was alien and indifferently hostile to human life. The jungle cared about the jungle, not about the people who foolishly ventured into it.

Or maybe it was that Dom's memories had colored her judgment and perceptions. She was no longer sure which were her own emotions and experiences and which were Dom's.

There was a deep grunt in the distance and Dom flinched. Then there came another grunt and the sounds of snapping. Goose bumps covered Laris's arms and something tickled at her nostrils. The horrid smell reached down through her sinuses to clutch at her throat.

Something cracked open and repulsion and fear began to bleed into her mind.

"What is that?" she gasped, coughing and trying not to retch. She peered through the trees, trying to see what Dom was watching so intently, but all that met her eyes was a black sheen and some vague but sinister movement of long things in the mud.

"The mudflats," Don answered as he quickly withdrew from her mind, closing the door upon his thoughts and memories. Immediately her heightened sense of smell and hearing began to fade.

Though accurate in the technical sense, Laris was certain that "mudflat" did not adequately explain the amalgam of evil odors and mental sensations that percolated through the black ooze and then crept outward on the rain-churned air. She had smelled death often enough now to know when it was about.

She had also been at an Everglades park when the alligators were being fed. It was one of the last vacations she had taken with her parents, and it had been unforgettable.

There were animals out there—big ones—and they were eating something. From Dom's distress she could imagine what—*who*—was being consumed. The only blessing she could find was that there was no screaming. Whatever poor soul was passing into the belly of the beast was already dead.

"Let's go," she said, feeling sick. No matter what Dom claimed, these old memories *could* hurt. Horror of this nature did not lose its potency because of time. And for him, this was more than some grotesque scrapbook of the macabre. This had been his life.

There was also the danger of running into a minion, or even Death himself.

Laris touched Dom's arm, shaking him from his horrified reverie. "The rain is easing and I feel a lot better," she lied. "We needn't wait here. Please, let's leave."

Dom looked down at her with blank eyes. It took him a moment to bring her face into focus and let go of whatever vision was playing out in his brain. Once he did rejoin the present, he immediately read the horror in her face and mind, and quickly nodded.

But instead of guiding her away, he expelled a slow breath and drew in another. He was like a swimmer preparing for a long dive in deep water.

"Dom?"

"Yes. We'll leave." But still he didn't move. She realized that though he had freed her, his recollections still held part of him in thrall.

Laris finally reached out and took Dom's cold hand. She began leading him down what passed for a trail on the rain forest floor.

Laris knew the instant they reached the edge of

Death's shadow. It would have been impossible not to notice the return of human discomfort: aching legs, stiff back, and stinging finger. And the disgusting, unending wet.

Also, she was entirely alone again with her thoughts.

Laris's shoulders slumped tiredly.

Dom shuddered to full wakefulness and halted for a moment on the other side of the shadow to take her in his arms and to offer wordless comfort.

"I am so sorry, *bella*," he said into her tangled hair.

"*De nada*," she answered, again recalling some Spanish. She held him in return, offering the only consolation she could.

They stood in the rain, unable to tell if some of the wetness on their faces came from tears.

"Your accent is purest Castillian," he told her, his voice the barest murmur of sound, barely audible above the rain.

"It should be. It's really *your* accent after all. It is part of me now."

Dom is part of me now.

As impossible as it seemed, standing there in his arms, Laris felt a stirring of desire. Something rolled over in her stomach and every muscle in her abdomen clenched. Tiny streamers of tingling warmth shot through her.

She almost laughed aloud. How crafty the body

was, seeking out pleasure even when her mind had told it of the grim dangers they faced.

"It's ridiculous, and I don't want you to think ill of me for this, but I want you," she said quietly.

"It is ridiculous . . . and I want you too."

She sighed.

He sighed.

"Attraction is an odd beast," Dom said, burying his face in her wet and snarled hair.

"And a horny one," she muttered, making him laugh silently. Beneath her hands she could feel his muscles gathering themselves. Warmth returned to his body. He straightened a bit.

"We have to go on now," he murmured. Still his arms did not loosen.

"I know. . . . Dom?"

"Yes, *bella?*"

"Do you think we are being tested? Were we led here on purpose?" she asked, recalling her morning rumination. "It seems too many awful things have happened to us just to be an accident. It doesn't feel like random bad luck. It seems like we are being driven toward a certain destination."

He was silent as he mulled the question over. "I hope not," he said finally. "Those kinds of tests generally end in disaster."

"But you said that . . . that the master builder wanted us to be together. For a reason. So maybe we should stop pretending that our travels are random.

257

He's trying to teach us something specific, isn't He?"

"Yes," Dom agreed, dropping his arms and stepping away from her. "He is trying to teach us—*me*—something. And I will figure it out. In the meantime, don't be frightened. He does want us to be together, so all will be well."

But that was only a half-truth. He had already figured out part of what was required. What the Great One wanted was for Dom to show enough faith that he would put aside his past and allow himself to fall in love, and because of that love, give his life—and Laris's—over to that faith.

Yet that wasn't all of it. Dom had already done that—and the Great One knew it. There was more. What was required now was a leap of faith that he could love and still bear it if that love was taken from him. That he could suffer another loss, but still go on. He had to accept the possibility of loss, and, should it happen, not seek total spiritual oblivion.

And He was surely willing to let them suffer anything in order to make it happen.

The possibility frightened Dom. It seemed an especially bad omen that there had been no sign of Enzo or Ilia since they left Death's shadow.

It had been centuries since Dom had been angry with the Great One and questioned his methods, but he was angry now. It was completely unfair that Laris should have to suffer to teach him a lesson.

* * *

The pythonian path they followed again began to climb, and it constricted until they could see neither sky nor what waited around the next turning. But though tired and breathless, neither of them complained or suggested that they go back and follow Death's seductive trail.

Eventually the rain eased. Glossy hummingbirds shook off their reserve and began flitting about them, warning the two humans away from their floral territories with angry chirps.

"There it is, our destination," Dom said suddenly, stepping out into a small clearing. He pointed. "That's the temple. We've come halfway around now and can see it."

"Oh, wow!" Laris looked across the basin and was filled with reluctant awe. She took Dom's hand. "I can't believe what I'm seeing. It doesn't seem real at all."

"But it is real, I assure you. And to our present life in the twenty-first century the temple remains here, unseen by Western eyes. In fact, I doubt that the natives even recall it anymore. And it's a fortunate find for us. This could be another portal. It's hard to tell in all this green, but I think I see another shadow."

Laris shook her head, even though she wasn't truly disagreeing with what Dom said.

The ancient temple was perched on the side of a cliff, clinging to its aerie with stony nails. All but the top reaches of the pyramid were lost in the green gloom that wrapped its base. There were some carved beasts perched near the building's crown, but beyond sensing that they were representative of some fierce protector, Laris could not tell what they were.

"Those stones are beautifully fitted," Dom said, draping an arm about her still damp shoulders. She could tell that his admiration was not as reluctant as her own but as sincere. "These buildings are all laid without mortar, but the fit between stones is so tight that a blade cannot pass between them."

"I don't really care if a blade can pass between them so long as we can," Laris said truthfully. Then: "Darn it all!"

"What?"

"Look at that! A lost temple! And right in front of us. Why *didn't* I bring a camera?"

Dom started laughing at the shared moment of humor, and took her hand. The sound was a tired one, but it filled Laris with momentary hope.

"I think it is time for us to eat. You look tired. Sit here and admire the unphotographable view. I am going to climb some trees and see about finding some more seeds and *dulces*. We need food to fend off the cold." He let go of her hand, taking his warmth with him.

Laris sank down on a convenient stone and did as Dom suggested. She badly needed a rest, and she would do her best to preserve the temple in her memory. Perhaps she could draw it once they returned home. It made her feel better to have a plan, however tenuous.

"I've learned my lesson. Never mind change for a pay phone. From now on I am always carrying aspirin, bug spray, and a camera."

Chapter Fifteen

Desiderio had watched Alfonso Menendez slip away from the others, and impulsively decided to follow him. A less suspicious person would have assumed that Alfonso was simply seeking some privacy to answer the call of nature, but Desiderio knew full well that Alfonso was not a private man.

There were only two things—or perhaps three—that would make this creature go off on his own: treasure, a woman, or food. Though Alfonso was as unintelligent as the clay from which one made adobe, he did have fine instincts for survival. Desiderio was willing to wager that at the moment a meal was more important than treasure, and that Alfonso had found a source of food, which he did not want to share with his starving companions.

Therefore it came as a shock to hear a soft, feminine

cry and Alfonso grunting loudly about killing a red-haired witch.

Disgusted at the thought of this creature making more trouble with the natives, Desiderio abandoned his stealthy pursuit. He rushed through the tangled undergrowth to the sounds of struggle, only to be momentarily struck dumb at the sight of a beautiful, white woman writhing beneath Alfonso's gross form.

He was hallucinating, Desiderio told himself. He had finally contracted a brain fever and was seeing fever illusions. There was no other explanation for a white woman being in the middle of the cloud forest.

But illusion or not, when the woman cried out again, he strode forward and pulled Alfonso off of the struggling apparition.

A damp and increasingly cold Laris sat for a long while on her rock and tried to enjoy the unusual silence of the cloud forest after the violent rain. She was exhausted mentally and physically—perhaps spiritually as well—and knew that she needed to regain some measure of strength before she could go on.

Unfortunately, the how of the matter evaded her. She was depleted in ways that she never had been before. Perhaps it was all the time they had spent in Death's shadow, but the fact was that she felt so empty of life now that she was not certain if she was truly human anymore. She was more like a filthy suit on a hanger than a flesh-and-blood being. She supposed that she should be grateful for the stiff, crusty dirt that grimed her clothes, and perhaps for her aching skeleton, for it was they that held her up, rather than her fatigued muscles or faltering will.

Something darkly iridescent fluttered at the corner of her eye, and she found enough energy to turn her head and look at the pretty, out-of-place insect.

Something about the moth's stuttering wings snagged her attention and sounded a vague alarm along her tired nerves. She had seen a similar moth twice before and been afraid of the thoughts it had brought to her. Only, right now she could not quite remember the details upon which she had been ruminating. She stared at it, puzzled, trying to recall some half-remembered dream.

The butterfly moved as if it were being buffeted by a wind so strong that its wings would be torn away. But there was no wind, no breeze at all, which made the ever-louder shivering of the plants behind her very odd.

The warning bell of her subconscious increased its volume, ringing insistently, racing her body's flight response ahead of conscious thought. Her muscles tightened, getting ready to spring away the moment the unknown danger presented itself.

Once considered, the soft rasping of leaf on leaf pressed menacingly against her ears. Her sluggish mind, only belatedly aware that she was hearing sound where none should be, ordered her to turn around and face the danger head-on.

One of Death's messengers had caught up with her.

Laris spun about just in time to see a leathery hand snatch at her face. She managed only a short, choked scream before being toppled to the ground, a human man's bony but hard body landing on top of her.

"*Bruja pelirroja!*" the voice accused. His rancid breath was like a blow to the nose, and the hard fist that twisted in her hair and forced her head back made her eyes tear.

Witch! Redheaded witch! That was what he was saying!

"No," she gasped, trying to heave him off of her. "I'm not a witch! Get off! Dom!"

He muttered something else that sounded like *muerto*—death. And Laris realized that he believed her to be a witch, a red-haired witch, and intended that she die so that her curse would be broken and he could escape the rain forest.

"I'm not a witch! Please!"

The man pulled out a badly rusted knife from his boot and waved the pitted blade before her face. His features cracked into a repulsive grin when he saw the terror in her eyes.

He sat up far enough to get the blade between them and slipped it under her blouse. He started to saw away at the stretchy fabric, snarling when it did not cut.

Realizing that he planned on a little rape before his murder, which gave her some time, Laris began fighting in earnest, her tired limbs finding a last reserve of strength in her intense revulsion and fear. She spent herself reckless, knowing that Death's shadow had to be racing toward her, bringing with it other dangers and horrors. Nails, teeth, fists, they were all used to defend herself, though to little avail.

The creature, annoyed with her struggles, finally tightened his knees, intent on squeezing the air from her lungs as he pulled at her blouse.

The world began to grow dark around her. Nausea flipped her stomach over and she knew that she had to escape this creature's obscene touch even if she died doing it.

In desperation, she picked up one of the small, palm-sized stones that littered the ground, and, using the rest of her strength, aimed a blow at the side of her attacker's dark head.

It connected, but she knew it was without much force.

"Damn it!" she swore to herself. "It wasn't supposed to happen this way! Dom and I were going to live in San Francisco."

Then the weight was suddenly gone from her diaphragm and she was able to draw a delayed breath into her aching lungs.

There were harsh words from another male voice,

audible even above her gasping and the ringing in her ears, and then there came a sharp snapping, something rather like a green branch being broken though Laris knew that it was not a tree limb that had been sundered.

A moment later Dom's blurred image was leaning over her. From his neck there dangled a small golden crucifix, which was the first thing her eyes focused on.

"*Senorita? Como esta usted?*" he asked, his voice rough with adrenaline, as he knelt and then reached out slowly for her. He touched her cheek with a shaking hand. "*Se haces daño?*"

"Dom, he tried to kill me. He just came out of the forest and tried to kill me. He said I was a witch. I think Death sent him." She wept, sitting up and throwing her arms about him, hugging his stained leather vest.

He stiffened for a moment and then put his arms around her, his hands running over her limbs and back as if to reassure himself that she was whole.

"*Madre de Dios!*" he breathed, and then something about *no entre sueños*.

"Why are you speaking Spanish?" she asked, sniffling. "You know that I don't speak it well."

"*Sangre de Christos,*" he breathed again, his tone of blank amazement finally penetrating her wall of shock.

Her nerves, her mind, even her body had been

tuned to Dom. She knew the exact pitch of his thoughts, the feel of his person, and something about him was slightly altered from when he had left her.

Once her attention shifted from her recent terror to Dom's strange alteration, several pieces of contradictory information reached Laris almost at once. Again, her body was ahead of her mind, collecting data and sending alarms to her exhausted nerves.

The first clue that something was seriously amiss with Dom was tactile; he shouldn't be wearing a leather vest. He had only a linen shirt with him.

"Dom?" She pulled back a little. "What is this thing you're wearing? Where did it come from?"

"*Como?*"

Her other senses awoke and flooded her with confusing messages.

Dom didn't smell right.

His hair was too long.

His voice was too deep and harsh.

His face was too browned and weathered, and he had a tiny scar near his left eye.

He was wearing a crucifix.

Laris recoiled from her rescuer with a small cry, and the man with Dom's face and cool eyes allowed her to roll away from him.

"*Cuadado! Esta un hormiguero,*" he warned her.

Laris glanced down and saw that she was in fact crouching on an anthill. She quickly shifted to her right, but didn't take her eyes off of the man who was Dom but not *her* Dom.

"It can't be," she muttered as she crab-walked farther from the busy anthill. She glanced again at his cross and then laid a hand over her own thundering heart. "How did you find me? This wasn't supposed to happen. We went the other way on purpose."

He continued to stare at her, looking bemused either at her language or her peculiar posture. Or perhaps the mere fact of her was cause enough for stupefaction.

"*Desiderio?* It is you, isn't it?" she whispered as she crouched with hands and feet braced, ready to spring away if he moved toward her. The shock of the situation stemmed the flow of frightened tears and forced her to think rationally.

The pale eyes widened at the sound of his name and his brows rose. His thin lips parted.

Before he could speak, there came the report of a distant gun. It wasn't loud, but the alien sound silenced the forest around them.

"Dom!" Laris gasped, staggering to her feet. How could she have forgotten about him and Rychard! She yelled louder: "Dom! Where are you? Answer m—"

In an instant Desiderio was beside her, a hand clamped to her arm and another over her mouth.

"*Que es eso? Quien esta aca?*" he demanded. *What is that? Who is there?*

Laris made a muffled and indignant protest at being restrained and muffled, and after a moment he took his hand away.

"*Silencio!*" he warned her. "*Quiere usted a morir?*"

No, she didn't want to die. But she needed to get to Dom right away. There had been a mistake. It was Desiderio who was supposed to die here—not Dom!

"It's Rychard! It must be," she answered quietly, trying to pull free of Desiderio's grip. She pointed her finger and made gun noises. "*Ricardo. Esta aqui.* He will kill Dom. *Vamanos* right now."

She hadn't thought that her pantomimed explanation augmented with pidgin Spanish would make any sense, but apparently it did. That, or he was reacting to the much hated name in the same manner as the Dom she knew.

"Wait, woman of England!" he commanded in heavily accented English. "Who does Ricardo kill? Are there many English here?"

"He's killing Domitien—Edom! You!" she answered desperately, not making any attempt to explain that she wasn't English. "It's that *Ricardo*—the one with black hair—and he always kills you. Remember?"

Desiderio seemed to look inward for a moment and then nodded slowly. Laris had the feeling that he was partly humoring her, but also partly moved to belief by her wild explanation.

"I go to see Ricardo and the English," he said. "*You* remain here."

"No. He'll kill you too. And I don't want to stay here with the ants and . . . *him*."

The horrid insects had already started to swarm over her attacker's body.

"Perhaps he will try and kill me." Desiderio smiled suddenly. "But he will not kill me soon. If it is Ricardo, I make a plan that he shall follow me into the jungle and I shall lose him there. You will be safe here until I return for you. Then we shall find the English."

"No! There are no English. It is just Dom and I," Laris objected again, frightened because there was no more shooting. What if Death had gotten confused and taken the wrong soul?

On the other hand, if presented with the choice, could she truly trade this man's life for Dom's? Could she hand him over to some blank-faced minion?

That brought Laris up short.

What if she *had* to chose?

She began to shiver. Taking hold of Desiderio's arm, she shook him.

"Listen to me! Dom needs me. He may be dying right this minute. You have to help me find him! But then you need to leave. Go far away from us—and stay out of the shadows."

"For why should I leave you?" Desiderio asked. "I wish to see the English."

"But you can't. There are no English."

They stared at each other, clasping each other's arms until someone cleared his throat.

"Of course I always need you, *bella*," Dom's voice answered carefully from the far side of the tiny clearing, interrupting her incipient hysteria. "But as I am not dying, and even if I were, I think that it would be ill advised for you to go chasing after Rychard."

Laris and Desiderio spun about to face Dom. Once again, Desiderio's eyes widened. He stared, speechless, at his less-battered twin who stood tensely over the ant-covered body of the man who had attacked Laris.

After a moment more of study, Desiderio dropped his own hold on Laris's arm and she was able to rush to Dom's side.

"It's you. You're all right," she said, testing his limbs for soundness before pressing close. Then: "I don't know how it happened, but it's Desiderio. He saved me from that awful man. H-he was going to k-k-kill me for being a witch."

"Alfonso Menendez. I always suspected that his blood ran yellow rather than red," Dom supplied, hugging Laris and watching closely as Desiderio slowly tied back his own hair with a bit of vine. After a moment, Dom pulled them both clear of the ants' growing trail. "He was quite a piece of work. I am glad that Des had the sense to kill him."

Laris shuddered some more as the delayed adrenaline worked its way through her body.

"This was w-worse than the snake dropping on me," she told him.

Dom stroked her gently, urging her to calm, but Laris knew his attention was divided. Scolding herself, she forced her hands to loosen their grip on Dom and her spine to straighten.

She took a deep breath and finally looked up at Dom. As she had suspected, his eyes were on his twin and not on her.

"He isn't dangerous," she assured him in a whisper. "Truly, he was being kind."

Dom nodded. After a moment more of study, he said something to Des in a rapid and unfamiliar dialect, but Laris got the word *ensueno*, which she thought meant dream or illusion.

Des laughed once and answered in his rough voice. The two men shared another glance and then Des bowed slightly. He smiled gently at Laris, his gaze lingering first on her face and then her hair.

He reached for his neck and pulled off his crucifix. Three steps brought him to Laris. He dropped the chain over her head and said something too rapid for her to understand.

"Amen," Dom answered.

And then, with a small shake of his head, Des turned toward the jungle and headed in the direction of the gunshot.

"Desiderio? Where are you going? Stop him!" Laris said urgently, shaking Dom's arm. As with Desiderio,

273

it appeared to have no effect. "Rychard will kill him. You know he will! And Death's shadow is that way. It'll be coming straight toward us now too."

"No. I don't think Rychard will get him. That isn't how Desiderio died." Dom shook his head. He looked down at the cross that hung at her neck. "Do you know, I always discounted what happened here as being nothing more than a fever dream. But apparently I truly did see you all those years ago. It is hard to credit it even now. . . . You have no idea how much I wanted to take you with me that day."

Laris was sure that there was some great significance to the fact of their meeting. It had something to do with what she had been thinking that morning, but she couldn't seem to wrap her brain around it.

Nor could she think what to say to Dom's contention that Desiderio had wanted her.

"What did he say to me?" she asked, touching the small crucifix he'd given her.

"He said: 'Gold is mute and useless to me now, but perhaps this may speak to thee. Let it guard thy heart.' "

"Oh." Laris swallowed and felt herself blush. "We can't stop him from going? Maybe find a door that would send him home to Spain?"

Dom shook his head. He didn't tell her what else Desiderio had said. What he himself had said, so long ago. *God save you, brother, from the fate of living without hope. God save you if she dies.*

"I think I hate history."

"We have to go," Dom said. "Desiderio may buy us some time, but Rychard is very close. We can't waste another instant circling this hill, looking for an easy way up. We are going to have to cut across here and go straight up the side. We'll eat lunch when we get to the top. The *dulce* trees will be closer then. It'll save time on climbing for food."

"We are going straight up? That?"

Laris turned to look at the man-made mountain and wondered where she would find the strength to do what must be done.

"Yes. I am afraid that we have no choice. Death's shadow is everywhere on the forest's floor. I kept encountering it while looking for food."

"Damn . . . You know, I'd give anything for a cup of coffee," she said tiredly. "I always feel better after I've had a little caffeine."

"I have something superior," Dom told her. He reached into his pocket and withdrew a handful of green leaves. "Chew on these, but don't swallow them. The natives use them to combat hunger and altitude sickness."

"Are they coca leaves?" she asked, taking one and placing it gingerly in the side of her mouth.

"I never knew the name," Dom answered, taking a leaf for himself. "I just know that they could disguise the ache of an empty belly."

Laris nodded and started to chew. The flavor

wasn't bad, only a bit bitter, but she didn't have to endure it for long. Her mouth went almost immediately numb.

Please let this work, she thought, addressing the Great One. *Give me the strength to do whatever I have to do.*

"I'm sorry, Laris. I know you are tired, but we have to hurry. I can tell that danger is closing in on us."

And it seemed that her prayers were answered, albeit in a strange manner. She no longer felt tired. The cold in her limbs and chest began to abate. Nature's leaves—or something greater—had provided her with the energy she needed.

She touched Desiderio's gift once, and though long out of the habit of entreating the Great One, she said a prayer for Des's well-being. Then she started after Dom, determined not to delay him as they crossed the rough, green space that separated them from the mountain.

She could sense that time was running out. Whatever the original plan for them might have been, she had felt marked, almost doomed, from the moment Death's minion touched her.

Perhaps it was this damning touch that had made Rychard able to track them.

Chapter Sixteen

A storm was coming, a dangerous one. It filled the air with a metallic green haze and had the servants muttering darkly about ill omens and curses.

Isabella reprimanded them gently, and then sent them back to work. But she, too, was worried about the dark bank of fearsome clouds that approached. She could not rid herself of the dreaded feeling that there were horrible cataclysms hiding in those awful billows.

In trepidation, she laid a hand against her growing belly and wished desperately that she had not sent Dominick away from their home.

Rychard was coming, but the thought of his presence brought no consolation to her. Nor would her brother reassure the servants, who took their cues from their master, and mainly disliked him.

277

Trying to calm herself, she turned her face into the jasmine blooming beside her and inhaled deeply of the scent that always reminded her of Dominick.

There was no path, only the stony ridge that climbed along the broken spine of the man-made mountain. It was surrounded by razor-sharp rocks whose broken upthrusts were only marginally softened with vegetation.

Dom had insisted that she go first so that he could catch her if she stumbled in her exhaustion. That his own balance was every bit as precarious and his exhaustion as acute was apparently irrelevant. He was the *man*; therefore he meant to follow tradition to the end, and plummet to his death with her in his arms if she could not be saved.

Or perhaps it was a chivalry born of the side effects of the leaves they were chewing. Perhaps they had given Dom more than energy, perhaps he truly believed that he was superman. Whichever it was, Laris was touched and also determined not to make any big mistakes.

She wasn't particularly afraid of the climb when they started out. She had no problem with heights, and a series of dance classes had taught her balance. Nevertheless, the way was uneven and strewn with slippery scree, so she went as slowly as she dared, and placed each foot with care before allowing weight upon it.

Watching for snakes and spiders also slowed her.

The final stretch of the climb to the top of the canopy of trees was worse, and required hands as well as feet and even a small amount of time on her stomach. Laris arrived on the next plateau bruised, dirty, sweat-covered, and panting with exertion. Her heart was also thundering in an alarmingly arrhythmic manner.

"Damn it." She squatted on the ground, folding in on herself, seeking to relieve some of the viselike constriction of her lungs and growing nausea in her chest.

"Laris?" Dom's head appeared.

Not wanting to worry him, she hauled herself upright and leaned against the sheer face of the square-cut stones, which made up the final tier of the pagan temple. She forced her breathing into a regular pattern.

She had never suffered from attacks of vertigo, but she was careful not to look over the side of the narrow ledge where she rested. There was no need to assault her eyes with the sight of the sheer drop into the green void when her head was already spinning from the drug and a lack of oxygen.

The rest of Dom arrived a moment later. For once, he was also breathing hard and showing signs of muscle fatigue. His pulse was thrumming like a trip-hammer, visible in his throat and temples.

"Rychard?" she asked.

"I don't see him." He didn't add that in the thickness of the rain forest's bower, seeing anyone was an impossibility.

"And Desiderio?" she asked, but more softly as Dom slumped beside her, resting his hands on his knees and taking slow deep breaths.

"No. No one is following us that I can see. And that is as it should be. We must not alter events if we can avoid it."

Laris nodded sadly. She looked down at Des's gift and then tucked it into her blouse.

"Let's rest for a moment more and then we will start looking for a way in."

"You are certain that there is a door here?" she asked, not really questioning him, but merely making conversation as a distraction from her body's woes. "It would probably be too easy if there were."

"The shadow comes here. There could be a door." Dom lifted a hand and pointed out to a darker trail of green gloom. "Though it wouldn't be the portal we came through when we arrived, it would still get us out of here."

Laris didn't like the idea of traveling any deeper into Death's labyrinth of portals, especially if they started visiting someone else's unfamiliar and probably equally dangerous life, but it was Hobson's choice. No other option offered itself to them. She was afraid of encountering another of Death's minions, but it was slightly better than watching Dom relive the horror of his time in the rain forest.

"I hate to risk using more of this drug," Dom said, looking at Laris's sweat-drenched clothing. "But I don't think either of us will manage the altitude and exertion if we don't."

Laris laid a hand against her chest and willed her heart to slow and even out its erratic beating.

"What's wrong?" Dom asked, immediately laying his own hand against her filthy shirt. The heat from his palm was reassuring. "Do you have a heart condition?" he asked, his voice uninflected as he felt her pulse.

Laris nodded reluctantly.

"It is a very minor mitral valve prolapse, just a small heart murmur. Usually it doesn't bother me at all, but the doctor said to be careful at high altitudes. I am fine for exercise. I am just supposed to avoid *exceptional* physical stresses, like weight-lifting elephants." She tried to make it a joke.

"But these conditions are hardly the usual ones for exercising, and we are definitely at high altitudes."

"These things are sent to test us," she murmured, but only half facetiously. "I'll be fine."

"Yes, they are meant to test us," he answered without smiling. "But perhaps there is something . . ."

Dom closed his eyes and concentrated. His hand seemed to grow even warmer as it pressed against her, and Laris felt her heartbeat moderating.

"Do you still have some sugar in your purse?" Dom asked, opening his eyes.

"Yes." Laris stared at him, convinced that he was a shade paler than he had been a moment before. He also had faint purple bruises beneath his eyes.

"Take that instead of the leaves. It should be enough to get you to the top if we have to climb some more. We won't use the leaves again unless we absolutely have to."

"Okay." She wasn't hungry, but Laris fumbled open her purse. Its zipper was caked with mud, and it resisted her tugging until she became violent. She added lightly: "I'm going to need a new purse as well as perfume. This one is hopeless. And my clothes too. They will never be the same."

Dom smiled, though clearly it was an effort.

"Aren't you glad now that you aren't hauling a camera too?"

"Very! Who would want to remember this place anyway?" Laris answered, tearing open one of the packets of brown sugar and pouring it into her mouth. She wished fervently that she had some water to wash the crystals down with. Though her body ran with moisture, her mouth remained as arid as the Atacama Desert.

"What a face!" Dom teased as she crunched up the hardened sugar. "You would think it salt you ate, not sugar."

"I can't feel or taste anything," she complained

through half-shut lips, stuffing the empty wrapper back in her purse. "Those leaves do worse things to my mouth than a trip to the dentist."

"Hm. I wouldn't know," Dom answered. "I haven't been to one in this century. I can say that my past experience with the tooth-drawers has left me with a preference for these leaves. Getting drunk before an extraction does not actually help much with the pain."

"I can well imagine that this would be better than booze," Laris admitted as she swallowed the last of the sugar. "But you needn't worry about that anymore. Dentistry has improved considerably in the last century. They don't get you drunk anymore."

He nodded. "I am counting on it. Surely many medical things have improved."

"Things have improved, period."

"Are you ready to go on?" Dom asked, straightening his spine with effort.

"Yes," she lied, also straightening.

They had a short search of the ledge but found no portals.

Dom looked at Laris's face and shook his head, but he nevertheless started for the steep, ladderlike stairs. They didn't have any choice but to keep moving. If they stayed where they were, they would die. He gestured for her to go ahead of him once again.

"What I don't understand is why some giant snake—or killer ants—haven't gotten him. Rychard,

I mean," Laris muttered, taking hold of the stair above her and starting her upward scramble. The stones were cold and immediately sucked the little remaining warmth from her limbs. "They managed to wipe out everyone else around here. He must be damned lucky, or been a native here in another life."

"I don't believe that there is such a thing as luck," Dom answered. "Just Fate."

"No luck? I guess we won't be wasting a lot of time in Las Vegas then." It was an effort to keep her voice even.

"Probably not if it is because you are feeling *lucky*," he agreed. "There are so many more practical ways to gamble in life."

"Yeah, like climbing up a snake-infested mountain," she muttered.

Dom actually laughed at that.

After a while, Laris noticed that there was some sort of pattern carved into the stones beneath her. She hadn't the energy to appreciate it aesthetically, but her hands were grateful for the new fingerholds. She supposed that she should be excited about actually touching human history, and perhaps keeping an eye out for artifacts, but there was barely enough energy in her muscles to keep her arms and legs moving. It might be her overwrought imagination or growing fatigue, but it seemed to her that each step was higher than the one before it. It was all she could do just to keep moving.

The gloom was oppressive, but Laris endured it until they broke out through the last layer of foliage canopy and into the hazy sunlight. Right on schedule, the clouds were moving in for their late afternoon storm and blotting out the sun before it could warm them.

"It's going to rain," she said, turning her head to look down at Dom. The action was a mistake, bringing on immediate dizziness. She quickly faced the stone in front of her and focused on its curved grooves.

"We're almost to the top," Dom assured her. "Another three minutes and we'll be there. There will be a place to take shelter so we won't have to get wet again. And if we are very lucky, we'll even find Death's doorway straightaway."

"I thought you said that you didn't believe in any such thing as luck," Laris reminded him, taking slow, deep breaths.

"I've changed my mind," Dom answered. "I have decided to believe in it after all. With faith, all things are possible."

"Not me," Laris answered, relieved when her fit of light-headedness passed off. "More than ever, I am inclined to believe in your bitch-goddess Fate. This much ill fortune takes careful planning."

"She's not a goddess," he replied. "But she certainly can be a bitch."

Laris nodded and continued to climb.

The next few minutes were a blur of gasped breaths and cramping muscles. It was all Laris could do to scramble over the last step, and she would not have made it without Dom's hands to boost her.

She rolled once to escape the very edge on the crumbling temple and then lay still. She closed her eyes and concentrated on breathing. It began to rain, but she didn't care. Movement was out of the question until she managed to get more air into her lungs.

"I don't recall," she gasped, turning her head so that the rain ran into her mouth but didn't actually drown her. "Did Job eventually turn on God?"

Dom lay down beside her. He rolled onto his side and put his arm around her, shielding her as best he could from the violent storm.

"He had questions, I'm sure."

"But did he get any answers?"

"Probably none he wanted to hear."

In Dom's arms, Laris found her breathing and heartbeat begin to moderate and she felt strong enough to open her eyes.

"Dom?"

"Yes."

"We made it. This is the top, isn't it? We don't have to climb anymore?"

"Yes, we made it." His pale eyes smiled at her. "Our escape is at hand."

"Good." Laris made to sit up. She needed Dom's help as her muscles had lost a great deal of their coordination. "Let's find our door and get the hell outta Dodge."

"I wish we had been in Dodge. I should have enjoyed seeing the Old West again. As I recall it, it was always warm."

"It doesn't rain much there either," Laris said, looking up at the sky. "I think the storm is breaking up. That was a quick one."

"A propitious omen." Dom got to his feet and then hauled her upright. He held her until he was certain that she had her footing. "Let's see what we have here."

"It doesn't matter. I feel ready for anything as long as it gets us out of here," Laris lied.

Dom shook his head as he looked around for the first time. His face settled into grim lines.

"Unfortunately, I think you may need to be ready, *bella*. This isn't an *Indio* temple."

"What?" Laris looked from Dom to the stone pyramid. Its facade was an ominous one. There were plenty of feathered serpents eating men, but there was also a selection of winged skulls and tall, cloaked shapes bearing scythes.

She tried to do some quick math—thirteen minions in a row at the base, then twelve on the next tier. Then eleven . . . and the temple had four sides . . .

"This is bad. What is this place?"

"I've never been here before, but I think it safe to

assume that we have arrived at Death's main place of business."

"And abandon all hope, ye who enter here," she whispered. Something caught at the back of her throat—a familiar and oddly frightening smell. Laris sniffed the air. "Do I smell jasmine?"

Chapter Seventeen

There was no funeral procession, only Rychard and the tiny body on the oxcart pulled by the sacrificial oxen by the shimmering light of a lopsided moon. Isabella had been lovely in life, but he thought her exquisite dead. He would never, never have to worry about her children usurping him again.

Almost he could hear her beautiful voice begging him to turn back, to take away the golden shroud—a costly but cold raiment, woven of thread so fine that it was nearly as transparent as yellow wine—and let her be buried with her mother.

But he would never do that. She was going into one of the forgotten tombs of the necropolis where no one would ever find her, and she was going in a manner befitting a daughter of a prince. He'd see her laid out, and then close the door on her phantom voice—and then he would forevermore disregard all memory of her and that northern barbarian, Dominick.

The area before the temple was a leveled terrace, unique in the surrounding terrain because it looked as if it might have been cleared by a bulldozer. Nothing grew here, not even moss. And nothing on the outside encroached upon the beaten earth.

"I wonder if it has been sown with salt." Laris wiped the rain off of her face. She didn't look back down at the army of minions. "Could this be where Death lives? Or is that a contradiction in terms?"

"Perhaps. Something happened here, something unnatural. Death's presence is very strong. It is as though the earth itself has died. Even the rocks feel drained and dead."

"Dead rocks. 'Every day, in every way, things just get better and better,'" Laris muttered between breaths, her previous semioptimistic mood rendered sour and shrunken by an empty stomach and too much adventure in the rain. It was difficult to feel the proper awe that the moment and place demanded.

Mostly, she felt angry that she had been led to false hope.

Dom did not reply. He took a step closer to the temple and raised a hand to the door as though testing the wind. When he exhaled slowly and shook his head, Laris stopped her complaining and concentrated on the atmosphere outside rather than the hunger and pain within.

She looked at the imposing door before them and tried again to quiet her breathing so that she might listen. It took her only a moment to tune in to Dom's reactions and sense what he was feeling.

"Damn it," she muttered. "This doesn't feel old like human old. It isn't a memory."

"Indeed. This is something else. It is something I've never seen before, but still horribly familiar."

It was somehow familiar to her, too, something from a nightmare. Though Rychard was somewhere close behind them and this was their only chance of escape from the carnivorous forest, still she did not want to pass through this portal. She was certain that something frightening, some devastating knowledge lurked in there, poised to spring itself upon them.

Reluctantly, she stepped to the wall and laid her hand against one of the few spaces not covered in hideous carvings. The rock was unnaturally cold.

"I had hoped that the climb was the worst of it," she said hollowly, glancing back at the door and thinking suddenly of Virgil's verse about Aeneas's entry into the underworld.

She would have made some joke about being caught in a bad opera, but the mood to jest had completely abandoned her.

Dom did not wish to enter the doorway either, for

he now knew exactly what waited on the other side. But he had no choice—*they* had no choice. He had to face his worst memory if he was to save Laris from the Amazon—just to save her, period.

And Laris would have to confront it too. The altitude was killing her. And Rychard was coming. She couldn't wait on the ledge while Dom went inside.

They would go in together, or they would die out here together. He wouldn't abandon her again.

That meant that he would have to do it. He would go back and face Isabella and what had happened to her because of the enmity between him and Rychard. This was something he had sought to avoid through all his lifetimes, hiding behind forgetfulness and rage, but he would endure it now because he valued Laris's life—and the slim possibility of their life together—more than peace of mind.

He would do it, he admitted, because he *loved* her. She was his to protect and cherish, his to sacrifice for.

A wise man had told him once that woman had been bestowed upon man by the kindly part of the Creator to reconcile him to the human condition, which was the lot of all men when they left Paradise and were physically separated from all that was spiritually lovely so that they might learn from their time on a physical plane. Laris was his connection back to the Great One. He had only to look at her face, to hear her voice, and he was reminded that there was a master builder.

This time he wouldn't willingly embrace Death and oblivion, because he had something he valued on the earthly plane. He would fight to save them both. He would even accept the guilt of what had happened to Isabella, if that was what it took to save Laris, to free her.

His only regret for what he was about to do was what the effect might be on Laris, for this life experience was her worst nightmare too. It was the moment that had defined her whole existence for the centuries that followed it.

"Dom?" Laris's voice was frightened as she stared first through the door at the scene beyond it and then at Dom's pale face. "I think I know this place. This may be different because it leads to one of *my* past lives."

"Yes." It was time to enter the confessional. He drew in a deep breath and strove for calm. "You do know it. It was there that you were destroyed by my cowardice."

"What? What do you mean?"

He refused to close his eyes against the guilt and the unwanted knowledge of who Laris had once been, but looking at her bewildered yet still trusting expression was almost more than he could bear.

He would not run anymore! He needed to have faith! Faith that she would love him even if she discovered the truth of what had happened to them. This was why his memories of this time had been plaguing him throughout this trip, why they had seeped back into his brain. It was time to take the leap.

"You do know," he told her. "Look inside yourself."

"I . . . I don't . . . know. . . . I don't understand." She reached for him even though it brought her a step closer to the hated portal. "Something is about to happen, isn't it? Something bad."

He didn't hesitate. Later she might hate him and be revolted by his touch, but Dom took Laris's hand and held it tightly, offering what comfort he could. And perhaps taking a little comfort too.

"Ready, love?" He stepped toward the door.

"I have to be, don't I?" she asked in a small voice. "This time it really is my life out there, too, isn't it? We're going to see *me*."

"Yes. And I am sorry. Because of Dominick, because of his—*my*—hatred of Rychard, and then my fearful, cowardly grief over what happened—we have to face this life all over again."

Laris's eyes examined Dom's face, searching out its expression and then looking to see what was waiting in his gaze.

"But this will make it better, won't it?" Her voice was small but urgent. "It will restore the balance somehow, and then we can leave?"

"I believe so. I pray so."

Laris's grip tightened, but her voice was steady when she answered: "Then I *am* ready. But let's hurry before I change my mind. I don't feel very strong anymore."

Dom kissed her chilled hand, and then trapped the caress between their palms.

"I'll help you all that I can."

They walked quickly through the tall portal and passed through a walled courtyard. Though there were lovely potted gardens all around them, there was no scent emanating from the phlox and snapdragons, and the colors of the plants were heavily muted. Death's shade had brought about an early twilight. Given the lingering miasmatic presence, they were not tempted to stop to admire anything as they had when visiting other places.

As short of breath as she was, Laris wondered if it would be possible to stop breathing altogether. She didn't want the unhealthy air filtering through her overactive lungs and seeping into her blood. Already it seemed to be chilling her and making her feel sluggish.

It made her feel dead.

They passed silently through an open and deserted gate that would require four strong men to move, and which bore the marks of a battle siege, and then walked out into the equally empty countryside.

A small frisson ghosted over her nerves, telling her that something was very amiss with this world.

"It's so still. Where are the people? The farmers? This looks like a stage set."

Outside the villa were orange and pomegranate trees planted in neat rows. About the grove were small mounds of flowerless geraniums and gardenias, and finally a few roses that were past their bloom and setting on hips, their vivid red bleeding through the gray haze and showing like drops of fresh blood.

Beyond that there were only the dark funereal pines, which stretched on to the horizon, and an unnatural, overcast sky. Laris stared uneasily at the green metallic cloud. A vague and alarming aroma of sulfur floated in the already thick air. A storm was coming.

That meant that it was autumn, the dying season. *There should be a breeze though*, Laris thought inanely. The fall meant easterly winds that harbinged the storm. She had always hated them. They brought with them the smell of smoke from the peasants' sacrificial bonfires where haulms and other things were burnt.

Laris looked about worriedly at this half-formed thought. The confusion of colors offered by such a garden would be beautiful in spring, but it was all fading now and entering the final stages of life. And the farther they ventured down the unpaved road, the more barren the scenery became. The world was familiar to her and yet not what she remembered. Her world had always been filled with noise and people. This felt dead—abandoned, forgotten.

She wanted to say something to Dom, but couldn't find her voice.

The only sound in this bleak earth was the soft scuff of their shoes in the dirt road as they overlaid their own prints upon the marks of unshod horses and wagon wheels.

Soon they passed through a stone quarry where there were squares cut into limestone walls. Most were sealed with recessed slabs of dark stone.

Pagan tombs. Laris had never seen them, but she had heard stories and recognized them for what they were.

"This is a cemetery," she said, clinging hard to Dom's hand. "Where are we? It looks a bit like Italy. . . . It feels like a very long time ago."

Dom looked down at her. In the unnatural twilight his lips appeared white, his entire face bloodless.

"This is Italy, but it is also the old kingdom of the people they call Etruscans. They lived here eight hundred years before the Carpenter was born. Their ways had a grip on the land for centuries, even after the Son came. And it was into this place of mixed religions and cultures that Dominick's wife, Isabella,. was born and raised a thousand years ago."

"Isabella." The name made her shiver. It was so close to the endearment that Dom used for her.

"And this is the necropolis where she was actually

buried. We are going to her grave. Her real one, not the tomb where they said she was interred."

"Why go there? She is dead."

"We must go because . . ." He paused, searching for an explanation. "I did not go before. I allowed her to go into the void alone. I gave up in despair when she was called away, and I allowed her to be taken from me without saying good-bye."

"I don't understand." But she was beginning to. "And why was she buried in this pagan grave if she was Christian? You didn't want that, did you?"

Dom shook his head once in vehement denial.

"Her brother did it, not I. But it was still my fault. I should have been here. Whatever my grief, I should have come to see my wife's burial. I could have stopped this from happening." His voice was fierce and full of self-loathing that he could not hide.

"Dom—" she said gently.

He interrupted her, speaking quickly as though he was afraid that he would not get it all out if he did not confess the entirety at once.

"There is a purpose in the rituals of death. It is not simply the comforting of the living, but a way of making the transition of the soul a complete one. But coming as I did from the north, the ceremonies of the south were alien and did not comfort me. In fact, they so repelled me that I did not stay beside her for the three days when her soul waited to pass on. I didn't even insist on a burial within her faith when

I suspected this might happen if Rychard took the body."

"Dom, don't." Laris stopped and turned to face him. She said urgently: "We don't have to do this. There is another road just a small way back. We can go that way—find another door."

"No. We do have to face this. This is the only road. You have to know the truth." His eyes were haunted, his voice relentless.

"But I don't want to know," she protested. "It doesn't matter anymore. Let the past stay in the past."

He shook his head. He didn't need to say what he was thinking, for Laris already knew. Dom was one who would commit himself to a path and would follow it to the limits of his not inconsiderable strength. He believed that this course was ineluctable, the will of the Great One, and therefore he would follow it.

"Nor do I wish you to remember it, but the matter is not for us to decide. The Great One wants you to know. You need to know so that you can heal. So you can truly be free to follow your heart. This is one lesson we cannot avoid."

"Heal? Heal what? I still don't understand. I don't feel wounded now. I'm happy. My life is wonderful. I have you, my career—"

"Yes, you have these things, but you are wounded still." He asked gently, kindly: "Have you never thought about why in all your lives you loved only me—why you clung so tenaciously to my love and would have no other?"

"No—but it doesn't matter. That was all *before*."

"Laris." Dom's voice was anguished as he touched her hair and then her cheek. "But it does matter. We have both been trapped by what happened here. I never let you—*her*—go. Isabella didn't understand my seeming abandonment, and she tried for life after life to reanimate my affections for her. You were never able to move on to a new love, not even when you lived in a life without my presence. And because of my vow never to love again, you could never truly return to me either. You have lived in limbo. In purgatory. And so have I."

Dom dropped his hand. His voice grew gentle even as the words themselves grew harsh: "Come. Let us break these shackles once and for all. Then we may move on."

Wanting to deny his hard terms, but fearing that Dom was somehow right, Laris allowed him to resume their journey.

Immediately memories began to crowd in on her.

Dom started talking again, his voice low and grim.

"Isabella's family was nominally Christian, and as such were supposed to place reliance upon God to direct their destinies. They were supposed to trust that Isabella's faith would mean entry into Heaven for their beloved and devout daughter and sister. But they were also an ancient people, proud, not far removed from old beliefs, and Isabella's eldest brother decided to follow the old ways instead of those of the humble new religion. This must have caused her great anguish while she waited transition. I thought that I could feel her, her fear and torment. How she must have hated me."

"Her brother?" Laris had a flash of something visual very like memory except that it came from someone else's eyes. "Rychard. He was her brother?"

"Yes. He was her brother." Dom's voice was flat but she could feel his emotions trembling beneath it. They were battering against his control, seeking to get out.

"After she was dead, Rychard took her body and adorned it in the old manner of preparing a sacrifice. He painted her with cosmetics and draped her in gold. He made a burnt offering and then he thrust her in a heathen tomb—"

"Stop! Enough!" Laris closed her eyes for a moment but opened them back up when the darkness didn't ease her dizziness. "Please. I feel ill—confused. There are too many voices."

Dom ceased speaking, but his tortured eyes were eloquent.

"I don't remember everything. It is all so confused. What happened to Isabella? How did she die? Was she alone?" Laris asked, sensing that she had been very alone for part of the time—lost in the cold and dark.

Dom drew a deep breath.

"She died young and in an unnatural manner. And she was not alone when she died, though she may as well have been for all the protection I afforded her."

"What?" Laris laid a hand against her stomach as remembered pain wracked her. "She was sick—so sick! And cold."

"Yes, sick unto death. The servants thought that she had eaten tainted food, but it wasn't that. She was given poison."

Laris gasped. "Poison? Who gave her poison?"

"Her brother."

Laris flinched, but she couldn't deny it. Inside she knew the truth. She remembered how it had felt, traveling through her body, chilling her as it went.

Dom laid a hand over her own and concentrated. Slowly the pain began to fade.

"Why?" she whispered, barely able to lift her feet now that she could see the large barrow ahead of her. The black space gaped blankly at them.

Dom's footsteps were also faltering.

"He did it because he could not stand that his sister loved his rival more than her own proud family. He could not accept that she would embrace her husband's religion. And finally he could not accept that she was going to give birth to his rival's child, that the child might be a boy who would inherit his family's lands because Rychard had been unable to conceive a child with his own wife or with any of the servants he bedded." Dom's face had thinned and paled.

Laris went cold with horror and tried to push the words away. Still, she felt her lips form words and heard her voice ask: "She was pregnant when he poisoned her?"

"Yes. And he did it because the last time the two of us quarreled, Dominick was stupid enough to taunt him with the possibility that it was *his* son who would inherit his family's lands when Rychard was dead." Dom paused before adding: "It probably seemed easiest for Rychard to kill the babe before it was ever born."

Laris closed her eyes again and tried to breathe evenly. It didn't help. It was as though she were breathing air without actual oxygen.

"But it wasn't a son, was it? It was a girl."

"Yes."

"What happened to the baby?" Laris asked, the second question wrenched from her against her better judgment.

Dom didn't want to answer her, but forced the words out with one great wrench. "She died. She was in labor for several hours trying to bring the child into the world, but she wasn't strong enough. We tried every antidote, but not knowing what poison he had used . . ."

"No," she whispered.

"And the midwife said that perhaps if she had not

been pregnant, she would have had the strength to combat the poison. She suggested trying to cut the babe from your womb, so that you might live, but you would not let her. I wasn't there to make the decision. You had to face it alone." The grief in Dom's voice was a unique torture, a horror more awful than Laris's own anguished memories that twisted her nerve endings until she wanted to scream.

They stopped walking just outside a giant square that was cut into the stone of the barrow. There was a small iron door, but it stood open. There was nothing, except their will, to prevent them going inside.

Laris stared at the opening with revulsion. Its edges were encrusted with a strange lichen that gave off a faint green glow. Out of the dark came a mix of odors, incense and decaying flowers, and death. It was desolate, lifeless; not so much as a bird's wing disturbed the stillness around them. There was no rustling in the trees, no wind, no sky. Their only companions were the dark clouds that pressed down above them, and they, too, were unmoving. It was not a world lost in somniferous dreams; it was one frozen at the moment of death.

Yet, in that instant she wasn't frightened by the dead that might be in the tomb, or the uncanny atmosphere that surrounded them. She was not even afraid of finally coming face-to-face with her poor cast-off shell. Her concern for Dom's silent torment so filled her that there was no room for any other feeling.

"My poor beloved," she whispered sadly, turning to face him. "Don't hurt yourself this way. We already suffered for this. Many times."

"All she ever asked of me was that I try to befriend her brother and that I not forbid him access to her." Dom bowed his head. "I let that monster into our home, but I did not try to forgive him. I did nothing to halt his hatred. Instead I encouraged him in his odium. And then I left Isabella alone with him."

"Please, love."

Dom shook his head. "And I have hated him— and myself—in every life since then. And now I remembered that you hated me, too. You hated me for what I did here and for not loving you when I was given the opportunity later on. I deserved your reproaches for my cowardice—all of them and more besides."

Laris bit back the words of denial hovering on her tongue and forced herself to answer logically. Dom was so wrapped in guilt and grief that he would not hear anything that was born of her own wild emotion. And she could not deny that in their many pasts there had been harsh words of reproach.

Anything she said now had to be the utter and complete truth. She took a moment to examine her thoughts and then spoke quietly.

"Yes, you encouraged his hatred. And that was

wrong. But *you* didn't force him to do anything. He and he alone decided to murder his sister. That guilt is his. Let him carry it."

"I should have been there," Dom insisted. "I should have stopped him."

"How?" she asked. "Were you omniscient? Did you know of his plans? Did you even suspect them?"

"No! Of course not!" he denied, appalled. "I loved her! I would have done anything to keep her safe!"

"Precisely. You didn't know. Dominick was a good person—young and foolish, maybe—but it would not have occurred to him that Rychard would murder his sister and her unborn child. The thought wouldn't occur to anyone sane. If any person should have guessed at his violent nature, it should have been Isabella."

"She was innocent!" Dom protested, instantly defending her. "She knew nothing of evil or malice. She would not have recognized it in him."

"Perhaps not." Laris drew in a slow breath. She was tiring. The end was close. "But I should have suspected. He had always played with poisons, killing animals, torturing birds. It was not in his nature to be affectionate to anyone. . . ."

"Laris—"

"It is odd. I realize now that this—this *memory*—has been here all along. You had it somehow locked up in both of us, but it existed, exerting pressure. And because we couldn't truly forget, it continued to shape our lives. We started repeating patterns and it went on ad infinitum. Talk about being blind! Why didn't we see it before? Why didn't *I* see it?"

"I don't know. Perhaps because I willed you to forget and you tried to please me, just as you always had."

"Could that be it? Could my blind acquiescence have set the pattern? If so, you should reproach me for I have hurt us both."

Dom shook his head, though not in denial of her words but rather her sentiment. Dominick would never blame Isabella for anything.

"It helped set the pattern. I fear what you say is true. But it is not your fault that you couldn't live with what I had become. Nor that you couldn't let go and live without me. That was all my doing—my stubbornness—that interrupted our lives." Dom held himself as though braced for a physical assault. "But now you know the truth of what happened and can make a change. You don't have to follow the pattern anymore."

"I can change, that is true," Laris said slowly. "I feel it. The memory is free now. We both know it for what it is. We understand what it has done, how it has shaped us, and we can change."

"Yes. Free will." His voice was bleak, and he clamped down on the pain to keep it from leaking out and touching her.

Laris shook her head at him, knowing precisely what he was doing.

"Dom, you have carried this version of events in your head for a long time. The guilt has almost become a sacred thing—something you feel should remain inviolate as an apology to Isabella for all that happened." Laris reached for him, laying a hand against his cheek. Emotion almost closed her throat. "I am not asking you to share this guilt with me. I know that you won't. So instead you must let it go into the past, Dom. Isabella never wanted this sort of devotion. Loyalty, like enmity, may be to the grave, but we shouldn't take it any further. Let it go back to where it belongs."

"I can't let go, not of the guilt. Don't you see? What I did was unforgivable. I hurt us both for lifetimes." He shuddered weakly. "I deserve to be punished forever."

"Do I?" she asked simply. "Love, you got it backward. There was a choice. In your grief you let go of the love that would have brought us happiness in our next life, and instead you kept the guilt. Both are bonds. They tie us. They will tie us until the end. Please reconsider what you are doing. We can still know joy."

He looked up sharply. His lips parted but he did not speak.

"This awful thing that has happened to us will continue to happen if you pursue this course of self-recrimination. You have shown me the truth, but it has not freed me because I still choose to share your life. I will be here to share in your fate, whatever it is. Your guilt is still tied tightly to me. Shall I have to suffer more?"

"No," he said hoarsely. "How can you ask me this? Of course I don't want to punish you."

"Are you certain?" she asked gently. "After all, I insisted that Rychard remain in our life. And I refused to let the midwife try and save me, so you were left all alone."

"No!" His voice was raw. "I never wanted to hurt you! Never!"

"Then listen to me! Listen to your heart and soul. You *can* let go of the guilt." Laris fisted a hand into his hair, standing on tiptoes to bring their faces closer together. "It is the tenet of your faith, then and now, that all things are forgivable if you truly repent. The Great One—if he ever blamed you, which I doubt— has obviously decided that you need to heal. That is why you and I were sent back. It is why even vile Rychard has been sent back again. I am certain that it is why we have all been given back our memories. We are supposed to make peace."

Laris tried to articulate her growing sense of urgency. It was difficult when her mind and body were being overtaken by a strange weakness. She didn't name the weakness aloud, but knew that it was Death coming for her.

Their time had run out.

"There isn't going to be any more punishment. The master builder is not that cruel. One way or another, it ends here. This is our last chance to make it right. And we haven't much time," she whispered.

Dom jerked his head in agreement. He felt it too. This was their last chance to make amends, to restore harmony and balance the scales.

"The chains work both ways, Dom. I won't be free until you are. If you love me, then you must let go."

"It isn't the Great One's forgiveness that I need." He looked into her eyes, his own gaze anguished. "It is Isabella's. She hated me then because I failed her. The part of you that is her must hate me now. You even said that you hated me."

"She did not hate you. I did not hate you. She was in pain, frightened and confused and grieved. But if you need the words, then have them. I forgive you, love. I forgive you for being merely human. I forgave you long ago."

He stared at her, stunned and unbelieving.

Incredibly, Laris laughed. The sound was weak but real.

"I love you, Dom. I always have. And I always will. That was never something that Isabella regretted. That was not something that was wrong. She would never have saddled you with this guilt. She wouldn't have done that even to her wretched brother."

"Isabella?" Dom's pent-up breath exploded. He

pulled her against him with trembling arms. He said into her hair, "No, you are Laris."

"I am both right now—and many others besides. And we all love you."

She held him close for a moment, listening to his heart, feeling the life force that was his soul and letting it mingle with her own. It was weaker than she had ever felt it.

"Dom, I have done my part. You must finish it, love." Laris hugged him fiercely though her limbs felt as if they were made of the heaviest stone instead of flesh. Her strength was ebbing, being sucked away. "Yours is the harder task. You must forgive your other, younger self. After that we can go on. This will truly be behind us. We can forget. Please try."

"I love you," he whispered.

He shuddered and held her tight. There was a moment of vertigo as something dark rushed by them and the earth seemed to shift on its axis. The smell of jasmine burst forth and then faded.

"Memory, get thee behind me," Laris whispered to the shadow. "Get thee behind us."

Something dark passed between them and the setting sun.

Feeling the last of the shivering tension fade away from his body, Laris slumped against Dom's heaving chest. Dom's own posture was one of exhaustion. They were barely able to hold each other erect as they struggled to suck the thick air into their lungs.

"Thank you, love," she whispered, turning her face into his throat and kissing the pulse that hammered there. His skin was clammy and pale, even in the red light that was the last of the daylight bleeding from the hazy sky. "It is finally done. We can go home now."

Dom shook his head. "Not yet," he whispered.

"What do you mean?" she asked.

"He means that it isn't done," said a cold, evil voice.

Fatigued, but not entirely surprised to see the third party that was tied up with their fate, Dom and Laris turned slowly to face Rychard. Around them, the world drained of all color and grew deathly cold.

"Rychard." Dom's voice was urgent, and he tried to straighten. "It can be done for you too. We can all put this behind us and move on."

Their nemesis looked more like a corpse than a living man, but he still held a gun in his right hand. And he still smiled crazily.

"No, it isn't done at all. But it will be once I've put her back in her grave. I didn't do it right last time. I let you live. But I won't make that mistake again."

Rychard raised his arm. The hand that held the gun trembled, but not enough to ruin his aim.

312

Chapter Eighteen

"What have I done?" he whispered.

Isabella stared up into Dominick's agonized face and tried to speak, but no words would form. The cold creeping through her body had frozen her lips and tongue. Her soul was leaving. She had no more time.

Dominick, I love you. Don't blame yourself, *she told him in her mind*, as her soul began its translation from earthly life into the hereafter.

A bright light appeared about her and she began to ascend. She looked about for the dark angel who had come for her baby, but none appeared. Suddenly her spirit stilled, unable to go on. Confused, she looked down and saw a chain of dark shadows that led from her heart to Dominick's bowed head.

"Forgive me, Isabella!" he cried.

Dominick—the chain! Let go, love. I forgive you. Let go.

But he didn't hear her.

Dom used the last of his strength to thrust Laris behind his own body and attempted to be her shield. It was a futile gesture if Rychard had more than one bullet left in his gun, but Dom made it anyway.

"Would you murder your sister again?" he demanded of Rychard. "She loved you."

"I'd kill the traitorous bitch in a heartbeat. But you can die first, if that is what you truly desire. It makes no difference to me."

"Rychard, stop!" Laris pleaded. "You're damned if you do this. You won't get another chance. This is a crossroads of destiny. Please make the right decision. Stop this insanity."

Rychard just laughed. "I've made my decision. Now you die."

Behind the bloodied murderer there rose an enormous shadow, which rapidly coalesced into a physical form. Dom, realizing what was happening, schooled his face to passivity, but he could hear Laris's shocked gasp as she saw who stood behind her brother.

Rychard heard it, too, and spun about to see who or what had crept up behind him.

"No!" he screamed, but Death was not deterred. He was wearing his uniform of office and carrying a scythe. He had gone to the trouble of altering his height so that he towered over all of them, and he wore his nightmare face. He was clearly out for a soul-harvest.

"Get away!" Rychard tried to back up but Death's bony hand shot out of his tattered black sleeve and grabbed Rychard's neck, lifting him off of the ground with frightful ease.

Terrified, Rychard tried to shoot the cloaked figure but the bullets had no effect other than to make the Reaper smile. The grin caused the hardened leather of his face to crackle as it creased. The eyes twinkled redly.

"Amateur. Allow me to show you how it's done," Death whispered in a terrifying voice that blasted her nerves with frost and paralyzed Laris into inaction. He leaned over Rychard's writhing form.

Death fastened his lips over his victim's still screaming mouth, nearly covering the lower half of his face. Rychard kicked twice, more spasms than planned movement, and then went limp. The Reaper's chest heaved violently as he inhaled and then was still.

Rychard's gun dropped to the ground.

"No, no, no, no," Laris whispered, unwilling to believe what she had just seen.

Death finally raised his head and allowed Rychard's corpse to fall to the ground. His eyes and lips were slightly reddened and his expression a bit languid.

"I've wanted to do that for the longest time,"

Death said, radiating satisfaction as he reached inside his robes and extracted a black lace handkerchief. He blotted his lips fastidiously and then refolded the linen.

Dom and Laris were too stunned to answer and too exhausted to run, so they stood in place, waiting to see what Death would do next.

"You will be glad to know that Rychard's soul is being recalled—permanently. He shall have eternal rest now." The creature's silky voice was soft but terribly unpleasant as it slid into their ears. Death patted his stomach. "The Great One has decreed that this model is hopelessly flawed and is to be destroyed immediately."

Laris moaned softly.

Death smiled again, an act that looked like it was tearing interior sutures in his sewn-up face. Laris, who was pressed against Dom's back, shuddered and locked her knees so that she would not fall to the ground.

"You, however, have made the right choices and been redeemed. Though you have caused some disorder among my minions, you are to be let go. So I shan't be seeing you again until—"

Dom held up his hand. "Please. I would as soon not know."

"And who can blame you?" Death laughed. "Your little songstress doesn't look interested in precognizant knowledge either. It's a pity, since I worked so hard to give a masterful performance, but I don't think that we are ever going to be good friends."

Laris thought Death's laugh was without any doubt the worst noise she had ever heard, and had to resist the childish urge to put her hands over her ears.

Dom, feeling her distress, turned and took her into his arms, urging her head against his chest. He frowned at Death. "Use a little tact, please."

"What exactly will happen to him? Rychard?" Laris forced herself to ask. She kept her eyes focused upward as she had no urge to see the body of the murderer who had once been her brother. Her memories of him animated by breath and a beating heart were horrible enough. She didn't want to recall the soulless shell huddled on the stony ground.

"Rychard?" Death considered her pale face with a knowing eye, and Laris wondered if he was planning on lying to her. Finally he said almost kindly: "Don't be concerned. He will have better treatment than he deserves. After all, he did one good deed before he died."

"He did?" Laris looked up at Dom's ashen face. "What?"

Unable to imagine Rychard doing anything helpful, her beloved simply looked back.

"Yes," Death said gently. "He forced the two of you together, and he gave Domitien time to reconsider his life course."

"A Judas goat?" Dom asked.

"But one who chose his own end. No one coerced him."

"I see. I guess that was accidentally helpful of him." Unable to stand looking at the Grim Reaper's smile any more, even in periphery, Laris turned her face into Dom's shirt. "Can we leave now? I'm very tired."

"Certainly, if you want. I have work to do too. *Requiescat in pace*," Death said, reaching down for Rychard and plucking the body up by its ankle. He started toward one of the tombs with his burden dangling upside down in his grasp. "You want that small wooden door over there to the right. Do watch your step. The floor is a tad uneven and I wouldn't want you to break your neck after all the trouble you've been through."

Dom snorted at this untruth.

"Once inside, go through the portal on the left. It will return you to your own time." Death belched once and muttered: "Disagreeable sod."

"Let's go, my love." Dom turned Laris so that his body blocked her view of Death. He did not think that she needed to see the Reaper's calloused treatment of Rychard's cast-off shell.

"Have a safe journey—and I'll be seeing you . . . soon," Death called after them. And then he began to hum Musette's song from *La Boheme*.

"That wasn't a very nice thing to say," Laris muttered, starting for the door Death had indicated. She didn't try to turn back and see what the Reaper was doing. It was bad enough listening to him butcher Puccini.

Dom shrugged.

"He has always had a warped sense of humor. It's an occupational hazard, I suppose. Just be grateful that he didn't ask you to sing for your freedom. He actually loves opera."

"Swell. Does that mean he is going to come and watch me perform?"

"Probably. At least when you do Italian opera. He isn't that fond of the French or German schools."

"You know him that well?" Laris asked, surprised. "Why would you? How *could* you?"

"I'm afraid I do know him," Dom answered. "Rychard and I were two of his favorite people. We always gave him a lot of work, and he preferred to handle our transitions personally."

"He did *that* to you?" she asked, appalled.

"No," Dom reassured her. "It's nothing like that. Usually we just walked to one of the portals. I think he was just . . . well, indulging himself. Rychard shouldn't have shot him. Death can actually appear quite unthreatening, especially with children."

"Perhaps, but I am still glad that I don't recall seeing Death at work."

Dom stopped outside the indicated door and sniffed cautiously.

"No bats."

"Thank heavens! I've had enough of nature's nasties."

They had to stoop to fit through the low door, but once they were over the threshold the intense cold and exhaustion fell away.

In fact, she and Dom felt wonderful. Their physical and mental well-being was restored, even energized. There was an almost sensual pleasure in the feel of the balmy air that caressed them, and in the smell of the ocean that glided in through the open door of the tiny tomb. They breathed life back into their bodies.

Unable to help herself, Laris glanced out the door to the right to see what was waiting there. It still amazed her that worlds that were long past and forgotten, and sometimes even buried beneath the earth and oceans, were available for them to see.

"Dom?" she called softly, peering out at the festive scene before her.

"No."

"But just look. I think it's a wedding."

"No." His voice was stern. "Do the words *death wish* mean anything to you?"

"Death is busy right now. And just look at this! It must be something from the Bible."

"He has minions, remember. And if there is a door to this place, then someone is dying."

"Don't be such a grump."

Sighing, Dom came to the door. He looked with

disfavor at the glorious view of the small emerald-green garden where a fountain played and the gaily robed and veiled villagers congregated under a pomegranate tree. In the distance there grew what looked quite impossibly like an acacia, and beyond that there was a small grove of gnarled olives. Their feathery gray-green leaves were casting small, shivering shadows on the ground.

"It's Byblos, twelfth century—one of the Frankish kingdoms. You can tell by the new fortifications." He turned his head toward Laris, studying her profile. He smiled at her eagerness but said deliberately: "It was a gorgeous place in its time, before it was lost to the Amorites and a half dozen other conquerors, but we aren't going out there. With our luck Salah al-Din will sack the town while we are trying to kiss the bride."

"Saladin? Here?" Laris had a brief vision of a tall, raptorlike man clad in a jewel-encrusted turban and bedecked in vivid silken robes and a cloak of spun gold. He rode through the streets on a coal-black Arabian with gleaming hooves. The warrior monk of Islam looked more than a bit like Valentino.

However, the rational part of her brain recalled the reality of bloody subjugation of the Holy Land by various zealots, and she sadly dismissed the romantic image. Cecil B. DeMille had had a lot of fun with his epic movies, but she would not actually want to see the sacking of Damascus, Syria, Iraq, or Jerusalem.

"Don't look so gloomy. You would think this was Masada instead of a wedding," she scolded Dom.

"It still could be," Dom answered. "Don't open any other doors."

He had a point. She also supposed that since they were traveling under Death's auspices they should be respectful of his instructions.

"Well, then, I suppose that if you can't kiss the bride, you will simply have to kiss me instead," she said, turning fully to face Dom.

As always, the sight of him made her catch her breath.

"There is nothing that I would like better—except kissing you in San Francisco." Dom drew her toward the left door. The delicate smell of evening fog rolled in on the floral-scented breeze, dewing their skin with the sea's familiar cool kiss.

"Ready?"

"More than."

Linking hands, they stepped out into the park and the lassitude of a warm, twenty-first-century evening. Laris inhaled deeply, grateful for once for the smell of car exhaust.

The sunset had spread itself out over the horizon and painted the park in copper and gold. The fog was not there yet, but Laris knew that it waited right off-shore in a great lavender bank, just biding its time until night fell, when it would creep silently ashore under the cover of darkness.

Above their heads sat two doves, clinging to the windmill's railing. One was silent but the other cooed happily.

"Thanks," Dom said to them. "We're glad to be back. However, in the future, *I would desire that we be better strangers.* Your cure was almost more deadly than the ailment. We'll find our own way from now on."

Laris stared hard at the birds, resolved to have a long talk with Dom about just who these two omnipresent avians were.

He finally turned from the cooing doves and focused on her. Perhaps it was a trick of the light, but she could swear that something about him had changed. It seemed as though some of the ice shield in his mind had melted and that she was now able to catch glimpses of the storms of unsuppressed emotion roiling within him.

And this view told her that not everything in his emotional makeup had changed. She could read the intent behind his clear eyes. He wanted to make love to her, to kiss and smooth away the brutality of what they had endured and replace the bitter memories with sweet hopeful ones.

And Laris was glad of that. It was far better to tremble with ecstasy than with fear and cold.

Cool fingers plucked at them, reminding them that night was falling.

"We must go," Dom said softly. "But first—"

"—a kiss," she finished, stepping into his arms.

He held her, enjoying the simple feel of her warm and supple body beneath his palms and allowing her to feel and enjoy the same.

"Yes, just one kiss," he said, tipping up her face and brushing his lips over hers.

Laris shivered and moved closer, wanting more of the featherlight touch.

Dom obliged, deepening the contact, kissing her as he had that first time when souls and hearts had been exchanged. Heat rose between them, burning away the ugly memory of Rychard's death, the brutal grip of the green hell where Desiderio had died, and all the painful and futile years of love denied.

Laris returned the tenderness, telling him with her lips and softest sigh that the past was ended and a new life begun. If his was a kiss of blessed oblivion, hers was the embrace of hope and promise for a future.

Dom shuddered and lifted his head slightly.

"This would be a good moment for you to tell me to stop."

"Why?" she asked, her senses drugged and able to feel nothing but the warmth of Dom's body and the craving it always awoke in her.

"Because it is nearly dark and we are still in the middle of a public park. Because we both desperately need to eat and bathe. And we have an audience." He gestured toward the birds.

"We need other things as well," she pointed out, but made an effort to rejoin the practical, physical world darkening around them.

"And we shall have them, after I am certain that you took no harm at Alfonso's hands."

Laris shook her head.

"I was merely bruised when I hit the ground. And, anyway, I think that everything was healed when we left . . . *there*. Besides, you know that Desiderio saved me before anything bad happened. The only casualty is my blouse."

"It is reassuring to know that I wasn't a completely unimaginative bastard back then. I didn't think that you were real at first."

"You were never a *complete* bastard." She smiled suddenly. "Except in Milan when you were El Conde's illegitimate son. What a jerk!"

Dom groaned.

"I knew that this would happen! I shan't have a single secret left."

"Not a one," she agreed happily.

Dom took her hand and started for the park's exit. "We are back home, and I predict that soon this city will be at your feet. But tonight you are all mine. Sing something for me, beautiful songstress. Fill up this night with something beautiful. There must be some song appropriate for the occasion."

"All right." Laris thought for a moment and then began to croon:

Melanie Jackson

Poor wandering one!
Tho' thou be footsore and weary,
Return to grace, thy steps retrace,
Take heart, take heart, take heart.

Dom laughed with delight. He had never enjoyed
Gilbert and Sullivan more.

Chapter Nineteen

The door closed behind them and they stood in the hush of their climate-controlled suite, their dirty shoes sinking into the thick rug that graced the gleaming marble floor of the room's foyer. They felt lucky to have made it through the lobby without being stopped by security. This wasn't the sort of hotel that allowed filthy vagabonds inside.

Laris looked from Dom to the door to the bathroom, clearly torn about which she wanted more.

"I won't make you choose," he answered, taking her hand and pulling toward the nirvana of the sunken tub and bohemian shower with four heads. "Actually, I guess that you will have to make one choice. What shall it be, bath or shower?"

Laris shook her head and a small piece of fern

frond fell to the floor. She stared at it in consternation and then dared a quick peep in the mirror.

"Oh, no! This is worse than I thought. It had better be the shower. I need to wash the Amazon out of my hair. I think I may be harboring some of those tree frogs in here." The words were meant to be light, but she shivered at the thought of what might really be clinging to her hair and body. "Ugh! You kissed this face."

"I did, didn't I? I wonder what I could have been thinking."

"I bet that it is more a case of which part of you was thinking."

Dom flipped on the overhead heat lamps and then turned the dimmer down a few degrees. The bright light and heat were welcome after their time spent in Death's gloom, but there was no need for ocular or dermal burns.

Laris moved at once toward the shower but Dom was there before her, turning on the taps and blocking the door with his body.

"Dom!" she expostulated, trying without success to push him aside. "Me first! I'm having a real hair emergency here."

"There's an energy crisis here in California. I thought that we should be thoughtful and shower together," he explained, his mouth prim but his eyes dancing.

Laris looked at the four showerheads all jetting water into the oversize stall and smiled at the rising steam. "I suppose that that would be the responsible thing to do," she agreed, sitting down on the edge of the tub and starting the process of prying her clothes off. "But I get the shampoo first."

"Of course," he agreed meekly, and sat down to remove his own clothes. "The honor of the first shampoo shall be yours."

Laris shrugged her sweater off and then considered where to begin. Her shirt was beyond all hope, not only filthy but punctured in two places where Alfonso's dull knife had managed to punch through the fabric.

Shuddering, she jerked it off and then cast it into the trash can. Her bra was likewise thrown aside. The delicate lace had torn in several places. France's finest was not designed for roughing it in the rain forest.

But Des's cross, nestled between her breasts, was still beautiful. The gold was battered on the ends and worn smooth on the back, but it still gleamed. So, not every memento of her visit would be cast aside. Laris touched it gently, blinking back a sudden flood of tears.

"It's all right, love," Dom said, gathering her into his arms and holding her close. "Cry for him, if you must. No one else did, so I am sure he would appreciate it."

Laris wrapped her arms about Dom, snuggling into his heat, but shook her head resolutely.

"No, I am done with crying. There isn't any need, is there? He isn't really gone since you are here. This is just leftover emotion, a hangover." She added: "And probably even that beastly murdering rapist has turned into an upright citizen by now."

Dom smoothed her hair but made no comment about Alfonso, since it was his belief that the man was reincarnating down the chain rather than up it and was probably a cockroach by now.

"You are right about the hair emergency," he said instead. The task of running his fingers through Laris's locks was more difficult than it had been that morning when they left the hotel. He didn't think that there were actually any seventeenth-century amphibians in there, but there was a lot of authentic ancient dirt and leaves clinging to her tangled tresses.

"I am aware of that," she said, biting his chest in mock vexation.

"No biting now. We'll get to that later. Let's get those pants off this gorgeous body and enjoy some water that's warm," he said lightly. His large hand patted her bottom. "Have I ever mentioned how much I love this slimmed-down body you have this time, especially your arse. In the past, your figure was more *belligerent*."

Laris lifted her head.

"You have mentioned my *arse* several times," she answered, deciding not to reprove Dom for the sexist words or gesture since they weren't in public. "And my body was never *belligerent*. It was *exuberant* and disdained restraint."

"As you like, *bella*. Here, let me help you with those trousers," Dom said, reaching for her zipper.

"You are too kind," she answered as he skimmed her panties down her legs as well.

"But always," he said, stepping into the shower and picking up the shampoo. "Now come here."

"I'm not sure that this is a good idea," Laris began, stepping out of her pants and eyeing the firm grip Dom had on the inverted shampoo bottle. "Speaking of exuberant, you do realize that one only needs a very small amount of shampoo to get clean?"

"I assure you that I am fully qualified to wash your hair. I have had lots of experience." He leaned over and pulled her into the stall.

Laris glowered at him and pulled her arm free.

"I don't want to hear any more about your *experiences*. That is all over with now, and there will be no more walks down memory lane with other women."

"Whatever do you mean?" Dom asked, looking innocent. "I merely wished to reassure you that I have washed my hair many times and know not to get soap in your eyes."

"Oh, it that what you meant?"

"Certainly. What else? Now come here before you hurt my feelings again." He grabbed her again and dragged her under the spray. Laris gasped and turned her face out of the stream.

"Dom! You aren't supposed to drown me either."

"Hold still, or you'll get this all over," he said, pouring out the golden hair soap with a lavish hand and spilling it all over her head and chest. "Now look what you've made me do. I'll just have to wipe it off."

Dom's hands were suddenly everywhere, swooping down her back, over her thighs, sliding across her breasts, tickling at her waist. She a made a token gesture of slapping them away, but truly did not mind his play as long as she *didn't* get soap in her eyes or he didn't start tickling the backs of her knees.

Eventually he did wash her hair and his own as well, but not until he had her breathing hard and tingling over most of her body.

"There! That's better. Clean as a whistle," he said, letting go of her. "You should have a little faith."

"Better than what?" she demanded as he abruptly abandoned her. "You are a real cad, you know that?"

When Dom smiled wickedly and turned his back on her to see to his own ablutions, Laris glowered. "I am rather Old Testament," she said to Dom. "None of that letting mercy season justice stuff."

He mumbled something as he rinsed his face.

Deciding that actions would explain her philosophy more clearly than words, Laris picked up the nearly empty shampoo bottle and returned his favor by helpfully "washing" Dom's body—though not too vigorously.

Her playful pauses over certain parts of his anatomy earned her a reproachful look, but she merely smiled at him, showing a lot of teeth.

"I hope you are pleased with your handiwork." Dom's voice was gritty.

"Not yet." Her smile widened as she ran a finger up the length of him. "But I expect that I shall be. Are you through playing in the water yet? Or shall we have another round of washing and teasing? I feel quite capable of going again."

Dom reached over and shut off the taps. He looked at her consideringly. "I'm older than you," he told her, his voice low and menacing. "And larger. And psychically stronger. Perhaps this would be a good time to sort out who is in control here."

Laris giggled at his growl. "That would also be cheating. No mind games in the bedroom." She shook a finger at him. "Besides, I thought that the — *um* —other matter was urgent for you."

"It is urgent, so what do you think about the vanity?" he asked, helping her out onto the bath mat and turning her so she faced the steamy mirror. "An interesting view, no?"

"With or without towels?" she asked, staring at their dripping reflections in the enormous glass that covered the wall. Steam had blotted out only the upper third, but there was still enough to show her that Dom was correct; he was a lot larger than she was.

The thought did not distress her. Dom's strength would never be turned against her.

"Frankly, it looks a bit dangerous. That's real marble and real slippery. Probably cold and hard too. I've had enough of discomfort for the time being."

"You have a point," he answered, reaching for the thick linens and wrapping one around Laris first and then choosing one for himself. "Safety first. And there are plenty of mirrors in the bedroom."

"Plenty," she agreed, turning to him with a smile. "So do let's get started before you lose—um, the *thread* of our conversation."

She reached out and snatched his towel away and fled for the bedroom.

Dom sprang after her, catching her after only one step. He caught her up in his arms and then tossed her over his still wet shoulder.

"Did you really say 'thread'?"

Laris laughed but didn't struggle against her captivity. Their bare skin was also very slippery, though not cold.

The urge to play fell away from them quickly once they were actually prone on the bed, Dom lying atop Laris with his weight suspended on his forearms and his legs resting between her own.

"There is something that I want from you, Laris. I want it very badly."

"Then take me—I'm yours!" she said lightly, but truthfully.

334

Dom shook his head. "Not that, you wanton wench. I am serious now. This is something that would also make the Great One happy."

Laris blinked and colored. She didn't want to think about the master builder when her thoughts were less than pure.

Dom smiled and ran a finger over her reddened cheek. "Such a sweet blush. But there is no need to be embarrassed."

"*Ha!* What is it that you want?" she asked, trying not to squirm against Dom's erection. It was difficult as he was lying between her legs and pressed tight against her where she could feel every pulse of his heart.

"I want your immediate capitulation, unconditional, irreversible, and irrevocable surrender."

Laris blinked again. Her mixed impulses jostled against one another while mind and body fought for supremacy. Mind came out temporarily ascendant, but it was a struggle as her body was not being gracious about the delay.

"I see . . . and how might I demonstrate this capitulation, supposing I was willing to grant you so complete a surrender?" she finally asked.

"By agreeing to marry me again," he answered promptly. "Immediately."

"I see," she said again, beginning to smile. "This is a case of you serving a jealous God and trying to please him, is that it?"

Dom shook his head, also smiling a little. "The Great One isn't jealous, but he does have some very set notions. A marriage would please and reassure him."

Laris looked at Dom, trying to decide if he was at all serious, and then asked: "And what about you? Would marriage please you?"

"Very much." He still smiled, but his words were sincere. "More than anything."

"And we have to do this immediately? I mean, *immediately* immediately?"

"Well, perhaps tomorrow would be soon enough," he conceded. He, too, could feel every pulse that beat against the welcoming heat that was Laris's seat of femininity.

"I shall think about it," Laris said at last. "I need to be convinced."

Dom tensed.

His actions were not meant to be provocative, but Laris shivered anyway.

"Laris!"

"This is a fine time to have a serious conversation," she complained. "But you started it."

"What do you mean, you need to be convinced?" He sounded huffy, and Laris had to bite back a smile.

"Well, there are one or two things we would have to work out before I could say yes."

"And what is that?"

"Well, I am afraid that in modern marriages there

actually *are* terms. The traditional ones are *love*, *honor, and*—"

"—*obey*," he said with a certain relish.

"—*cherish*," she corrected. "I think that I might be willing to settle for these, as long as you throw in the whole 'in sickness and health, in prosperity and adversity' shtick."

"Well . . ." Dom's eyes gleamed. "It is a hard bargain, but I think I could manage that much in the way of vows."

"Good. Then that just leaves one other thing to clear up."

"What else?" Dom shifted again. This time, she was fairly certain that he did it on purpose. "We can honeymoon in Las Vegas and gamble all day, every day, if that's what you'd like."

"Thank you, but that isn't what I was chiefly concerned about."

"No?"

"No." Laris raised her legs and wrapped them around Dom's hips. She added tauntingly: "I just want to be sure that you are in fact still potent and capable of the rigors of marriage. This has been a long and trying adventure, and there is simply no other way of knowing if the trauma of it has affected you."

"I see." Dom growled at her: "Do let me put your mind at rest."

He looked down at her breasts with their nipples of deep rose, then up the slender column of her throat, and then back at her beloved face.

"No, we won't have any problems with this," he said, lowering his mouth to hers. "You should be able to follow my *thread*."

He slid down her body, kissing the curve of her shoulder, grazing her breasts, and then to the hollow of her navel. It was a traditional erogenous zone, but it awoke more of Laris's sleeping nerve endings and made them sing out with desire.

Gently, he stroked up the plane of her thigh and then touched her auburn curls. He bent his head and touched her with the tip of his tongue.

Laris's breath broke and her body tightened, arching slightly off the bed. He swore, though many inches away, that he could hear the thundering of her heart as it galloped after desire.

Heat pulsed through her body and he heard her moan his name, a new sound to him, not as musical as a sigh but every bit as moving.

"You'll give me a heart attack," she warned. "Have a little mercy."

Dom lifted his head. "That would be quite a feat at sea level. And, anyway, I thought we were doing Old Testament this evening. That means justice, not mercy."

"Please." She held out her arms to him. She added: "To forgive is divine. You can evolve."

Dom paused for a moment, torn between two conflicting desires, but it was inevitable that one would win over the other.

He flowed up the length of her body, caressing as he came, savoring the soft skin that made Laris so recognizably female. His impulse was to ravage, to bury himself in her heat and softness and let her take the world away.

He throttled a groan and told his body and imagination to be patient.

His imagination he could command, because it had a reality every bit as splendid as anything it could create, but his body was not so easily deterred. It demanded that it be given what it desired. And how could he argue against it when her own desire was evident in the heat that pressed against him in undulating waves?

Her hands moved over his body, restless and encouraging in their touch, urging him to complete the union. They found his shoulders, the plane of his back, then its small, then his buttocks. There they nipped.

"Dom! Stop teasing."

He groaned and closed his eyes. Slowly he eased his way inside her body, refusing to rush through the pleasure of joining every fiery inch of their bodies.

Laris's hands traveled back up his body and laced themselves into his hair.

"Yes, oh, yes. But faster!"

Laris's voice was deepening, and he was pleased for

the training that made her so expressive. He opened his eyes to gaze at her, wanting to see the dilated pupils that would blot out the softer irises and the telltale perspiration that dewed her face.

Abandoning restraint, he surged into her. She cried out softly, and he lowered his mouth to hers where he nibbled and drank in her cries.

The heat of their joining overflowed, spilled out over their skin, and overran their senses. Time went away, there was no place, no reality other than the fire burning between them.

Such conflagrations could not be long denied. Laris's rapture burst free, exploding over them in a convulsion that could not be ignored.

Dom's body, happy to follow where she led, permitted itself a sympathetic detonation and threw itself gladly into the cataclysm. He tucked an arm beneath her hips and arched into her as the convulsions traveled up his body and into her own where she absorbed them with another soft cry. The soft sound told him that the sweet fire had burst over her again.

Laris clung to Dom, their bodies absorbing the last of the shock waves that passed between them, and shivered slightly in the aftermath of the eruption. His weight upon her was as sweet as his skin was salty where she kissed him on the neck.

For a long time they did not speak, just rested together while their breaths and heartbeats returned to normal, and their minds rejoined their bodies in their hotel room in San Francisco.

Dom finally stirred and made as if to roll aside, but Laris wrapped shaky legs about him and urged him to be still.

"Not yet," she murmured.

"You'll end up flat as a mat," he said, kissing her cheek and then the corner of her mouth.

"Just a few moments more—for balance. There were so many moments when I doubted that I would ever hold you again," she confessed softly.

Dom raised up enough to look down into her eyes and reality returned to him in a rush. This wasn't a dream, a long-smothered wish. Laris was real. She was here and she was his. It was another kind of shock to his system, and as with his climax, it also traveled the length of his body and made him shiver with pleasure.

"What is it, love?" she asked, putting arms around him and urging him back down upon her. "You look so shocked. Is something wrong?"

"No. I . . ." Dom could not at first find the words to explain his gratitude for her generosity of spirit that had waited for him for a thousand years. There weren't enough words to tell of the intense pleasure she gave him by just *being*.

But then he recalled the right phrase from another millennium. It wasn't everything he needed to tell her, everything that he wanted to share, but it was the crux, the heart of what he felt.

And it translated beautifully into English.

"I love you," he said simply.

Laris sighed happily.

"I've waited so long to hear you say that."

He looked at her for a moment more. Physical desire had been appeased, but he was still hungry for her in other ways. He wanted more of her voice, her touch, her dreams, her life.

"I love you, too, you know," Laris said, smiling. "But please, lie down again."

Contented for the moment, Dom allowed her to pull him back down and run her delicate hands over his back and to wind themselves in his hair. He tucked his face into the curve of her throat and listened to the torrent of life that ran through her body.

"You would probably object to the suggestion that I cut my hair," he murmured and Laris again ran fingers through his damp locks.

"You do and I'll cut mine," she warned him.

Dom chuckled and, shifting to one side, moved a hand between their bodies. He touched between her thighs. "Now that would be a great pity."

"That isn't the hair I meant," she scolded, but started to smile. "You just aren't going to be typically postcoital and sleep, are you?"

Dom raised up on an elbow again and smiled down

at her. "There is nothing half so wonderful on the planet as being in your arms, *bella*, and heaven knows that I crave sleep. But I have to admit that I am now lusting after something else."

"Oh." She tugged warningly on his hair. "It better not be called Portia."

"Don't be so brutal and untrusting, woman. I merely want some dinner. And not just any dinner. A superlative one. Sole *meuniere*, a spinach salad, saffron rice, and a cold chenin blanc, and perhaps for a finish a *crème anglaise* and brandy . . ."

Laris's eyes shone in the dim light from the foyer. "Not for me. I want steak. Make that a prime rib, medium rare. And asparagus—"

"With sweet butter?" Dom suggested.

"Of course. And au gratin potatoes."

"With chervil."

"And chocolate mousse torte with coffee and whipped cream!"

"Your every wish is my—and Henri's—command," Dom answered, reaching for the bedside phone and pushing the button for room service.

He at last noticed that there was a message light blinking in annoying flashes, and was fairly certain that it was good news for Laris from the San Francisco Opera Company.

But the world, even when it came bearing glad tidings, could wait just a while longer. Dinner and the consumption of the best celebratory champagne were more important.

After all, he and Laris only got married once every millennium.

Epilogue

Enzo settled on the fountain rim across from Ilia and permitted himself a satisfied smile.

"That worked out rather neatly," he said, picking up a teapot and pouring a pale green brew into two saucers. He dropped a bit of silvered mirror into Ilia's and passed the plate. "And none of the Host died in the battle."

Ilia snorted and looked over at the wounded doves who were sheltering in the ever-blooming jacaranda.

"They certainly suffered enough to put things to right with Dom and Laris."

"Life is suffering from time to time," Enzo said piously.

Ilia snorted again.

"Human life is suffering. Ours is one of endless duty and joyous worship."

"Come on, my friend," Enzo chided, pouring his own tea and likewise putting a bit of mirror in the saucer. "Admit to the happiness of this occasion."

"Laris has been made an offer from the opera company?" Ilia asked. He eyed his reflection in the bottom of the dish and then swooped down to take a drink.

"Can you doubt it? Of course she has." Enzo eyeballed his own reflection and then also bobbed down for a sip. He sighed happily.

"That should please Death. He likes San Francisco but preferred the Met for theatrical productions." Ilia smiled in a way that made him look totally unlike a Victorian cherub. "That won't please Dom at all."

Enzo tut-tutted.

"Our only failure on this occasion was with Rychard. Such a shame when one of the Great One's experiments doesn't work out."

"I don't know. Once in a while, I think that a little evolution is a good thing."

"Ilia!" Enzo pretended horror. "That is the rhetoric of the enemy."

"Well, no one ever said that they were stupid. And I don't see them as the enemy. Scientists are simply slower than the rest of the world at selecting the proper standard of judgment. If they had been given any talent for painting or music, they might not go so far astray."

"That is astonishingly broad-minded of you," Enzo said admiringly.

"They are educable. If they live long enough," Ilia added.

"So, my friend, are you at all curious about what is waiting in Dom's future? Shall we bend the rules and have a peep?"

"No," Ilia said firmly. "Unless—have you already looked into the glass?"

Enzo ruffled. "Certainly not. But I have heard a rumor that the Great One has two souls being prepared to send to Laris."

"Twins—but so soon? What of her new job?" Ilia betrayed his affection for Laris by his dismay.

Enzo smiled inwardly. "Oh, no! They shan't be sent immediately. After all, they will require a great deal of work before they are ready for the twenty-first century."

Ilia turned horrified eyes on his friend.

"It can't be—surely the Great One is not resurrecting Rychard?"

"Of course not! Don't be absurd."

"Sorry," Ilia said, taking another drink of his tea. "That was foolish of me. When the Great One has ruled out a personality type, well, that is the end of the matter. I was—*What?*"

"Well, usually that would be true. But he is so

pleased with how Laris turned out that he has decided to play around a bit with an older musical model in the hope that she, too, can be saved."

"Not *Portia?*"

"Yes, I fear so."

"And he is sending twins?"

"That is the plan."

"Poor Laris! And do you know, I almost feel sorry for Domitien too?"

Enzo didn't comment, but simply finished his tea. He set aside his cup and said: "I am needed in London. Do you want to come?"

"No," Ilia answered. "I have something else to do."

"Very well. I'll see you at the equinox."

"Certainly. Good-bye for now," Ilia answered, watching his friend launch himself into the sky.

After Enzo's form had shrunk to a pale dot, Ilia went over to the scrying glass and, making a minute adjustment to the rings that surrounded it, he leaned over and peered into the crystal depths.

An image formed immediately.

"Did you ever think that we would see our girls' faces looking back at us from a music store?" Laris asked Dom as they sat side by side on a bench in Golden Gate Park. Her lovely faced had aged only a little and her beautiful voice not at all.

"I didn't doubt that they would have a career in music and be successful at whatever they chose. After all, they have their mother's gifts," Dom answered.

The hand of time had also been gentle with its weight on him. There was true silver mixed in the pale blond now but his face was unlined and his eyes were still clear.

"What I never thought to see was the day that they would finally settle down and marry." Dom shook his head. "That frightful redheaded temper has terrified more than one man before he could see the loving heart beneath it."

Laris nodded and laid her head on Dom's shoulder.

"I'll admit that I had doubts too. They have always looked a lot like me, but in temperament they always seemed more like—"

Dom turned his head and silenced her with a kiss.

"It's a tempting game, but don't think about it."

Laris smiled and shook her head.

"That was sweet but sneaky. So do you think Enzo and Ilia will come to the wedding?"

Dom shrugged, as he put his arm about Laris and urged her to cuddle closer. "That is hard to say. They have been around for all the other big events in the girls' lives. I imagine they will be at their wedding if it is at all possible."

Ilia looked over at the complicated marking that circled the glass, translated it into the earth's lunar calendar, and then made a note of the date.

He couldn't speak for Enzo, but he certainly planned on being at *this* wedding.

Author's Note

Since I have been asked about this, I want to state for the record that *Dominion* is not biographical. It is a work of fiction that speculates about reincarnation, and being that it is fiction, I have taken the liberty of bending the rules of geography, time, space, physics, biology, zoology, botany, and various other scientific disciplines to suit the needs of the plot.

For the sake of simplicity I have given my characters similar names for each incarnation. The hero, Domitien, is also Dominick, Dorran, Desiderio, etc. The villain, Rychard, is also Ricardo, Rhys. The heroine, Laris, is Laura, Lotty, and so forth. These previous incarnations, excepting Desiderio, are encountered only in the past-life segments at the start of each chapter and there is no need to keep track of them in order to follow the plot.

Also, though it pains me to admit it, I have no firsthand knowledge about Death's musical or reading preferences. Nor have I ever seen Fate's dreadlocks. I just made those parts up.

NIGHT VISITOR

MELANIE JACKSON

All self-respecting Scots know of the massacre and of the brave piper who gave his life so that some of its defenders might live. But few see his face in their sleep, his sad gray eyes touching their souls, his warm hands caressing them like a lover's. And Tafaline is willing to wager that none have heard his sweet voice. But he was slain so long ago. How is it possible that he now haunts her dreams? Are they true, those fairy tales that claim a woman of MacLeod blood can save a man from even death? Is it true that when she touched his bones, she bound herself to his soul? Yes, it is Malcolm "the piper" who calls to her insistently, across the winds of night and time . . . and looking into her heart, Taffy knows there is naught to do but go to him.

___52423-6 $5.50 US/$6.50 CAN

Belle
Melanie Jackson

With the letter breaking his engagement, Stephan Kirton's hopes for respectability go up in smoke. Inevitably, his "interaction with the lower classes" and the fact that he is a bastard have put him beyond the scope of polite society. He finds consolation at Ormstead Park; a place for dancing, drinking and gambling . . . a place where he can find a woman for the night.

He doesn't recognize her at first; ladies don't come to Lord Duncan's masked balls. This beauty's descent into the netherworld has brought her within reach, yet she is no girl of the day. Annabelle Winston is sublime. And if he has to trick her, bribe her, protect her, whatever—one way or another he will make her an honest woman. And she will make him a happy man.

___4975-9 $5.99 US/$7.99 CAN

Amarantha
Melanie Jackson

'Tis not Robert Burns's legendary elfin knight who greets Amarantha upon her arrival at her folklorist uncle's Cornish mansion, but the dark and wild-haired Tamlane Adair. The Scotsman's languorous movements enthrall her, and the rumors of his nighttime rides across Bodmin Moor only heighten the virile man's mystery. His voice is like satin or silk, sliding over her, clothing her in blissful delirium. Listening, she can almost forget the Jacobite rebellion that has cost her so much. In Tamlane's green eyes, Amarantha cannot help but see the danger of the Cornish coast...and in his arms, its wonderful promise.

___4900-7 $5.99 US/$6.99 CAN

MANON
MELANIE JACKSON

Alone and barely ahead of the storm, Manon flees Scotland; the insurrection has failed and Bonnie Prince Charlie's rebellion has been thrown down. Innocent of treason, yet sought by agents of the English king, the Scots beauty dons the guise of a man and rides to London—and into the hands of the sexiest Sassanach she's ever seen. But she has no time to dally, especially not with an English baronet. Nor can she indulge fantasies of his strong male arms about her or his heated lips pressed against her own. She fears that despite her precautions, this rake may uncover her as no man but *Manon*, and she may learn of something more dangerous than an Englishman's sword—his heart.

Lair of the Wolf

Also includes the eighth installment of *Lair of the Wolf*, a serialized romance set in medieval Wales. Be sure to look for future chapters of this exciting story featured in Leisure books and written by the industry's top authors.

___4737-3 $4.99 US/$5.99 CAN

IONA

MELANIE JACKSON

Isolated by the icy storms of the North Atlantic, the isle of Iona is only a temporary haven for its mistress. Lona MacLean, daughter of a rebel and traitor to the crown, knows that it is only a matter of time before the bloody Sasannachs come for her. But she has a stout Scottish heart, and the fiery beauty gave up dreams of happiness years before. One task remains—to protect her people. But the man who lands upon Iona's rain-swept shores is not an Englishman. The handsome intruder is a Scot, and a crafty one at that. His clever words leave her tossing and turning in her bed long into the night. His kiss promises an end to the ghosts that plague both her people and her heart. And in his powerful embrace, Lona finds an ecstasy she'd long ago forsworn.

___4614-8 $4.99 US/$5.99 CAN

KIMBERLY RAYE
A STRANGER'S KISS

Alex Daimon is the incarnation of desire, the embodiment of lust, the soul of carnality. For centuries he has existed to bring down the just and the wicked alike, to corrupt the innocent. Thus comes he to the bed of Callie Wisdom, the young heir of the witch who bound him to Darkness . . . and the girl is ripe for possession. He means to do what he's done so many times before—seduce and destroy. But looking into her crystalline eyes, Alex wishes that Callie might see some end to his curse. And introducing her to passion, Alex wonders if this time, instead of his kiss drawing his victim down into darkness, her love may not raise him up to the light.

__52462-7 $5.99 US/$6.99 CAN

Dorchester Publishing Co., Inc.
P.O. Box 6640
Wayne, PA 19087-8640

Please add $2.50 for shipping and handling for the first book and $0.75 for each additional book. NY and PA residents, add appropriate sales tax. No cash, stamps, or C.O.D.s. All Canadian orders require $5.00 for shipping and handling and must be paid in U.S. dollars. Prices and availability subject to change. **Payment must accompany all orders.**

Name _____

Address_____

City_____ State _____ Zip _____

E-mail _____

I have enclosed $_____ in payment for the checked book(s).

☐Please send me a free catalog.

CHECK OUT OUR WEBSITE at www.dorchesterpub.com!

Dark Angel

Cassandra Collins

It's pouring rain the night Scarlett first sees him standing outside the diner window, and when lightning illuminates his features, she knows the handsome stranger has come for her.

Jake has been sent as a guardian, but there are powerful forces threatening his charge. He has faced them before but this time, he will be the winner. His arms will encircle Scarlett's sweet body, and the protection he offers will lead him to paradise.

The fallen angel and the troubled beauty share one destiny, one love, and the hope that in each other's arms, they just might find heaven.

Dorchester Publishing Co., Inc.
P.O. Box 6640
Wayne, PA 19087-8640

_____52414-7
$5.50 US/$6.50 CAN

Please add $2.50 for shipping and handling for the first book and $.75 for each additional book. NY and PA residents, add appropriate sales tax. No cash, stamps, or CODs. Canadian orders require $5.00 for shipping and handling and must be paid in U.S. dollars. Prices and availability subject to change. **Payment must accompany all orders.**

Name: _____

Address: _____

City: _____ State: _____ Zip: _____

E-mail: _____

I have enclosed $_____ in payment for the checked book(s).

For more information on these books, check out our website at www.dorchesterpub.com.
_____ *Please send me a free catalog.*

Enchantment
KATHLEEN NANCE

The woman in the New Orleans bar is pure sin and sex in a stunning package. And for once, hardworking, practical-minded Jack Montgomery lets himself be charmed. But no sooner has he taken the beautiful stranger in his arms than he discovers his mistake: Lovely, dark-haired Leila is far more than exotic; she is a genie. When he kisses her, heat lightning flashes around them, the air sparkles with color, and a whirlwind transports him out of this world. Literally. Trapped with Leila in the land of the Djinn, Jack will have to choose between the principles of science that have defined his life and something dangerously unpredictable and unsettling.
